A DANGEROUS KISS

"If you shrink from me in terror, Miss Middleton, no one will believe we are conducting a flirtation."

"You merely took me by surprise."

"Stand, Miss Middleton."

"Why?"

"There is no need in progressing any further if you cannot be depended upon to uphold your part of the charade."

"I will do well enough, sir."

"Oh?" he taunted softly. "Is that why you are cowering in that seat as if you fear I might ravish you at any moment?"

"I do not fear you."

"Then stand."

"Very well." She thrust herself to her feet, relieved when her less than stable knees held her upright. "Are you satisfied?"

"Not nearly," he murmured.

Keeping her gaze firmly ensnared, Hellion stepped forward to gently cup her face in his hands. With an odd fascination his thumb brushed her lower lip over and over until his head at last lowered and his intention became clear.

He was going to kiss her.

His lips were warm and shockingly possessive. With infinite patience, he explored the taste and shape of her mouth. Then, lightly his tongue stroked until her lips instinctively parted in invitation .

DEBORAH RALEIGH

SOME LIKE IT WICKED

ZEBRA BOOKS
Kensington Publishing Corp.
www.kensingtonbooks.com

ZEBRA BOOKS are published by

Kensington Publishing Corp.
850 Third Avenue
New York, NY 10022

All Kensington titles, imprints, and distributed lines are available at special quantity discounts for bulk purchases for sales promotion, premiums, fund-raising, educational, or institutional use.

Special book excerpts or customized printings can also be created to fit specific needs. For details, write or phone the office of the Kensington Special Sales Manager: Attn. Special Sales Department. Kensington Publishing Corp., 850 Third Avenue, New York, NY 10022. Phone: 1-800-221-2647.

Zebra and the Z logo Reg. U.S. Pat. & TM Off.

ISBN 0-8217-7855-2

First Printing: September 2005
10 9 8 7 6 5 4 3 2 1

Printed in the United States of America

CHAPTER ONE

From the diary of Miss Jane Middleton, April 21st, 1814:

Dearest Diary,

I have discovered since my arrival in London that attending a fashionable ball is rather like being a player in a theatre production.

To begin with, everyone is expected to know their character and their precise stage directions.

Older gentlemen, who are notoriously hard of hearing, are placed well away from the orchestra so they may bellow at one another without disturbing the dancers.

Matrons and dowagers are situated in a prominent position so that they may comfortably dispose of the reputations of the various guests.

The young, dashing blades and débutantes blessed with natural grace and beauty are allowed their privileged place in center stage as they flirt and twirl about the dance floor.

And last, and perhaps least, the unfortunate

wallflowers are gathered together in a discrete, shad-owed corner, rather like a forgotten, ill-tended garden.

Woe be it to any player who does not meekly submit to his or her proper role . . .

Miss Jane Middleton was frankly miserable.

She hated London. She hated the thick, black air. The narrow, crowded streets. The endless noise. The arrogant, utterly shallow Ton. And most of all, she hated the painful, torturous humiliation of what was politely termed the "Marriage Mart."

Who could have suspected that it would prove to be as delightful as having a tooth drawn?

Without a mother to warn her of the pitfalls, she had simply presumed that all maidens traveled to London and were introduced to a number of gen-tlemen anxious to discover a wife.

She possessed no great expectations.

She knew she was plain of feature and far too out-spoken for a maiden. She was also three and twenty, well past the age of a proper *débutante.*

But she did possess a sizeable fortune as well as an unentitled estate in Surrey that would surely be a temptation. It seemed reasonable that she could dis-cover a kindly disposed gentleman who would wel-come such material possessions.

How could she have suspected that she would be so swiftly judged and found wanting? Or that because she was not a Diamond of the First Water she was ex-pected to politely remain in the corner, ignored and forgotten by the various gentlemen?

Really, it was enough ↑
in frustration.

And it did not help to h.
made the source of amuseme
who had achieved social success.

Shifting uneasily upon the har   ıe
seat, Jane stoically attempted to igno.   pretty
maidens who had halted next to the   .ıı of wallflowers who had been thrust into a darkened corner.

Over the past few weeks she had endured any
number of snubs, insults, and cruel taunts from
Miss Fairfax and Miss Tully. They seemed to take
particular delight in torturing those poor maidens
already suffering beneath society's disdain. She had
swiftly learned the only means of enduring their
rude taunts was simply to pretend that she did not
notice them.

Almost on cue, the tiny, blond-haired Miss Fairfax loosed a shrill giggle as she pointedly glanced
toward Jane. "Really, Marianna, is it truly not pathetic? To just imagine an entire evening spent
without one gentleman asking for a dance or even
bothering to make his bow in your direction. How
utterly embarrassing it must be for them."

The taller, raven-haired Miss Tully wrinkled her
nose as if she had caught a whiff of some particularly nasty odor. "You would think that they would
eventually realize that they are unwelcome."

Jane clutched her fan until she feared it might
snap. Inwardly she allowed a delightful image to
form of the two maidens being tumbled into a
large, putrid midden heap.

Or perhaps roasting over a fire. Slowly.

"If only it were possible to ban them. It would be

n good, after all," Miss Fairfax twittered. ly they cannot enjoy an evening of being nubbed and ignored?"

"Perhaps they do not possess the wits to realize that they are so ill-favored that they will never attract the notice of an eligible gentleman? After all, they are desperately persistent."

"True enough, although I fear that persistence will not be enough to lure a partner to this dismal corner."

Miss Tully gave an unpleasant laugh. "Well, perhaps Pudding-faced Simpson. Or poor, doddy Lord Hartstone. It is said he requested a potted plant to honor him with a waltz last week."

Miss Fairfax gave a dismissive sniff. "Not even he is so doddy as to desire a dance with that lot."

Jane bit the side of her lip until she drew blood. Oh yes, she definitely wanted them roasting over a slow, hot fire. With an apple stuck in their shrill mouths.

It was not that she often concerned herself with what others might say. After all, she had been flouting convention since her father had insisted that she be trained to take over his numerous business concerns. But the scandalous disapproval had never struck a nerve. She had known deep within herself that she was perfectly capable of performing as well as any man.

This, however . . .

This disdain struck far too close to the truth, she grudgingly acknowledged. After several weeks she still had not attracted the attention of a respectable gentleman. Or any gentleman, for that matter. If the truth be told, they avoided her as if she carried the pox.

At the moment it seemed more likely that she would sprout wings and fly than find a husband.

"True enough," Miss Tully drawled, and then thankfully she was distracted by a movement across the crowded dance floor. "Oh, oh. Look, 'tis Hellion."

With a nerve-wrenching squeal Miss Fairfax was bouncing on her toes to catch sight of the current toast of London society, Mr. Caulfield, a devilishly handsome gentleman who managed to send every woman in London fluttering like a batch of witless butterflies.

"Are you certain?"

"I am hardly likely to confuse him with any other gentleman, am I?" Miss Tully demanded in tart tones.

"No," Miss Fairfax was forced to agree with a dramatic sigh. "What other gentleman could possibly be so elegant or so handsome?"

"Or so rakishly charming."

"How utterly delicious he is."

"A pity he never pays heed to *débutantes*. That is the sort of husband I desire."

The blonde slid her companion a sly glance. "My mother says that a clever female could capture his elusive attention. He is after all a man, and as capable of tumbling into love as the next."

Predictably Miss Tully frowned in a sour fashion. It did not appear that friendship could be allowed to interfere in the all-important hunt for a husband.

"I suppose that you believe you are clever enough to win his heart?" she scoffed.

"We shall see." Miss Fairfax gave a shrug before wrapping her arm through Miss Tully's. "Come, he will certainly never stray toward these wretched creatures. Let us stroll closer to him."

Together the two maidens set off in determined pursuit of Mr. Caulfield and Jane allowed herself to glare at their retreating backs.

Really, it was bad enough to endure being ignored, shoved aside, and at times given the cut direct. But to be taunted by two maidens without a breath of sense between them was beyond the pale.

She was in control of a vast fortune, she managed her own estate, and she had earned the respect of hardened businessmen who would have sworn that a female was incapable of caring for her own pin money.

It was unbearable that she should be judged less worthy than those twits simply because she did not possess a scrap of beauty.

In dire need of a moment's respite from the choking heat and ill-disguised glances of disdain from the vast crowd, Jane rose to her feet.

Gads, she would give up half her fortune for the opportunity to return to the quiet peace of Surrey.

"A few weeks in the country would surely not be so dreadful, Biddles. There are certain to be a few odd companions rattling about and, of course, there is always the pleasure of avoiding such tedious balls as this." The gentleman simply known as Hellion leaned against the wall in a corner of the crowded ballroom.

There were any number of rumors as to how he acquired the title.

Elderly gentlemen were convinced it came from his aggravating habit of shocking society with his outrageous antics. In the past ten years he had disrupted a ball at Carlton House by bringing with him a monkey that had promptly stolen Lord Marton's wig and sent poor old Lord Osburn into a fit of the vapors. He had attired his mistress as a young blade and audaciously brought her to several gentlemen's clubs. He had made an appearance in a particularly bawdy play and only last year appeared at his uncle's wedding attired in the deepest mourning.

Elderly women were convinced the name came from his habit of ignoring respectable females and openly preferring the companionship of seasoned courtesans and wicked widows.

Young ladies, of course, believed it was his devilish beauty. He was, in truth, indecently handsome. Golden hair that shimmered like the softest satin was carelessly brushed toward features carved by the hand of an angel. His brow was wide and his nose aquiline. If there was a hint of arrogance in the high, prominent cheekbones and square cut chin no one had ever been heard to complain. Even his form was magnificent in its chiseled perfection.

And his eyes . . .

Those black, wicked eyes.

The eyes of a rake, a rogue . . . a sinner.

It was little wonder maidens sighed in rapture when he glanced in their direction. And young gentlemen futilely attempted to ape his elegance.

Only Hellion knew the precise day he had acquired the notorious title. It was a day that would be forever branded upon his mind. And one that he had no intention of revealing to anyone.

"My dear Hellion, have you taken utter leave of your senses?" The small, sharp-featured gentleman

drawled softly at his side. "You know how I detest the
country. All that fresh air and mud. It cannot possibly be good for a gentleman's constitution. That is
not even to mention the danger of all those filthy
cows that are always lurking about. Who can say when
they might decide to bolt and trample some innocent victim?" He gave a delicate shudder. "No, no. I
fear that I cannot possibly leave London at the height
of the Season."

Hellion lifted a restless shoulder. He had no
more desire than his companion to flee town
during the fashionable month of April. Still, what
could he do? His countless creditors were becoming positively vulgar.

"As enchanting as I find London to be, I fear it
might not be quite so lovely from behind the walls
of Newgate."

Lord Horatio Bidwell, more affectionately known
as Biddles, lifted a brow. "Surely matters have not
progressed to such a dismal state?"

Hellion grimaced. In truth, he had managed to
land himself in a devilish coil. Certainly not the
first occasion, but by far the most tedious.

"I assure you that I have found myself at point-
non-plus," he confessed in low tones. "I have never
made a habit of living within my income, which to
be honest is hardly adequate for a fishmonger, certainly not for a gentleman of fashion. My extrava-
gances hardly mattered as long as I remained the
heir apparent to the Earl of Falsdale. Creditors
were delighted to court my favor and I was just as
delighted to accept their generosity. But now . . ."

The flamboyantly attired Biddles lifted a dainty
handkerchief to his nose. To all the world he ap-

peared no more than another ridiculous fop that lit-
tered society. Only a select few were allowed to realize
the shrewd, near brilliant wits behind the silly image.

"But now that the current earl has chosen to
take a wife young enough to be his granddaughter,
your role as heir apparent has become considerably less secure?"

Hellion struggled to maintain his air of casual nonchalance. Who would have thought his pompous
prig of an uncle would choose to wed when he was
near to sixty? Or that he would select a bride barely
out of the schoolroom?

It would have been humorous to see the old
windbag making a twit of himself over a mere child
if it hadn't made Hellion's life a sudden grief.

"Quite odious of him, I must admit," he retorted
in determinedly calm tones. "He could at least have
possessed the decency to choose a bride who was
not quite so obviously capable of producing the
next heir. Since the wedding I have been besieged
by frantic bill collectors demanding payment."

"The old earl cannot be trusted to take care of
such nasty business?"

Hellion stiffened in distaste. He would flee abroad
before he crawled on his knees to his uncle. "No."

The pale eyes narrowed with swift comprehension.
"I see. If your uncle cannot be depended upon then
you must turn your attention to other means of acquiring the necessary funds. Gambling, of course, is
far too unpredictable, unless one happens to possess
a talent for cheating. And I have discovered to my
own dismay that the lottery is not at all a reliable
means of holding off the vultures." There was a

moment's pause. "Ah, but of course. There is one certain means of repairing the empty coffers."

"Indeed?" Hellion smiled wryly. "And how is that?"

"Why, all you need do is to turn your attention to the numerous *débutantes*. There seems to be an endless gaggle of them and more than one will bring with them a sizeable dowry. Some of them in fact possess an embarrassment of riches. You could be comfortably settled within a month if you wished."

Hellion glanced about the elegant guests with a shudder. To his shame, he had briefly considered the notion of marrying a fortune. It would certainly put an end to his current troubles and ensure that his notorious appetite for the finer things in life would remain appeased.

But somehow the notion had made him shy away in unease. Since his parents' abrupt death he had never intimately shared his life with another. He had no siblings, no close relations beyond his odious uncle. And in truth, he did not desire such an intrusion. Not when he was perfectly satisfied with the undemanding, transitory relationships he enjoyed with his mistresses and friends.

The devil take it, he was not about to become responsible for another's happiness. Especially not a romantic, starry-eyed woman who would no doubt expect him to hand her his heart on a platter. It was unthinkable.

"I am not about to put myself on the block to go to the highest bidder," he denied in firm tones.

Biddles eyed him with a faint smile. "A charming description of the Marriage Mart."

"But accurate."

"It would solve a number of your troubles."

"And bring further troubles." His lips twisted as he took note of the various chits giggling and flirting about the room. "How should you like to be leg-shackled to one of these goose-witted maidens for your entire life?"

"Egads, that is not humorous, Hellion. I must insist that you do not even jest about such a notion," Biddles retorted in horror.

"Precisely. Which means I shall have to discover another method of acquiring the funds that I need."

"Perhaps I can be of help."

The soft, decidedly female voice came from behind the large urn, and both Hellion and Biddles stiffened in shock as a small dab of a girl abruptly stepped into view.

Hellion glared at the woman in embarrassment. Good God, did she possess no manners? Did she not realize just how vulgar it was to hide in shadows and pry into a gentleman's secrets?

Not that he could entirely blame her for preferring the shadows, he unkindly concluded. She certainly possessed no beauty to put upon display. She was too slender and too dark for the current fashion with curls unbecomingly scraped from her gamine countenance and skin more olive than alabaster. Her only saving grace appeared to be the large blue eyes, although they met his gaze squarely rather than from beneath lowered lashes as was only proper.

"Who the devil are you?" he growled.

"Miss Middleton," she retorted, not seeming to be at all intimidated by his simmering anger. "Forgive me for intruding, but I could not help but overhear your conversation."

Hellion thinned his lips in displeasure. "Could

not? How extraordinarily odd. Were you stuck to the floor? Or perhaps you forgot how to place one foot before the other so that you could politely move away?"

She at least possessed the grace to blush. Hellion noted the dark color did nothing to enhance her plain features.

"No, I was not stuck to the floor, nor did I forget how to walk," she surprised him by admitting. "In truth, I deliberately remained to listen."

Caught off guard by her honesty he furrowed his brow. "Why?"

She seemed to hesitate, as if debating within her own mind before slowly squaring her shoulders. "I believe that we may be of service to one another, Mr. Caulfield."

"Service?"

"I . . ." She glanced over her shoulder at the guests who even now were sending speculative glances in their direction. "I have a proposition for you."

Hellion stilled.

A pox on the chit.

Did she think she could use his secret to force him into marriage? She would not be the first woman to use such despicable methods to try and acquire him as a husband.

"You are mistaken, Miss Middleton," he stated in cold tones. "There is no proposition that a virgin could offer that would possibly interest me. I have no patience with *débutantes* or their tedious attentions."

"I am well aware of your preference for more sophisticated ladies," she retorted wryly. "Indeed, all of society is aware of your unfortunate . . . habits."

"Then what do you want?"

"The proposition I wish to offer you is one of a business nature."

Hellion did not believe her for a moment. What could this chit know of business? She must think him daft.

"Then once again I must disappoint you, Miss Middleton. My only business is pleasure," he drawled.

Something that might have been distaste rippled over the tiny countenance, but startlingly the features swiftly hardened with determination. "I am willing to offer you five thousand pounds."

Hellion gave a choked noise.

It was not often he was caught so completely off guard.

Five thousand pounds? It was a veritable fortune.

Certainly it would put an end to his most pressing creditors. And most importantly of all, allow him to avoid the painful necessity of turning to his uncle for charity. But even as the dazzling thoughts were spinning through his mind, his common sense was whispering that such a fortune never came without a price.

He folded his arms over his chest as he regarded the maiden with a brooding intensity. "Very well, Miss Middleton, you have my attention."

She did not appear overwhelmed by his capitulation. Instead she once again glanced over her shoulder. "Perhaps it would be best if we conducted our conversation in a place that is less crowded."

Hellion hesitated.

To be alone with a maiden could spell certain disaster. One scream and he would find himself hauled down the altar before he could bolt.

Still, he could not deny he was intrigued. If she

were another seeking to trap him into marriage, she was at least the most original. And he had no doubt he was far too wily to be caught. No matter how clever the trap.

"Your notion has merit," he agreed with a rather mocking smile. "One can never be certain when there might be a sly eavesdropper lurking about the shadows."

The blush returned, but her pointed chin tilted to a determined angle. "Yes."

"Then shall we repair to the gardens?" he suggested, holding out his arm.

She hesitated only a moment before lightly placing her fingers upon his sleeve.

Hellion deliberately glanced toward Biddles, who had all but disappeared into the shadows. With the slightest nod of his head the flamboyant dandy slipped through the crowd. He would be waiting in the garden to avert any unpleasant surprises.

In silence Hellion led his odd damsel toward the open balcony. He did not doubt his choice in companions would be the fodder for the gossips on the morrow. It did not trouble him unduly. He had been upon the tongues of the rattles for years.

Once on the balcony he continued down the curved staircase until they were at last in the relative privacy of the shadowed garden. Although Hellion had seen no hint of Biddles he possessed full faith he was nearby.

"Well, my dear." He drew to a halt turning to regard her in the faint wash of moonlight. "This is as private as we dare."

Her hand abruptly dropped from his arm and he heard the sound of her rasping breath.

So, she was not nearly so confident and self-assured as she liked to appear. The notion pleased him. He far preferred to be the one in command of any situation.

"Yes." Her hands briefly fluttered, as if she were not quite certain what to do with them before clasping them together at her waist. "I . . . did you know we have been introduced before this evening?"

Hellion lifted his brows in disbelief. Surely to heaven she had not lured him out here to chastise him for forgetting a previous introduction? Hell's teeth, he was introduced to an endless parade of *débutantes* every evening. Not even he was rake enough to recall them all.

"Then it appears I owe you an apology, Miss Middleton. My deepest regrets for my wretched memory."

Surprisingly her lips twitched with a wry humor. "I did not reveal our previous encounter to badger for an apology, Mr. Caulfield. I simply wished to reveal my dilemma."

"Dilemma?"

"You are not the first gentleman to have forgotten an introduction to me," she confessed in low tones. "To be brutally frank no gentleman recalls my name. Or if they do, they attempt their best to pretend as if they do not."

His brows rose. "Surely you must be mistaken?"

"Oh no, I am a practical woman, you see. I realize that I am old enough to be upon the shelf and that I have no claim to beauty. I suppose some might even consider me a fright. Even worse I have never developed the sort of silly charms that gentlemen seem to prefer. I do not giggle or flirt or pout. I am outspoken and prefer honesty to flirtation."

Hellion was arrested by her blunt honesty.

What other woman would so baldly claim her lack of charm? Especially to an unattached gentleman. She was either the most original maiden he had ever encountered, or she was unhinged.

His attention fully captured he regarded the strange, elfin face. For the first time he noted the full sweetness of her lips and the pure lines of her features. No, she would never be considered a beauty, but there was a measure of charm that would not be ravaged by time.

"I see."

"My hope was that my fortune would allow potential suitors to overlook my numerous faults. Even if the money does smell of the shop."

He gave a choked sound of disbelief. "You desire to be wed for your fortune?"

She shrugged, her straightforward gaze never wavering. "As I said, I am practical. Can you foresee any gentleman tumbling into love with me?"

Hellion bit back the charming denial that rose to his lips. This Miss Middleton was not just another twittering *débutante*. She would never accept the shallow lies that formed the usual conversations in society.

She was not a beauty. She was not lushly formed. Still, she was clearly intelligent and eccentric enough not to be a bore.

And there was that startling, sensual mouth . . .

A mouth that would no doubt bring endless pleasure to a gentleman with the patience to tutor her in the delights of passion.

"Who can say what the future might bring?" he at last hedged.

"I do not have the patience to await such an unlikely event." She abruptly stepped closer, her large eyes oddly luminescent in the moonlight. "I wish to be wed while I am still capable of producing children. That is why I requested to speak with you."

Unease prickled over his skin. There was an unmistakable expression of determination upon her countenance. She was a woman upon a mission. And at the moment he was standing directly in her path.

His eyes slowly narrowed. "You have decided to buy a husband and your thoughts turned to me?"

"Yes."

The dangerous fury threatened to return.

Had she thought of purchasing him simply because she had overheard his impulsive confession of being on the dun? Or did she presume every male must be for sale?

"I suppose that I should be flattered, Miss Middleton," he retorted in dark tones. "But to be frank I am not yet so desperate that I must put a price upon myself."

Her own brows drew together. "What?"

"I will not wed you, my dear. No matter what your fortune," he said in concise tones.

Without warning she gave a sudden laugh. Amazingly the gamine features seemed to light with a rather enchanting mischievousness.

"Oh no. I do not want to wed you, Mr. Caulfield."

"No?"

"Certainly not," she said firmly. "What I have in mind is a kind, comfortable husband who will be content at my estate in Surrey. One who shares my interest in business and hopefully will be a friend as well as a companion. I have no desire for a . . ."

"A what?"

"A rake," she said baldly.

Well.

That certainly put him nicely in his place. Hellion was not certain whether to be relieved or insulted. All he did know was that this bewildering creature increasingly intrigued him.

"It appears that I am being uncommonly dull-witted this evening, my dear. If you do not wish me as a husband then why did you seek me out?"

"Because I am a wallflower."

He blinked. Gads. Perhaps she was unhinged.

"A wallflower?"

"It is the term used for those unfortunate maidens who cannot hope to tempt a gentleman into asking her to dance or even to strike up a conversation."

"I am familiar with the term," he said dryly.

She drew in a deep breath. "Yes, well, since my arrival in London I have been relegated to dark corners and placed next to elderly gentlemen at dinner. Such a position makes it impossible for me to encounter the gentlemen who might desire to wed me."

Although vaguely familiar with the clutch of maidens who routinely lurked in the shadows of whatever room they entered, Hellion never gave them much thought. Of course, he rarely gave any proper woman much thought.

"Rather hard luck, but you will eventually discover a gentleman you desire."

"And how precisely am I to do that?" she demanded, her hands dropping so that they could ball in frustration at her sides. "There appears to be no more hideous fate than to be seen in the company of a wallflower. I am rather like the plague."

"The plague?"

"Avoided at all cost. I suppose they fear my unpopularity is contagious."

He choked on an unflattering laugh. "Surely you exaggerate?"

"I only wish that I did," she said in grim tones. "Thus far I have been approached by one rakehell who is so desperate for wealth he would wed the devil himself, and a gentleman old enough to be my grandfather. All other suitors pretend that I do not even exist."

Hellion studied the small, somber face. It was obvious that her adventure to London had proven to be a terrible disappointment. And yet, she had not given in to despair. There were no tears, no melancholy.

Only that unmistakable air of determination.

"And what service do you believe I can perform?"

"I wish you to strike up a flirtation with me."

"I beg your pardon?"

"It has not escaped my notice that you are the undoubted leader of society."

"An empty title I can readily assure you, my dear," he said dryly.

"Hardly empty," she argued, her tongue reaching out to wet her full bottom lip. The gesture revealed she was not utterly unaware of the unconventional nature of their conversation. And unexpectedly sent a tingle of sharp heat through his thighs. Damn. Why the devil was he suddenly imagining those lips pressing to his skin, teasing and skimming ever downward? It was startlingly erotic. "If you are seen to speak with a woman or offer her a dance she is swiftly surrounded by a bevy of gentlemen hoping to follow your lead."

Hellion abruptly cleared his throat. "I believe that you greatly overestimate my power."

"Not at all. Only last evening you were seen to take Miss Valstone to dinner and she was nearly mobbed when she returned to the dance floor."

Hellion was polite enough not to mention Miss Valstone was considerably prettier than poor Miss Middleton and a consummate flirt.

"Surely you do not believe that a flirtation with me will allow you to become the toast of the Season?" he questioned gently.

She smiled in a knowing manner, as if able to read the disbelief he attempted to disguise. "I am not a fool. I assure you my only hope is to leave the shadows long enough to discover a gentleman that I can respect enough to wed. My wealth must count as some inducement."

Somehow her calm assumption that her only charm was in her bank account brought a frown to Hellion's brow. "You would respect a gentleman who would wed you for your fortune?"

She lifted her hands in a dismissive manner. "Marriages based upon need rather than affection are not so uncommon. Indeed, my own mother came from an aristocratic family who had fallen upon difficult times. The marriage was proposed by my grandfather to restore their faltering estate even though my father was a merchant."

"Such marriages may not be uncommon, but I would hardly think it would be the desire of most maidens."

A reminiscent expression softened the tiny features and deepened the blue of her eyes. "Although it was not a love match my parents did develop a deep friendship that was unwavering until their death. In truth, I believe their respect for one another was far more vital and enduring than any passing fancy could have been. And quite necessary considering . . ."

His frown deepened. "Considering what?"

A brief silence descended at his abrupt question, as if she judged whether he was truly interested or simply being polite. At last she gave a faint shrug.

"You must know that being from such different social positions ensured that they were not accepted in either. My father was not welcome among the aristocracy, and my mother made those among the merchants uneasy. It was . . . awkward for us to say the least. Still, they were happy together. And that is what I desire."

Hellion slowly stiffened. Her words echoed far too close to his past. The isolation. The loneliness. The fear that there would never be a place in the world where he could truly belong.

Then he abruptly realized that unlike him, this woman had determined upon her path and was prepared to do whatever was necessary to achieve her goal.

A wholly unexpected pang of envy struck deep within Hellion.

It was absurd.

This poor chit had been a spectacular failure in society. She, herself, admitted that she was a wallflower. She was even forced into the ignoble position of purchasing her husband.

And yet . . .

And yet there was absolute courage in her bold scheme. She was not content to allow failure to steal her dream. Rather than scampering home in embarrassment, as most young women would have done, she simply had considered the matter and determined upon a daring path.

Could he claim such valor? Did he confront the troubles in his life with such admirable spirit? The very fact that he shied from even pondering the disturbing questions made him shift in unease.

Unaccustomed to being anything but utterly assured in the company of a woman, Hellion briefly allowed his gaze to sweep over the tidy, rigidly formal garden. He lingered just a moment upon the marble fountain that shimmered in the moonlight before at last drawing in a deep breath.

Only then did he return his attention to her watchful gaze.

"Miss Middleton, while I respect your very logical approach to marriage, I fear I cannot be a partner in your scheme."

Her expression gave nothing away as she continued to regard him with that unwavering gaze. "May I inquire why not?"

He gave a lift of his shoulder. "I have always made it a strict policy never to dally with *débutantes*. They are a complication I do not desire. If I am suddenly seen to be paying court then all of London will presume that I am chasing you for your fortune."

The blue eyes widened, as if considering his position for the first time. "Yes, I suppose that is true.

No one would be foolish enough to believe you consider me a desirable flirt."

A reluctant laugh was torn from Hellion. "You are very blunt."

A measure of amusement touched her dark countenance. "Yes, I suppose I am. Like you I prefer to avoid complications. Unfortunately, it is not a trait that is much admired in a female."

"No, I suppose it is not," he agreed, reluctantly accepting the ridiculous, unwelcome pang of sympathy for Miss Middleton. What would she do if he refused to help her? Return home? Or worse, approach another gentleman who might take unfair advantage of her obvious naiveté? "You are quite set upon this scheme, Miss Middleton?" he abruptly demanded before he could halt the words.

Her features hardened before she gave a firm nod of her head. "I wish to wed this Season, Mr. Caulfield. I do not believe I could endure another London Season. In truth, I would rather face the gallows. If that means offering you five thousand pounds to make me noticeable to eligible gentlemen, then so be it."

His full lips twisted. "You have no assurance that my meager attention will provide you the opportunity that you seek."

That smile that seemed to glow from her very heart abruptly returned. "Any investment is a gamble. I am willing to take the risk."

"You are a unique woman, Miss Middleton," he said softly.

"Then you will accept my proposition?"

Hellion paused.

He should tell her no.

It was not that he truly feared being labeled a fortune hunter. It had merely been a convenient excuse. After all, there was little shame in choosing a wife that would bring wealth to a family. It was, in fact, expected of many gentlemen, even if delicacy prevented mentioning such a boorish subject.

And heaven above knew he was in desperate need of the blunt. Still, he was far too cautious to take her words at face value.

A young virgin was always trouble.

Marriage trouble.

"I will consider it," he at last conceded.

"Thank you." She briefly laid her fingers upon his sleeve before offering a small curtsy. "I must return before I am missed."

With swift, rather inelegant motions she had turned to make her way back up the stairs to the balcony. Hellion's lips twitched as he watched her retreat. She moved like a stable boy, he acknowledged wryly. And yet . . .

For all her lack of grace and traditional beauty, there was something about her. A vibrancy of spirit. A purity of purpose. And a passion for life that an experienced gentleman knew would be echoed in the bedchamber.

Ah, yes. She would be no passive mouse to close her eyes and bear the touch of a man. She would be a willing recipient who would give as much as she would take.

"A most intriguing proposal." A voice drawled from behind him.

Turning about, Hellion regarded Biddles as he leaned negligently against the trellised arbor.

"You heard all?"

Biddles negligently removed a rose petal clinging to his shocking-pink coat. "But of course."

"And your thoughts?"

"Five thousand pounds could provide a certain measure of comfort."

"As long as Miss Middleton is to be trusted."

The long, pointed nose twitched. "You have reason to believe that she is lying?"

Hellion briefly glanced up to watch Miss Middleton disappear into the ballroom.

"Not at all, but after having been hunted by desperate maidens and marriage-mad mamas for the past ten years I have learned to err on the side of caution."

"Most wise," Biddles murmured, although there was a glimmer of amusement in the pale eyes.

"I would prefer to assure myself that Miss Middleton is precisely who she claims to be."

"Ah, and how do you propose to do that?"

Hellion folded his arms over his chest, a slow smile spreading across his face. "Oh, not me, my dear Biddles. You."

Biddles gave a vague blink. "Me?"

"If there is a secret to be discovered concerning Miss Middleton you are precisely the man to ferret it out."

Biddles lifted his hand to press his fingers to his chest in mock surprise. "Why, Hellion, I am wounded. What could a fribble like me discover?"

Hellion gave a short laugh. This man was the most devious spy England had ever produced.

"I have no doubt that you could discover the size of her slipper to her favorite color within the hour. What I wish to know, however, is if her fortune is as large as she claims, if she has any scandals in her past, and if she has confided in her friends a desire to have me as her husband."

"You believe this to be a trap?"

Hellion grimaced.

The problem was he did not know what he did believe.

Miss Middleton fell into no recognizable mold.

She was bold, intelligent, and clearly capable of taking command of her life. She also managed to strike a cord of sympathy within him that he was not at all certain he wished to acknowledge. It would be sheer folly not to take the proper precautions.

"It would not be the first trap I have encountered."

"Anything else?"

"Yes," Hellion retorted with sudden resolution. "I want a secret."

Biddles stilled, his nose twitching. "A secret?"

Hellion's smile twisted. "My friend, you should know me well enough by now to realize I never bet upon a hand without holding the winning card. I desire a means of controlling Miss Middleton should she prove to be untrustworthy."

Without warning Biddles threw back his head to laugh with delight. "What a devious mind you possess, Hellion. It is no wonder I am so terribly fond of you."

CHAPTER TWO

From the diary of Miss Jane Middleton, April 21st, 1814:

P.S. Dearest Diary,

I have come to the unmistakable conclusion that maidens possess an uncanny fascination for those gentlemen who are utterly unworthy of their regard.

If a man is considered as steady in nature with proper manners he is swiftly disdained as a stiff-rumped fellow. If he is studious or inclined to deep thought he is a bore. If he is shy or retiring he is insufferably dull.

But present a maiden with a gentleman who offers shallow charm to genuine regard, who prefers cards to her comfort and who is certain to break her heart, and she will flutter in anticipation.

It is a sad statement upon the depth of the female heart . . .

* * *

She would not swoon.

Firmly placing one foot before the other Jane Middleton made her way across the crowded ballroom to her familiar seat in a shadowed corner.

She was aware of the curious gazes that followed her deliberate progress and battled to keep her features unreadable. Of course, there was nothing she could do about her awkward blush, she acknowledged.

Or her shaking knees.

Or pounding heart.

Or ghastly fear she had just made a complete and utter ass of herself.

Without warning her lips twitched with her irrepressible humor. What if she had made a fool of herself? It would certainly not be the first occasion since her arrival in London.

In the past month she had tumbled from one disaster to another, including spilling punch upon doddy old Lord Crocker when he had pinched her backside, and nearly maiming Mr. Smith during her one and only waltz.

Her smile faltered as she edged toward the area unofficially set aside for the poor, misbegotten wallflowers.

Spilling punch upon a gentleman or trodding upon his toe could hardly be compared to offering a veritable fortune to a notorious rake for use of his skills at flirtation.

Finding her seat Jane abruptly sat down with a faint groan.

Dear heavens, what had she done?

Thankfully she had no opportunity to ponder the madness as a plump woman with a halo of golden curls and mischievous blue eyes slid into the seat beside her and slapped her arm with an ivory handled fan.

"Why you sly minx," she said with chiding tones.

Jane smiled with fond amusement. Miss Anna Halifax was her one and only friend in London.

Unlike the other gaggle of wallflowers, Anna made no effort to scorn the other maidens stuck in the dark corners, as if she were somehow above the indignity of being relegated to the fringe of society. Indeed, she accepted her dreaded fate with a wry humor that eased Jane's own frustration.

If not for Anna, she was quite certain she would have fled for the security of Surrey within days of her depressing arrival in London.

"Good evening, Anna."

"Do not good evening me," Anna warned, her pale face alight with curiosity. "I want to know precisely what you are up to."

Jane blinked in genuine bewilderment. "I haven't the least notion what you mean."

Anna gave an impatient click of her tongue. "Do not be coy, Jane Middleton. The entire room is whispering of your tryst with the delicious Hellion. I could just choke my aunt for dallying over her ridiculous turban and forcing me to miss the excitement. As if one turban is not as hideous as another. I demand that you tell me all."

Jane felt a blush rise to her cheeks. Never having been the object of gossip she had no notion just how swiftly it would sweep through a room. The realization was daunting and just a trifle unsettling.

She shifted upon the cushion of her seat, finding

it suddenly too hard for comfort. "There is nothing to tell."

The blue eyes framed by too pale lashes for true beauty abruptly narrowed. "On second thought I believe I shall choke you. Did you or did you not leave the room upon the arm of Mr. Caulfield?"

"Yes."

"Why?"

"What did you hear?" Jane deftly evaded.

"Oh, some silly nonsense that you tossed yourself at his feet and he was forced to remove you from the room to avoid an unpleasant scene."

It was precisely what Jane had expected. There could be no question of the rakish Hellion deliberately seeking her out and luring her from the ballroom.

The sky was more likely to topple to the earth.

Or pigs learn to waltz.

Her lips quivered with wry humor. It was all so typical of her predicament since arriving in town.

"I suppose it is not entirely nonsense," she reluctantly admitted.

Anna did not bother to hide her surprise. "What?"

"I did approach him and request to speak with him."

The surprise remained, but a wicked hint of amusement sparkled in the younger woman's eyes. "Jane, how deliciously naughty of you. I did not believe you possessed the audacity."

"Neither did I," she readily admitted, not about to reveal that it had been mere chance that had led to her impulsive decision.

If she had not been walking by that urn at that precise moment and overheard his stark confession of floundering in debt, the ludicrous notion would never have occurred to her.

Certainly it would never have come to mind that he could be tempted to provide her assistance.

His financial straights, however, was not a subject she would reveal to anyone. Not even her dearest friend.

"What did you say to him?" Anna demanded, clearly delighting in the brief stir of excitement in their undoubtedly dull routine.

Jane paused. She was unsure she wished anyone to know of her audacious stupidity. On the other hand, she was now familiar enough with Anna to realize she would not rest until she had learned the truth. The woman could be as tenacious as a bloodhound.

"This must remain between the two of us," she warned.

Anna abruptly grimaced. "And who would I tell? My aunt possesses the wits of a slug and you are my only friend. Of course, there is my endless flock of admirers, but . . ."

Jane gave a low chuckle. "Very well."

"Yes?" Anna obediently leaned forward, her round countenance set in expectant lines.

"I offered Mr. Caulfield a proposition."

A scandalized delight abruptly appeared in the blue eyes. "Why, Jane, you are naughty. Very, very naughty."

Jane once again shifted upon the cushion. Really, one would suppose that if she were to be condemned to the corner, a hostess could at least provide a decent seat.

"Not that sort of proposition," she retorted,

perhaps more sharply than she intended. "A business proposition."

A measure of the delight faded from Anna's face. "I knew that it was too good to be true. With you it is always business," Anna complained. She found Jane's fascination with handling her vast fortune incomprehensible. Jane on the other hand was never so happy as when she was contemplating a new investment. "What was the nature of this proposition? Coal mines? Silk? Spices?"

Jane clutched her fan and stiffened her spine. "I offered to pay him five thousand pounds if he would strike up a flirtation with me."

Silence.

For the first time since Jane had been introduced to the gregarious woman, Anna appeared struck dumb.

She opened her mouth once, then twice before she could at last find her voice. "What?"

Uncomfortably aware that she had managed to shock even this unshockable woman, Jane gave a restless shrug.

"Anna, I am weary of being stuffed into dark corners and treated as if I carry the pox," she said in unconsciously defensive tones. "I will never encounter a suitable husband unless I am allowed to mingle among the gentlemen. I had to do something. Even something desperate."

There was another pause as Anna considered her explanation. Slowly she gave a nod of her head.

"And what better means of being thrust into the center of attention than to be the current interest of the most notorious rake in London?" she said, a smile spreading across her countenance. "Brilliant, absolutely brilliant."

Jane did not feel brilliant.

Indeed, with every passing moment she felt more and more like a perfect dolt.

Again.

"I thought so at the time; now I begin to wonder if I have taken complete leave of my senses."

Anna waved aside her words. "Did he agree?"

"He promised to consider the notion."

Anna abruptly sat back in her seat, appearing nearly as bemused as Jane felt.

"Well, well. A flirtation with Hellion. What a perfectly marvelous notion." She aimlessly toyed with her fan, then suddenly sent Jane a twinkling glance. "What is he like?"

Unprepared for the question Jane discovered herself floundering.

What was he like?

Despite her skittering nerves, or perhaps because of them, she had been sharply aware of the man known as Hellion. Not just because of his masculine beauty, although that was certainly enough to steal the wits of any woman. In the moonlight his carved features had possessed an unearthly perfection and his hair had shimmered with silver satin. Even the dark eyes had taken on a sheen of mystery.

But it had been more that slumbering danger that enshrouded him that had made her pulse leap and her mouth dry. There was no sense of peace in that lean countenance and those haunting black eyes. Instead, a restless power crackled about him. As if he were frustrated deep within.

Suddenly aware that Anna's gaze had narrowed

in a speculative fashion at her hesitation, she gave a vague shrug.

"He is handsome and charming, of course."

"That much I already know," Anna pointed out in dry tones.

"Very well. He is surprisingly intelligent and less vain than I would have expected."

"And wickedly seductive?" Anna prompted.

A renegade tremor raced through Jane.

Even knowing he possessed no interest in her had not prevented her own traitorous awareness. Just being near him had sent a rash of electric sensation over her skin.

What would it be like if he had truly desired her?

If he had allowed those elegant, wicked hands to caress her? And he had kissed her with a hunger she could only dream of?

A dark, forbidding excitement bloomed deep within her.

One she was swift to crush.

Had he touched her, she would no doubt have melted to a puddle of gibbering insensibility, she acknowledged with self-derisive amusement.

"Oh yes, he is quite wickedly seductive."

Anna cocked her head to one side. "What are you not telling me?"

Jane heaved a small sigh. There was no means to hide anything from this perceptive woman.

"There is something . . . dangerous about him," she conceded.

"But naturally. Every successful rogue is delightfully dangerous. It is what stirs the female heart."

Jane gave a firm shake of her head. "Not just a

danger to a maiden's innocence, although I do not doubt that he is a master of seduction."

"You fear he might be of a violent nature?"

"No," Jane denied, not for a moment believing the man would harm a lady. "It is more a sense of a deeper restlessness. Beneath all his charm, I do not believe he is truly happy."

Anna gave a disbelieving snort of laughter. "How on earth could he not be happy? He is a gentleman endowed with wealth, position, and indecent power over society."

Jane discovered herself reluctant to share her odd awareness of Hellion's vulnerability. It seemed an intrusion of his private self that he kept hidden from the world.

"Perhaps it is merely my fancy," she said in determinedly light tones. "After all, we only spoke for a few moments."

Easily sensing her reluctance, Anna sent her a teasing smile. "Did he attempt to kiss you?"

Jane readily chuckled at the absurd question. "No. Despite the moonlight and beauty of the garden, he was not overcome with passion. Quite astonishing, is it not?"

"No doubt he is allergic to roses," Anna suggested.

"No doubt. And there was, of course, a faint hint of a breeze."

Anna nodded wisely. "Ah well, there is nothing worse than a breeze to cool a gentleman's ardor."

"Yes, indeed."

Opening her fan, Anna slowly waved it in a negligent fashion. An odd glimmer glowed in her eyes.

"My dearest Jane. I am quite proud of you, you know," she at last said in abrupt tones.

Jane was taken aback. "Proud?"

"You have rebelled in the most glorious fashion."

Strangely embarrassed, Jane gave an uneasy laugh. "You are mad. I have behaved with a shocking lack of propriety."

Anna leaned forward with a somber expression. "No, you have taken command of your situation. Society thrust you into the position of ridicule, but you refused to accept its harsh judgment. Instead you have boldly decided to use its absurd vanity to your own advantage. If Hellion acknowledges you as a worthy woman then all will rush to follow his lead, just as they rushed to condemn you with disdain. You are a champion for all wallflowers."

Anna had clearly become noddy, Jane decided as she regarded her friend in shock.

"Absurd. I am merely a woman desperate enough to attempt any foolishness. And I am still far from certain that he will agree to my request."

There was a faint stir across the room and Anna turned her head to regard the two gentlemen entering from the balcony.

"Ah, here comes the devil now. And Lord Bidwell."

Jane refused to allow her unruly gaze to cling to Hellion's elegant form. It was bad enough society presumed she had all but accosted the man. She would not also add insult to injury by gaping at him like a looby.

Instead she studied the slender man at his side.

"An odd gentleman," she murmured, noting the brilliant pink coat and burgundy pantaloons.

"Undoubtedly," Anna agreed in a distracted tone.

Returning her attention to the woman at her side, Jane was startled by the arrested fascination upon her countenance.

"What is it?" she demanded.

"What?"

"You are regarding Lord Bidwell in quite a queer manner."

Anna's gaze never wavered from the pointed, rather intriguing countenance. "Do you know, I suspect that Lord Bidwell is not quite the fribble that he would have others believe."

"Why do you say that?"

"More than once I have noted him hovering behind plants and furniture."

"Hovering?" Jane demanded with a lift of her brows.

"Well, he usually is pretending to adjust the buckle upon his shoe or even to have fallen asleep in a corner, but I am quite certain he was attempting to overhear the conversations of those close to him."

It seemed absurd.

Why would a lord of the realm behave in such a disreputable manner? (Jane conveniently forgot her own recent role as blatant eavesdropper.) Surely Anna must be mistaken.

Then she abruptly stiffened, a sense of dread clutching her stomach.

"Good heavens," she breathed.

With obvious reluctance Anna turned to regard her with a questioning gaze. "What is it?"

"Lord Bidwell was standing with Mr. Caulfield when I approached him. I was so nervous I paid him little heed."

"He manages very well to fade into obscurity when he wishes."

"Yes." Jane pressed her hands to her stomach. "And now he returns to the ballroom with Mr. Caulfield."

It took only a moment for Anna to follow her fearful reasoning. "You believe he might have been listening to your conversation?"

"It is possible." Jane gritted her teeth as she considered the horrid implications. "Blast it all. What if he tattles of my ridiculous scheme? I shall be utterly ruined."

Anna gave a slow shake of her head, her brow furrowed. "I think it far more likely that he will attempt to blackmail you. He is notoriously without a feather to fly with."

Jane gave a choked cough, not at all enamored at the notion of being held a virtual hostage by the nasty little rogue.

"Thank you, Anna, that is most reassuring."

As if realizing her words had hardly been a comfort, Anna abruptly reached out to pat Jane's arm in a comforting motion.

"Do not fear, Jane. I shall deal with Lord Bidwell."

"Really? And how will you accomplish such a feat?"

Anna took a moment to consider her various options before a slow, decidedly smug smile curved her lips.

"Clearly we shall have to be more clever than he is."

"Pardon me?"

"Do not concern yourself, Jane. I shall devise some scheme of keeping that inquisitive nose out of your business." Anna's sweet features abruptly hardened with resolution. Her eyes, however, shimmered with a strange glow. "I have always longed to pit my wits against another. This will be the perfect opportunity."

Jane was quite certain that she had never seen her friend quite so animated before.

"I think you must be deranged."

Anna gave a rueful chuckle. "No, just so wretchedly bored that I would willingly roll dice with the devil to relieve my tedium."

Against her will Jane's gaze turned to regard the golden-haired, black-eyed Hellion.

A shiver raced over her skin.

A premonition?

Or simple feminine lust?

Impossible to say.

"I believe that dicing with the devil is precisely what we are about to do."

Several hours later Hellion left the smoky card room and came to a sudden halt.

Across the thinning crowd he could see the slender form of Miss Middleton sitting in neglected isolation. There was nothing in her serene composure to indicate she was in any way miserable, not unless one studied the manner in which she tightly grasped her fan. Hellion, however, possessed the oddest sensation— he could physically feel her smoldering frustration.

A frustration that only deepened as a group of dandies swept past her seated form, never even noting her presence.

Hell's teeth. On how many occasions had he passed her by with the same blithe arrogance?

Perhaps two or three dozen occasions? His lips thinned as his heart was struck by a pang of guilt.

What was the matter with him?

He never took note of eligible maidens.

Oh, to be sure he occasionally asked one to dance or escorted her down to supper. He knew his duty to his hostess. But never could one claim he had sought her hand more than once, nor that he had made any indication he desired more than a passing acquaintance.

Still, he could not utterly deny a sense of discomfort at the sight of Miss Middleton forlornly watching the dancers glide across the floor.

Bloody hell. She was obviously worth a dozen of the giggling, prancing chits upon the dance floor. And to a gentleman who appreciated genuine warmth to shallow beauty, far more desirable.

His brooding gaze swept over the delicate profile, lingering upon the satin mouth before lowering to more closely survey the slender form. She would not do for a man who enjoyed the more lush curves, but his practiced imagination could easily judge just how perfectly the delicate breasts would fit into his hands.

"Ah, Hellion, I hope lady luck has been kind with you this evening?" Biddles drawled, appearing at his side with that unnerving silence.

Hellion swiftly smoothed his features, not about to reveal his uncharacteristic interest in an innocent chit.

"She was fickle as ever," he retorted. In truth he had won more than he had lost, but the difference would not have fed a mouse.

"A true lady," Biddles retorted with a faint smile.

Hellion shrugged. "I thought you had escaped to the comfort of your mistress."

A lacy handkerchief appeared in the thin fingers as Biddles dabbed at his nose. "A charming notion. Unfortunately I had to offer Barbette her *conge*."

"Indeed?"

"It was inevitable, I fear. She had decided to end her liaison with the French ambassador, you see."

"Gads, surely that is good news?"

"Good?" Biddles regarded him with chiding astonishment. Rather as if he were a dim-witted child. "What possible use can she be without providing the delectable means of knowing when the ambassador is properly occupied so that I can read his correspondence in peace?"

Hellion was shocked in spite of himself. "Good Lord, she tells you when she is to have a tryst with the man so that you can slip into his house and read his private papers?"

Biddles gave a bland smile. "It has been a most profitable arrangement."

Hellion could only admire his audacity. "Well, I suppose it is a pity that it has come to an end, but surely the woman possessed other attractions?"

"The usual." Biddles gave a negligent shrug. "I very much fear that I have reached the advanced age where I desire more than a body paid to be willing."

An echo of restless dissatisfaction threatened to race through Hellion. Dissatisfaction he was swift to smother.

No, damn it all. He enjoyed his beautiful courtesans. What gentleman of sense would not? They were beautiful, well trained in the arts of seduction, and best of all wise enough not to badger a gentleman when he was in need of peace.

If perhaps he discovered himself biting his tongue at their shallow chatter, or wishing that he could discover one mistress that he desired to share more with than a swift coupling, it was simply a reflection of his current troubles.

It had nothing at all to do with loneliness. Or the sense that he was constantly searching for something just beyond his reach.

"If you say," he forced himself to mutter in what he hoped were careless tones.

Perhaps not careless enough, as Biddles regarded him in a knowing manner. "You will discover soon enough."

Hellion narrowed his gaze in a silent warning. This was not a subject he was willing to discuss. "That I very much doubt, my good friend. So, you had no other delights to tempt you on this fine evening?"

The twinkle returned to the pale eyes. "Actually I had several, but I was rather rudely coerced into discovering information on Miss Middleton, if you will recall."

Hellion gave a startled lift of his brows. Not even he had expected such quick results. "You cannot have succeeded so swiftly?"

"Surely you did not doubt my skills?"

"Skills? You must be a sorcerer to have conjured information with such speed."

Biddles offered him an elaborate bow, his lace handkerchief fluttering in his fingers. "My talents are boundless, my good sir."

"They must be. What did you discover?"

"To begin with, I have firmly ensured that Miss Middleton is indeed a considerable heiress."

Hellion was not unduly surprised. A claim of fortune was all too easy to disprove. The fact his own straightened circumstances were not yet common knowledge was simply because no one had made the effort to discover the truth.

He winced at the horrid thought.

"How considerable?" he demanded.

"Rumors claim one hundred thousand pounds."

His heart nearly stopped. "Good Lord."

"There is also a tidy estate in Surrey that is unencumbered."

"An heiress, indeed," Hellion breathed.

It was a fortune far greater than even the one he had expected as the Earl of Falsdale. Far greater. It seemed impossible to believe that some young buck had not yet swept her off her feet. Could they all be so shallow?

Biddles gently cleared his throat, bringing an end to Hellion's brief distraction.

"As far as scandals I can discover none. To be honest, few others have paid enough heed to her arrival to spread any gossip."

"A typical wallflower," he said dryly.

"Yes."

"Have you encountered any of her friends?"

Biddles gave a regretful shake of his head. "She appears to have only one, a Miss Halifax, and she disappeared before I could approach her."

"A pity."

"I shall speak with her before the week is out."

Hellion folded his arms over his chest as he turned

his head to regard the solitary female form in the corner.

"Then all that remains is her dark secret," he murmured.

"I do not perform miracles, Hellion," Biddles protested. "Such information will take time to acquire."

"Not too much time," Hellion retorted in low tones.

"Then you are going to accept her proposition?"

A tingle that might have been anticipation raced through his body. He was uncertain when he had made his decision. Or even precisely why he was about to agree to the audacious proposal. All that he did know was that he could not turn his back upon Miss Middleton's plight.

A rather worrisome realization.

"How could I possibly refuse?" he muttered, his gaze remaining firmly fixed upon the woman who had managed to do what no other had ever done before.

Capture his jaded interest.

CHAPTER THREE

From the diary of Miss Jane Middleton, April 25th, 1814:

Dearest Diary,

It must be said that there is something utterly reassuring about numbers.

After all, life is such a muddled, unpredictable affair. It never seems to matter how well one plans a day or the future, there are always unexpected, unpleasant surprises. It can be as small as rain on a day one has scheduled to go riding, or the realization that the yellow gown one has ordered makes one appear rather like a summer squash. Then there are the horrid surprises, such as the realization that a promise made upon the grave of a beloved father is destined for failure.

Ah, but numbers . . .

They are precise. They never alter nor deceive.

Two plus two will always be four.

It is a truth that one can depend on. Today and forever.

A most reassuring notion.
Which is no doubt why it is far more enjoyable to
devote a day to balancing ledgers than mingling
among the masses.

The note arrived shortly after breakfast.

After devoting three days to convincing herself that it was decidedly best that Hellion had chosen to forget her proposition as the ravings of a lunatic, Jane discovered her heart halting in shock.

The note promised nothing more than that he would call upon her at three o'clock. Jane, however, was certain that he would not have chosen to actually seek her out unless he was considering her wild scheme.

It was a knowledge that sent her heart galloping and her palms perspiring.

She should send a message informing him that she had changed her mind. She should at the very least send the excuse that she was ill and unable to see him. That would give her the opportunity to ascertain she was not suffering some horrid brain fever that was causing her to act the buffoon.

But on each occasion she determined to put the gentleman off, she discovered herself wavering.

What did it matter that her decision to offer the daring proposition had been more an impulsive urge than a well-calculated scheme? Or that it had been utterly unlike her to take such a risk without considering all the numerous implications?

Did she have any option?

There was no avoiding the unpleasant truth she was failing miserably at her attempt to discover a suitable husband. Did it make more sense to devote the remainder of the season in dark corners, hoping some gentleman tripped over her feet or became so desperate he would force himself to take a wife he neither admired nor respected?

The thought sent icy shivers through her body.

She had made a promise. One that she could not abandon.

Sucking in a deep breath she allowed the memory of her father's broken frame as he was carried to the house form in her mind. He had been barely clinging to life, and yet his thoughts had been solely upon her. Grasping her hand he had choked out his fear at leaving her on her own. Tugging her close, he had whispered in her ear.

"My sweet child, for all my success and achievements, my greatest happiness has always come from having a wife who was my true partner and a daughter whom I love with all my heart. I have taught you all the skills to command your inheritance, but not to gain contentment. Fortune is meaningless. A family is the true treasure. Please, Jane, promise me that you will seek a husband who can be your companion. A man to share your laughter and tears. A man who can give you the children you deserve. I cannot bear to think of you alone. I cannot bear it . . ."

What could she have done but accept the pledge? She would have promised anything to ease his desperate fear.

Now she could only hope that there was one gentleman in all of London who could offer her at least a measure of friendship.

Seeking to ease her tangled nerves, Jane closeted herself in her large library. There was nothing more soothing than a few hours devoted to the vast investments she controlled.

What could be better than watching the progress of a once-abandoned coal mine as it was transformed into a profitable success? Or pouring over the information she was gathering upon a posting inn she was considering having built?

It was fascinating, exciting, and her one true passion in life. Let other maidens worry over the cut of their gown or the number of gentlemen who paid them respect. She would always prefer the blood-tingling pleasure of pitting her wits against fickle profit.

She was still busily scratching out a list of questions she intended to hand over to her business partner, Mr. Samuels, when the door to the study was pushed open.

Presuming that it was a servant to warn her Mr. Caulfield had arrived, or even her distant cousin, Mrs. Shelling, whom she had brought to London as her companion, Jane did not bother to glance up for a long moment.

It was only when a rash of prickles raced over her skin and the faintest hint of male cologne tantalized her nose that she abruptly lifted her head to discover Hellion leaning negligently against the doorjamb.

The quill dropped from her fingers as she rose awkwardly to her feet.

She had depended upon a few moments to compose herself after he had been announced, although she was not quite certain how she intended to accomplish such a feat.

Perhaps several large shots of brandy.

Or barricading herself in her chambers.

Now, however, she could do no more than force a stiff smile to her face and hope she did not appear as ruffled and ill at ease as she felt.

"Mr. Caulfield."

Thrusting himself away from the door he offered her a slight bow. "Good day, Miss Middleton. I trust you received my note?"

"Yes, yes of course. I commanded Reeves to have you shown to the front parlor."

His lips twitched as he strolled toward the large desk. "Ah, you must be referring to the starchy butler who greeted me at the door. In his defense he did attempt to lead me to the parlor, but I assured him that you would prefer that I join you here."

Attired in a charcoal coat and breeches and white waistcoat he appeared dangerously appealing. The early afternoon sunlight slanted through the window to shimmer in his golden hair and crisply outlined the elegant perfection of his features. And those eyes . . . they smoldered with a wicked temptation that could have made a saint swoon.

Her heart momentarily faltered. This was madness. What did she know of such worldly gentlemen? What did she know of any gentlemen?

A sudden impression of a hare blatantly toying with a smiling fox rose to her mind only to be swiftly banished.

No. She was no hare. And she had no need for intimate knowledge of gentlemen. This was a business arrangement. Nothing more. And she knew all there was to know about business.

"I see."

He halted beside the desk, then audaciously perched his elegant form upon the corner. A decidedly worrisome smile curved his lips.

"I realize it is rather unconventional to meet you without a proper chaperone but I presumed that you would prefer our conversation to be conducted in privacy. There is bound to be a measure of . . . intimacy in our discussion."

His charm was a potent, nearly tangible force. Tangible enough to send a warm flutter of awareness sweeping through her stomach.

Jane briefly wondered if it was so well rehearsed that he used it without thought or if there was a deliberate reason for his effort. Whichever it was she would be a fool to ever underestimate its power.

"You need not have concerned yourself with Sophia," she retorted in brisk tones. "She is quite incapable of hearing a word unless it is shouted directly in her ear."

"Ah." He lifted his shoulder in a careless fashion. "Still there is always the risk that we would be interrupted by one of your callers. I prefer to have you to myself."

She barely choked back a wry laugh. The only caller she had received since her arrival in London was Anna, and she had specifically warned the young woman that she would be occupied with Hellion on this afternoon. There was a greater opportunity that the French would invade than that her door knocker would be availed upon.

"A most unlikely occurrence, but I suppose we can be as comfortable here as anywhere. Would you care for refreshments?"

"No, I thank you." He watched as she gingerly

perched upon the edge of her leather chair, then, with a deliberate care, he glanced about the library. His brows rose slightly at the distinct masculine atmosphere of the leather furnishings and shelves that were filled from ceiling to floor with research books. The small tables upon the Oriental carpet were nearly hidden beneath the numerous newspapers and quarterly magazines that she scoured daily. On the window seat she had a pile of architectural drawings for her newest posting inn scheme. All in all it was a room that was well used and not at all for fashionable pursuits. "A handsome room, but an unlikely place to find a young woman on such a lovely afternoon."

Jane met the curious gaze squarely. She had determined when coming to London that she would not hide or apologize for her peculiar habits.

"I spend every day in this room," she stated in firm tones.

The dark gaze returned to her rather defensive countenance. "Every day?"

"My father left me a number of investments upon his death. It takes a great deal of effort to oversee them."

There was a momentary pause as he continued to study her with a piercing intensity. "You are in control of your father's inheritance?"

She smiled wryly at his barely hidden astonishment. At least he had not tumbled off the desk or recoiled in horror. After all, a woman who claimed a head for business was a decided oddity. Rather like a dancing bear.

"Of course I am. I assure you my father properly trained me to take over his position, although neither of us could have predicted I would need his training at such a young age."

"It is hardly the usual occupation of most young ladies," he murmured.

"So I have been told." She could not halt the faint tartness in her tone. "It is yet another reason I am considered a wallflower."

Rather surprisingly the expression upon the handsome features was more pensive than outraged. As if he found her occupation a mere curiosity.

"And yet you continue your work rather than handing it over to your man of business?"

She gave a startled blink at his abrupt question. It was not at all what she had expected. "I would never trust another with my fortune. Besides, I find such work a pleasure, not a burden. I far prefer an afternoon with my accounts than purchasing yet another gown I do not need."

"Strange, indeed."

Her lips abruptly thinned. He was not nearly so charming as she had thought. "I trust you did not come here simply to insult me?"

"Forgive me. I did not mean to be insulting. It is simply that I am far more accustomed to those who prefer to idle their days upon pleasure."

"Those such as you?" she demanded sharply.

He abruptly froze, as if she had unwittingly scored a hit. His lips twisted as he gave a mocking nod of his head.

"Such as me."

Feeling a ridiculous prick of guilt at having seemingly touched a wound, she squared her shoulders.

This was business. It was time she began regarding it as such.

"Perhaps we should turn our attention to the reason for your visit?"

"By all means." That heart-melting smile returned, although with an effort. "As you no doubt have surmised, I have decided to accept your proposition."

It was precisely what she had surmised. And what she had prepared herself for the entire day. So why was her breath abruptly caught in her throat and her heart flopping like a fish out of water?

"I see."

His eyes narrowed at her faint words. "Unless you have changed your mind?"

"No, no. Of course not."

"Good."

So this was it. She regarded him with a bemused gaze, unable to decide if she were thrilled or horrified by the realization that her scandalous proposition was being accepted.

Perhaps she was both.

"Yes, well I suppose you will desire your money. Would you prefer a bank draft taken to your home? Or I could have it delivered to your man of business if . . ."

"We can discuss such details later," he interrupted without warning, a faint hint of displeasure revealing his reluctance to consider the fact that he was taking money from a woman. Jane tucked the information in the back of her methodical mind. She would have to take care not to injure his male pride.

"Of course," she smoothly agreed.

His gaze slowly roamed over her countenance. "First I wish to discuss our upcoming charade. It is important that we both understand what to expect of one another. I suppose you wish to begin our flirtation at once?"

"I . . . yes." She busied her less-than-steady hands by searching for the piece of parchment she had been scribbling upon earlier. This was business, she silently reminded herself. Just business. And a good thing it was, a voice in the depths of her mind mocked back. She could not survive a real flirtation. Not with this dangerous man. "The sooner the better. In fact, I have already made a list."

"I beg your pardon? Did you say a list?"

"I fear it is a habit of mine. It is a very good means of keeping things tidy in my mind."

"I see." He made no effort to reach for the paper in her hands. Instead that wicked black gaze remained firmly upon her face. "And what is upon this list?"

"I have noted down the various invitations that I have received. As you might have suspected, my father's connection to the shop keeps me from being among the more exclusive entertainments, but there are still several to choose from. This way you will know where you may find me any given night."

"A wise notion, no doubt."

"I have also made notations next to those events that are more likely to attract eligible gentlemen."

"Of course."

Although there was nothing to be detected upon the deceptively angelic features, Jane was quite certain that he found a great deal of amusement in her methodical approach to their flirtation.

"I have also made a list of those things you might be expected to know of me," she grimly plodded onward.

"Ah. And what things would that include?"

"The names of my parents and grandparents, details of my home in Surrey . . ." Her words broke off as he gave a deep, rumbling laugh. Really, men were the most mysterious of creatures, she seethed as she glared into his lean countenance. "What is so amusing?"

That devilish, fascinating smile flashed at her spurt of annoyance. "Obviously you have not indulged in many flirtations."

"I thought that we had already established that fact. It is, indeed, the reason you are here," she retorted stiffly. "Why is that so humorous?"

He paused to allow his black gaze to roam freely over her tidy violet gown and plain features. "My dear, if I truly were conducting a flirtation with you, my very last interest would be in the names of your parents or details of your estate."

Ridiculously, a shiver raced through her at his husky words. They seemed to hold a wealth of meaning far beyond her understanding.

"Oh." She awkwardly set aside her list. "What would your interest be?"

He slowly stood, his gaze searing into her wide eyes. "Your favorite flower, your preference in perfume, if you desired to be kissed upon your neck or the soft curve of your breast."

Jane hurriedly placed her hands in her lap to hide their trembling. Kissed upon the neck? Her . . . breast? Did gentlemen do such things?

It sounded utterly decadent. And far too plea-surable for her poor, untutored heart to bear.

"Oh."

"I would know if your hair is as soft as satin and whether your lips taste of passion. I would know the feel of your skin better than yourself," he re-lentlessly continued, boldly stalking around the desk. Then, without warning, he abruptly swiveled her chair so that he could place his hands upon the padded arms, effectively trapping her. Her throat tightened as his beautiful countenance lowered until it nearly touched her own. Her heart tight-ened as his warm breath stroked her heated cheeks. She dared not consider what else was tightening as tingles of excitement raced through her blood. "And, of course, whether your curves were perfectly formed to fit beneath my body."

She abruptly sank back into the unrelenting leather. "I take your meaning, Mr. Caulfield," she breathed unsteadily.

Hellion pulled back to regard her with glittering eyes. "If you shrink from me in terror, Miss Mid-dleton, no one will believe we are conducting a flir-tation."

The fact that he was absolutely correct only in-creased her sense of discomfort. She was supposed to be considering this as a business deal. Not as a nervous virgin being exposed to her first taste of passion.

"You merely took me by surprise."

His brows lifted as he straightened and stepped from the chair. "Stand, Miss Middleton."

"Why?"

His expression was far too determined for her

liking. "There is no need in progressing any further if you cannot be depended upon to uphold your part of the charade."

Why the . . . toad! Uphold her side of the bargain? She had never failed at a business transaction yet. And she wasn't about to start now. No matter how dangerous her heart warned this gentleman might be.

"I will do well enough, sir."

"Oh?" he taunted softly. "Is that why you are cowering in that seat as if you fear I might ravish you at any moment?"

"I do not fear you."

"Then stand."

He had effectively challenged her pride. What else could she do?

"Very well." She reluctantly thrust herself to her feet, relieved when her less-than-stable knees held her upright. "Are you satisfied?"

"Not nearly," he murmured.

Keeping her gaze firmly ensnared, Hellion stepped forward to gently cup her face in his hands. He used no force but Jane was powerless to pull away as his fingers stroked slowly over her cheeks and down to trace the curve of her mouth. With an odd fascination his thumb brushed her lower lip over and over until his head at last lowered and his intention became clear.

He was going to kiss her.

The knowledge entered her foggy mind the same moment his mouth softly touched her own. Then there was no possibility of thought.

His lips were warm and shockingly possessive. Not demanding but rather compelling as they sweetly pressed and nibbled. With infinite patience he explored the taste and shape of her mouth, as if she were a rare treat that must be savored with infinite care. Then, lightly his tongue stroked until her lips instinctively parted in invitation.

An odd, intoxicating pleasure coursed through her blood, making her light-headed and as dizzy as if she had just consumed a fine bottle of champagne.

Oh, this was dangerous, she fuzzily acknowledged. Wickedly, delightfully dangerous.

Murmuring soft words of encouragement, Hellion stroked his lips over her heated cheek and down the length of her jaw. The dazzling sensations raced through her, distracting her from the fingers that determinedly stroked down the arch of her neck, and then audaciously lower to sweep over the curve of her breast.

She might not ever have noted those roaming fingers if a shocking jolt of desire had not clenched her stomach when he captured the tip of her nipple and gently rolled it to an aching peak.

That she could not help but note.

Abruptly wrenching away she regarded him with a wary gaze. "Mr. Caulfield, I would allow no man such liberties," she managed to retort in breathless tones.

He appeared perfectly composed as he regarded her flushed countenance. Perhaps those black eyes were a trifle darker, and his breath a tad shallow, but there was certainly none of the flustered bewilderment that she was experiencing.

Annoying man.

"No man?" He arched a golden brow. "Then I

suggest you forget your notion of acquiring a husband, my sweet."

"I . . . well, certainly I will do my duty once I am wed . . ."

"Duty?" He gave a low chuckle, a far-too-knowing expression upon his countenance. "Did it feel like duty when you were shivering and moaning beneath my touch?"

Jane abruptly stiffened. Had she shivered? Perhaps even moaned out her pleasure?

Dash it all. This was like no other business she had ever conducted. How was she to keep control of the situation when he was able to reduce her to a quivering half-wit with the slightest touch?

"Enough," she commanded as she sucked in a steadying breath. "I believe you are having sport with me."

"Not yet, but I assure you I would like to have sport with you," he murmured with a deliberate glance toward her disheveled neckline. "For such a tiny thing you are surprisingly delectable."

"You . . . Is this how you behave with all innocent maidens?"

His lips twisted with wry amusement at her accusation. "Of course not, but then I have never set up a flirtation with an innocent woman. If I did, however, I am certainly male enough to desire more than a chaste kiss upon your fingers. Much more."

She did not doubt that for a moment. There was a restless sensuality about him that was nearly tangible. A sensuality she could still taste upon her lips.

"This flirtation is pretense only," she reminded

him in stern tones. "There is no need to handle me in such an . . . intimate fashion."

He arched a brow at her stern reprimand, his gaze returning to her tingling lips. "Miss Middleton, whatever my faults, I am no easily duped school lad. I know when a woman is enjoying my touch and for a moment there you were more than delighted with my intimate handling," he softly mocked. "Indeed, I expect with a bit more coaxing you would have been pleading for more of my intimate handling. A charming notion, is it not?"

Her mouth dropped open at his audacious claim. "Mr. Caulfield . . ."

He abruptly held up a hand as he noted the angry flush upon her cheeks. "No, no, my dear. Let us not wrangle. I am simply attempting to ascertain that you will not swoon the first occasion I approach you in a crowd."

She gave a loud sniff. "Do not be absurd. I never swoon."

"There is also the undoubted fact that there is an unmistakable air of awareness between two people attracted to one another. It is in the glances they exchange and how they seek to touch one another whenever possible."

"I wish to be seen as an eligible lady, not a trollop," she informed him sourly.

He did not appear impressed by her logic. Instead he crossed his arms over his wide chest and offered her a flat stare.

"Let us get one thing straight from the beginning, Miss Middleton. You might be all that is clever when it comes to numbers and lists; however, you are a rank amateur when it comes to flirtations. I, on the other hand, am an expert, which I presume is the reason you chose to hire me."

"Yes, but . . ."

"Then allow me to know what is best when it comes to this proposition."

Her lips thinned. "You are very arrogant."

"And you are a managing shrew who will never discover a husband if you do not halt your habit of taking command of every situation," he retorted without apology. "No gentleman desires a wife who is determined to run roughshod over him."

Her mouth opened to slay him with her tongue when she grudgingly swallowed the hasty words. Although strong willed and blunt of speech, she was not so obstinate that she couldn't admit when she was in the wrong.

It was true that she did possess a forceful nature and habit of demanding that others bow to her will. It no doubt came from the fact that she had been thrust into her father's position at such a young age. The grim battle to maintain control over her destiny was not an easy one. And one that she fought almost daily.

She gave a restless shrug. "It is difficult for me. I am accustomed to being in command."

The elegant features abruptly softened at her reluctant concession. "Then perhaps it would be best for you to return to Surrey, my dear. No gentleman worth his salt will tolerate being led upon your leash."

She abruptly stiffened at his words. "No, I cannot."

His gaze narrowed at her sharp refusal. "Why? Is being wed truly so important? You have what most maidens only dream of possessing. Security, wealth, and an independence that is rare for a woman."

Jane grimaced. In truth she was for the most part quite content with her existence. What woman would not be? As Hellion had pointed out she possessed a rare freedom for a woman. Why would she desire to burden herself with a demanding husband?

The answer was quite simple. Deep in her heart she knew that her father had been right. She was alone. Desperately alone.

"I made a promise to my father upon his deathbed. And indeed, I find as I grow older I desire to have a family. My home in Surrey is an empty place without my parents."

There was a long pause as he considered the resigned determination etched upon her countenance before he gave a slow nod.

"I see."

"Do you still intend to help me?" she demanded.

"That depends." He stepped forward and placed his hand beneath her chin so that she could not avoid his glittering gaze. The faintest shiver raced through her at his warm touch. "Will you follow my lead? Will you allow me to decide how this flirtation is to proceed?"

Better prepared on this occasion Jane did not flinch from his touch. She could not, however, entirely control the beat of her unruly heart.

"Within reason."

The aquiline nose flared with irritation at her refusal to hand over complete control, then, without warning, he gave a sudden laugh.

"Blast it all, you are a stubborn wench."

She offered him a wry glance. "No, just wise enough not to give free rein to a notorious rake."

A disturbing heat sparked to life in the devilish eyes. "My dear, surely you do not believe your virtue is in jeopardy?"

Her breath threatened to disappear entirely as a prickling awareness filled the air. "I believe you are a very, very dangerous gentleman."

He smiled, slowly and wickedly, as his fingers moved to stroke the unsteady line of her mouth.

"And you, my sweet, possess curves that were meant to fit into a gentleman's hands and lips that might very well drive me mad."

It had been a simple matter to slip into the elegant town house.

Far too simple, Biddles acknowledged with a faint sigh as he busily rooted through the various correspondences that had been left in a drawer of a satinwood table. Since his return to London from the Continent his various skills had become sadly rusty.

And he had become wretchedly bored.

What the devil was the fun in attending social events to overhear the tedious conversations of French immigrants? Or even the handful of diplomats that had flocked to town? What was the pleasure in shadowing the occasional Napoleon sympathizers who did not possess the wits to keep their mouths shut when they were in their cups?

Even the few coded messages he had intercepted and then altered to confuse the enemy had been child's play.

He desired a challenge. Something that would

demand a true test to his undoubted intellect. Something that would put an end to his jaded apathy.

With another sigh Biddles glanced through a stack of letters that Miss Middleton had tidily stored in the desk. At least Hellion had provided some measure of distraction. Although it did not seem likely that the staunchly prim maiden would possess a dark, hidden secret, there was always the faint hope. He was all too aware that some of the most respectable members of society possessed shocking habits.

Some that shocked even him.

Discovering a packet that had been pushed to the very back of the drawer, Biddles removed it with a faint flare of hope. The heavy vellum was different from the routine letters from acquaintances in Surrey and the invitations to various events. Perhaps this would offer a measure of interest.

Glancing covertly about the peach and ivory room, Biddles nearly missed the soft tread of approaching footsteps. Someone was slipping toward the drawing room and taking great care not to be heard.

With swift motions he tucked the packet beneath his brilliant emerald jacket, but there was no time to close the drawer to the table before a young woman whisked into the room.

Biddles easily recognized the plump, rather pretty friend of Miss Middleton from the ball. His momentary unease faded. Just another frivolous maiden, he assured himself. Certainly no danger to his current scheme.

Then, rather astonishingly Biddles watched as

her pale eyes carefully scrutinized the entire room, swiftly detecting the open drawer and his proximity to the table. There was even a hint of shrewd perception that glittered in that searching gaze.

"Why, Lord Bidwell, whatever are you doing here?" she demanded as she moved to stand directly before him.

Smoothly slipping into his role of a twittering dandy, Biddles offered an elegant bow. "Ah, Miss . . . Halifax, is it not?"

She did not appear remarkably charmed. "Yes."

"A most delicious surprise." He reached out to boldly claim her hand and lift it to his lips. The practiced motion allowed him a full view of her low bodice and the stunningly provocative fullness of her ripe curves. He felt an unexpected jolt of awareness. "I cannot tell you how often I have longed for our paths to cross."

Expecting the fluttering confusion of most untried maidens, Biddles was surprised when she regarded him with a bland smile. "Is that so?"

"Can you doubt me?"

"Oddly enough, I recall our paths crossing on numerous occasions, my lord. Could it be that you simply did not notice?"

Biddles gave a choked cough. Perhaps he had underestimated this woman. A rare occurrence, indeed.

"I would never be such a cad as not to notice a lovely young woman," he smoothly countered. "Although I must admit that I had not until this moment noticed just how astonishingly lovely a woman you are. My dear, you quite take my breath away."

Her brows slowly lifted. "Your breath? Why, sir, I do believe that you must be attempting to flatter me."

Biddles discovered his gaze lowering to those soft, mouthwatering curves. "Not at all, I assure you. Rarely have I beheld such temptation."

"Flattery, indeed." Her smile hardened as she abruptly turned to regard the open drawer. "Were you searching for something in particular, Lord Bidwell?"

Biddles stiffened, the end of his pointed nose twitching as his gaze flicked back to her wide eyes. Well, well. There was definitely more to this chit than most.

He found himself regarding her with a decided interest.

"I merely seek paper and quill to leave a note for Miss Middleton. It appears she is occupied at the moment and unfortunately I must leave for an appointment."

"A pity," she murmured, clearly not believing his clever explanation for a moment. "Was it anything of importance you wished to discuss with Miss Middleton?"

"No, no. A trifling matter."

"Perhaps I could give her a message?"

He slowly smiled, acknowledging her swift wits. "Just that I hope to see her at Lady Lanberger's this evening. And you as well, my dear."

Her brows arched. "And that is why you called?"

"It is surely as good a reason as any other?"

"If you say," she grudgingly conceded.

"I do, indeed." He offered another, slightly deeper bow. "Now I really must be on my way. A gentleman's day is so wretchedly filled with appointments and whatnots. I am sure you will understand my haste. Until tonight."

Not waiting for her response he slipped from the room, then cautiously moved toward the back of the hall. He could not exit through the front door without explaining to the startled butler how he managed to enter in the first place. Besides, he possessed a rather fond preference for stealing through back doors.

He did pause, however, as he reached the servants' chambers.

Miss Halifax.

Hmm. He might just have to keep an eye on that one. She was far more wily than most, and clearly suspicious of his arrival at Miss Middleton's. It would never do to have her interfering.

Besides which, if he were perfectly honest with himself, she had intrigued him. Upon more levels than one. An unwitting smile curved his lips.

Suddenly his life did not seem quite so dull.

CHAPTER FOUR

From the diary of Miss Jane Middleton, April 26th, 1814:

Dearest Diary,

Obsession with fashion among society has always struck me as being vastly absurd.

We condemn the notion of torture for even our most dangerous prisoners, and yet we willingly, nay gladly, subject ourselves to endless pain and discomfort in the name of beauty.

Gentlemen poke and stuff themselves into whalebone corsets that squeeze their innards and turn their countenances purple. They pad and stuff the coats that are always distressingly tight. Then, as a crowning glory, they waste the better part of the day in tying the perfect cravat that is destined to droop within moments of entering a crowded ball.

Women, of course, are even more foolish.

Not only do we devote more hours a day to changing our gowns than to actually wearing them, we need allow our evil maids to inflict bodily damage as they wrench unruly curls into obedience. As if that is not enough, we cannot seek our beds at night without smearing our faces with some vile concoction that promises smoother skin, fewer freckles, and a maidenly glow.

To think what could be accomplished if society devoted as much thought and effort to the betterment of England . . .

Well, perhaps not.

Considering the distressing lack of true intelligence among society it is perhaps best that they remain entertained with such frivolous pursuits. The betterment of England should not be left to someone who believes that all of life must halt until he achieves the perfect gloss upon his boots.

"Ah, Hellion. I presume that tonight is the night?"

Reluctantly wrenching his gaze from the door where he was watching for the arrival of Miss Middleton, Hellion offered his friend a distracted grimace.

"I would hardly have made an appearance at this tedious musicale if it were not."

Biddles cast an amused glance toward the clutch of *débutantes* nervously pacing at the front of the narrow salon. It was well known among society that only condemned family members, desperate mushrooms, and those unfortunate enough to discover themselves without any other invitations attended such musicales.

"The arias will no doubt sound sweeter with the knowledge they are bringing you a tidy fortune," he murmured.

"Perhaps not sweeter, but at least tolerable. Have you seen Miss Middleton?"

"So anxious, my friend?" Biddles demanded with a hint of amusement.

In truth, Hellion discovered that he was indeed anxious to begin this strange flirtation. A most peculiar realization.

Well, perhaps not so peculiar, he acknowledged as an unwitting smile curved his lips. During his last encounter with Miss Middleton he had been more than pleasantly surprised to discover that she was just as intriguing as he had initially suspected.

Not only was she intelligent, but also she was bold in nature and quite capable of facing the world without the slightest fear. There was nothing clinging or weak about this woman. And yet, there was a rather charming vulnerability beneath her brisk air of efficiency.

And there was that kiss . . .

Whoever would have thought that a gentleman of his vast experience would be so completely caught off guard?

But he had been.

The kiss had been intended to teach the stubborn chit that he would not be treated as her salaried toady. He did not pander or fawn to anyone. Not even for the undoubted fortune that she offered.

Perhaps it was not truly honorable to use his skill at seduction to bedazzle the poor woman, but at the time he had been at the end of his patience. She would swiftly learn that he would not be bullied. Either he would be allowed to be in command of this flirtation or he would walk away.

Unfortunately she had neatly turned the tables upon him.

During that brief kiss that had been meant to place her under his spell of enchantment, he had stirred to life a most potent desire within himself. Her lips had been warm and so sweetly innocent. And her body had fitted with exquisite perfection against his own. Even now he could vividly recall the feel of those soft breasts and her fresh, clean scent that had reminded him of spring.

He gave a wry shake of his head.

A surprising woman, indeed.

Still, he was not about to admit as much to his friend, who was even now regarding him with a sly smile. It had been unnerving enough to feel sympathy for Miss Middleton. Now to realize he also felt desire was something he intended to keep well hidden.

The ruthless gentleman would make his life intolerable.

"The sooner this begins, the sooner it will come to an end," he retorted in an offhand manner, wincing at the sudden screech of a violin. "And the sooner I can return to tossing invitations to musicales into the rubbish bin where they belong."

"Yes." That sly smile remained. "There is no doubt that it will be rather a trial upon you for the next few weeks. I do hope that your nerves can bear the strain."

"A trial?"

"Well, you will be forced to endure the more tame social entertainments that are proper for a *débutante*, and of course, make the occasional effort to drive her through the park or call upon her at home."

Hellion gave an indifferent shrug. "I am prepared to make the necessary sacrifices."

Biddles lifted a lace handkerchief to dab at the point of his nose. "And then there will be all the tedious gossip that will haunt you. There are far too many gentlemen envious of your popularity, and vindictive females who did not manage to capture your elusive attention, not to stir rumors that you are so desperate for a fortune you must pursue a mousy chit who still smells of the country."

Hellion's lips tightened at the unflattering description of Miss Middleton. He felt an unaccountable urge to give his friend a sharp shake.

"I thought you approved of my accepting Miss Middleton's proposal?" he said instead.

"But of course I do," Biddles protested. "I simply desired you to be prepared for what is certainly to come."

"You of all people should know that I have yet to concern myself with what others say about me."

"True enough," the smaller gentleman conceded. "Do you have any further warnings?"

"Ah well, there is always the tedium of making conversation with a giddy, giggling *débutante*."

Hellion couldn't prevent his sudden laugh. Obviously Biddles had never spent any time in the company of this particular *débutante*.

"I can assure you that Miss Middleton is neither giddy nor does she giggle. In truth she is distressingly sensible."

"A sensible female?" The pale eyes glittered with humor. "Surely you jest?"

"It does seem unlikely, but she is not at all the usual female." Hellion smiled wryly. "Did you know she is in control of her fortune and personally handles her father's investments?"

Biddles mused over the words for a long moment. "How terribly odd. Who would have thought such a thing from a mere mouse?"

"Mouse?" Hellion lifted his brows in mocking amusement. "She is a shrew with the tongue of a rapier and a habit of expecting others to pander to her will."

"Egads." Biddles shuddered with horror. "That is worse than a giggling maiden."

"Actually, she is not so difficult to manage once you properly instruct her as to who is in command," Hellion countered, his expression unconsciously softening with recollections of his delicious instructions.

"Indeed?" Biddles narrowed his gaze. "And what was the precise nature of these instructions?"

"Ah, now that is a matter I am not prepared to discuss with even you, my dear friend."

Biddles chuckled but there was a hint of warning in his expression. "Just ensure your instructions do not land you in the nearest church, Hellion."

Oddly Hellion did not even flinch at the warning. "I have full faith that you will keep such a hideous prospect from occurring."

"Do not be so smug in my abilities, Hellion. Thus far I have discovered nothing of value."

Something in his tone had Hellion raising his brows in surprise. "But you have discovered something?"

"Just some rather obscure contracts that I wish to pursue."

"Contracts?"

Biddles shrugged. "It is all I possess at the moment."

On the point of discovering more of these seemingly mysterious contracts, Hellion was halted as he felt a peculiar tingle arrow down his spine. He knew before he ever turned that Miss Middleton had entered the room.

Slowly shifting so he could view the door, he watched as she entered with a younger woman and a turbaned matron. A rueful smile curved his lips as he noted the plain blue gown and how her hair had been hastily knotted at the back of her head. Clearly Jane Middleton had not devoted her hours to dazzling him with her beauty, he acknowledged. He would wager his last quid that she had waited until the last moment to pull on a gown and dash from the house.

The realization should perhaps have been annoying. Without undue arrogance he was well aware that many women dedicated hours to their appearance in the mere hope of capturing his roaming gaze. He was, after all, Hellion.

But rather than being irritated, he discovered his smile widening at her disregard for his opinion. She challenged him in a manner he had never before experienced.

Hearing a faint chuckle at his side, Hellion reluctantly turned to discover Biddles regarding him in open amusement.

"What is so humorous?" he demanded.

"Merely that you are quite convincing in your role as a prospective suitor. I have never seen you so . . . eager."

For the first time in a decade Hellion was forced to battle an urge to blush.

"Five thousand pounds can make any gentleman eager," he retorted with a defensive stiffness.

"As you say." The amusement remained annoyingly intact. "Shall we join her?"

"We?" Hellion frowned. He might dearly enjoy the company of Biddles, but not when he possessed an opportunity to secure a moment alone with Miss Middleton. "I do not need you to hold my hand. I am quite capable of conducting a flirtation without your assistance."

Biddles gave a derisive sniff. "As appealing as the notion of holding your hand might be, dear Hellion, I was thinking more in terms of charming Miss Halifax. I have reason to believe that she harbors a suspicion of my intentions toward Miss Middleton."

Hellion chuckled at the hint of pique in his friend's voice. "Biddles, anyone of sense harbors suspicion of you."

"Very amusing," he retorted dryly. "I fear her wariness may prove to be a hindrance to my investigations."

"Ah. And you hope to charm her suspicions away?"

Biddles made a wretched attempt to appear humble. "Well, it is one of my finer talents."

"Along with modesty," Hellion mocked. "Let us go."

Not bothering to wait for his preening friend, Hellion moved with purposeful steps toward the woman who had settled in the shadows of a corner.

More than one hand reached out to attempt to detain him but he easily shrugged them aside, his gaze never wavering from that dusky, elfin countenance. He was almost at her side before she at last sensed his approach and turned to regard him with wide eyes.

With his most potent smile Hellion reached to bring her fingers lightly to his lips. "Miss Middleton."

He convinced himself that a telling shiver raced through her at his touch, but there was nothing to detect upon her tranquil countenance.

"Mr. Caulfield, what a delightful surprise," she murmured.

"A delight, indeed." He stepped closer than precisely proper. Instinctively his blood heated at the warm, spring scent of her. "I had begun to give up hope you would make an appearance."

With a tiny tug she freed her fingers from his grasp. "I fear I became involved with negotiations for a plot of land and was quite late in returning home."

He arched his brows in genuine surprise. "You left me waiting while you haggled for a parcel of land?"

That smile that illuminated her entire face abruptly appeared. "It was a very important parcel of land."

"Shrew," he chided, although he could not prevent his own lips from twitching. This woman appeared to be an expert in deflating a gentleman's pride. Thankfully he possessed more than his fair share of arrogance. His gaze swept over the tiny features, easily noting the strain she was battling to hide. "You seem tense. Is anything the matter?"

She gave a grimace, her gaze covertly shifting toward the gawking crowd across the room.

"Everyone is staring at us."

His brows lifted. "Surely that is what you desired?"

"Yes, of course. It is just . . ."

"What?"

She gave a restless shrug. "I suppose I have been relegated to dark corners for so long that I find it unnerving to be the subject of such unwavering interest."

"You will soon become accustomed," he assured her, regaining command of her hand so that he could lay it firmly upon his arm. "Shall we take a turn about the room?"

There was a momentary pause before she was sucking in a deep breath. "Very well."

In silence they moved from the shadows and strolled at the fringe of the room. Even Hellion was aware of the shocked gazes that followed their movements and the sudden twitter of disbelief that fluttered through the air. His attention, however, remained firmly upon the stiffly held form at his side.

"Miss Middleton," he murmured softly.

With obvious reluctance she lifted her gaze to meet his own. "Yes?"

"We are not marching into battle. A stroll should be a slow, elegant affair, not a mad dash."

"Oh." She awkwardly slowed her headlong rush. "Sorry."

"And I do wish you would smile," he continued, lowering his head so that he could speak directly into her ear. "My attentions are supposed to bring you delight. At the moment the guests could be forgiven for believing that I have given you a sour stomach."

She gave his arm a sharp pinch. "There is no need to be rude."

He abruptly covered her hand with his own, giving her fingers a retaliatory squeeze. The shrew would have him black and blue if he were not careful.

"Smile, Miss Middleton," he commanded.

Pulling back she offered him a wide, patently false smile. "There. Are you satisfied?"

"Now you appear foxed. Or daft."

"Why you . . ." The eyes more gray than blue at the moment flashed with a dangerous fire before she unexpectedly gave a reluctant chuckle. "Mr. Caulfield, you really are the most aggravating of gentlemen."

"The most?" He offered her a teasing smile. "Well, I suppose I should take pride in excelling at something." He paused, considering how best to ease her lingering nervousness. "Tell me of this parcel of land you desire."

She regarded him in startled surprise. "You cannot be interested?"

He shrugged, wondering if he should be offended by her obvious belief he had no interest beyond the frivolous. Of course, she would not be far wrong, he ruefully concluded. Thus far he had done precious little to improve his mind, or his fortunes.

"We must talk of something," he retorted, his eyes abruptly darkening. "Unless you would rather that I gaze at you in silence like a moonstruck looby?"

She gave a predictable shudder. "Good heavens, no."

"Then tell me."

"Very well. I am considering constructing a posting inn."

He gave a choked noise. "You?"

Her smile was wry at his obvious dismay. "Well, I do not intend to cut the stones or lay the planking myself. I only intend to provide the financing."

Alertly steering past the clutch of matrons regarding them with near trembling curiosity, Hellion forced himself to shove aside his natural prejudices. This woman had already proven that she was well out of the usual mold.

"Do you know anything of owning a posting inn?"

"I have done a great deal of research, but more importantly I have hired those who have actual experience." Her expression became reminiscent. "My father taught me to pay for the best and then to stay out of their way so that they can do their job properly."

Hellion discovered himself intrigued despite himself. He had always considered the business of trade rather sordid and fit only for those who possessed few ethics. He was a gentleman, after all.

But the sheer passion that Miss Middleton devoted to her work was irresistible. How would it be to care so deeply for something in his life? To be able to lose himself completely?

"So you provide the capital and then step aside?" he demanded. "That does not seem like my managing Miss Middleton."

She cast him a wry glance at his accurate guess. "Not precisely. First I must make a detailed budget of what I predict might be the potential revenue of any investment I might decide upon. Then I determine the various costs from the initial investment to the daily cost of keeping the enterprise in operation. There are also the unexpected expenditures, such as repairs, accidents, and thefts. Once I have calculated the profit I must ensure that it is greater than my investment. There is little use in tossing money into a losing enterprise."

"Gads, you make my head ache," he protested with a startled laugh. "Surely you cannot enjoy such tedious tasks?"

She flashed him that enchanting smile. "It is far preferable to spending my days shredding the reputations of others or being tortured by my dressmaker."

He deliberately drew her to a halt in the shadows of a nearby alcove. His hand lightly teased over the fingers upon his arm.

"There are other entertainments to delight a young woman," he protested in smoky tones.

Her eyes swiftly narrowed in suspicion. "What sort of entertainments?"

"If you enjoy art I can always procure a private viewing of the Duke of Northumberland's collection. Or we could visit the British Museum," he retorted with mock innocence.

"Perhaps."

"There are also the Tower and Westminster Abbey to visit. In the evenings we can attend the theatre and Vauxhall. Oh, and of course, Astley's. That is not even to mention the endless celebrations that are being planned since the abdication of the Corsican Monster."

She grimaced at his light words, not appearing at all impressed with the thought of being escorted about town on his arm.

"Now you are making my head ache. I should be exhausted by such a hectic schedule."

He allowed his gaze to openly roam over her up-turned countenance and down to the modest neckline of her gown. It took very little effort to recall the feel of her nipples as they had hardened against his thumbs. Suddenly his skin felt flushed with a disturbing warmth. He wanted to tug her through the nearby door and find a place of privacy. He wanted those lips eagerly exploring him and stirring his passions to raging life. He wanted to press her close to his body and allow his muscles to harden with pleasure.

Instead all he could do was move close enough to breathe deeply of her sweet scent.

"Ah, you prefer more relaxing entertainments?" he whispered in roughened tones. "Good. So do I. The mere thought of further exploring the taste of your lips holds infinitely greater appeal than a tedious night at the theatre."

A delightful blush crept beneath her cheeks. "Sir."

He gave a low chuckle, not missing the frantic pulse that beat at the base of her throat. She was not indifferent to him. No matter how she might wish to hide the truth.

"Now, my dear, you appear like a woman who is being properly flirted with. Your cheeks are flushed and your eyes are sparkling with maidenly confusion."

"It is annoyance, Mr. Caulfield," she crisply retorted.

"Not entirely annoyance, I think. I have not forgotten those sweet moans when I kissed you."

She hardened her features as she took a deliberate step backward. "I believe you enjoy taunting me."

His own smile faded at her sharp words. "There is a difference between taunting and teasing, my sweet," he informed her firmly. "I do not mock your innocence, or the delightful discovery that you are not indifferent to my touch. It shall make our time together considerably more pleasant."

Her expression remained wary. "More pleasant for whom?"

His blood threatened to boil as he considered all the various means of pleasing this woman. There were many, many means, all of them delicious.

And why should he not, a renegade voice whispered in the back of his mind? He would have to take care, of course. He would not forget that she was an innocent woman. A rather rare species for a man such as himself. But there were any number of ways to conduct a seduction without actually taking her virginity.

It would be his pleasure to teach her the delights of passion.

"For the both of us," he swore in low tones. "That I promise."

Anna hid her smile as Lord Bidwell minced beside her on their way to the refreshment table. His red coat and yellow waistcoat were perfectly suited to ensure his image of frivolous stupidity, and as the crowning glory he had produced a Chinese painted fan to slowly waft before his pointed nose.

For most people it would be easy to dismiss him as a twit. What gentleman of sense would ever prance about in such a fashion?

But Anna was far too perceptive to miss the shrewd intelligence in the pale eyes and the restless energy that flowed through his slender form.

He would make a dangerous adversary, she acknowledged with a tiny thrill of excitement. And a true test of her wits.

Waiting until they were well away from Anna's foolish aunt, Lord Bidwell at last turned to regard her with a vacant smile.

"Tell me, my dear, have you known Miss Middleton for long?"

Anna assumed the rather foolish expression of most *débutantes*. "Oh no. We only met when she arrived in London for the Season."

He fluttered the fan in a nonchalant motion. "You seem to be very close for such a short acquaintance."

"Do we?"

"Yes, indeed." He slanted her a sidelong glance. "Such a charming young lady."

"Very charming."

"And quite talented," he gamely persisted despite her seeming stupidity. "I understand she possesses a most remarkable head for business."

Anna batted her lashes. "Why Lord Bidwell, are you interested in learning the mysterious arts of trade?"

The pale eyes twinkled, as if sensing her deliberately vague responses. "Egads, no. What would a frippery fellow like me do with such knowledge? I far prefer to concentrate upon important matters."

"Important matters? What sort of important matters?"

"The buckles of my slippers and the delightful new walking stick I am having commissioned. For a gentleman it cannot be stressed enough how vital a dashing walking stick is to his ensemble."

"Of course." Deciding it was time to rattle the clever little sneak with a dose of his own medicine, Anna came to a sudden halt. "Oh, look. It is Monsieur LaSalle."

There was only the faintest of stiffness in the slender gentleman as he came to a standstill beside her.

"So it is. Are you acquainted with the gentleman?"

"No, but I have noted you always take a great interest in him."

"Me?" The fan was abruptly snapped shut. "How absurd. I do my best to avoid the horde of French immigrants who have invaded London. They are so very provincial, you know."

She met his mocking gaze squarely. She desired this gentleman to realize that she would not simply step aside and allow her friend to be injured.

"Then you did not meet with him in the library during Lady Hulford's ball and then again in the garden after Mrs. Wallace's *soirée*?"

There was a long shocked silence before Lord Bidwell narrowed his gaze in a dangerous manner.

"Have you been spying upon me, Miss Halifax?"

"I am merely observant, Lord Bidwell." Anna tilted her chin, blatantly revealing a decided lack of fear at his subtle warning. "And quite devoted to Miss Middleton. I would not take kindly to any threat to her happiness."

An emotion that was impossible to define rippled over the narrow face. Not anger, thankfully. Perhaps a measure of surprise. And even a hint of challenge.

Then quite unexpectedly a genuine smile curved his lips. "I see."

"I hope that you do," Anna retorted, a frown tugging at her brows. There was something rather disturbing about that smile. Almost predatory. "Now if you will excuse me, I must procure some champagne for my aunt."

"But of course." Lord Bidwell performed a flourishing bow as he raised her fingers to his lips. "I concede this skirmish to you, my dear. However, I shall be better prepared on the occasion of our next delicious battle. Until then."

Anna forced herself to turn and walk away at a dignified pace. Her heart, however, was pounding at a rapid rate.

Dear heavens, what had she done?

It was one thing to bravely imagine herself matching wits with the sly, overly clever gentleman. To prove to him that she was equally swift of wit and quite dangerous in her own right.

It was quite another to realize she had managed to divert his attention from Jane directly onto herself.

Dicing with the devil, indeed.

CHAPTER FIVE

From the diary of Miss Jane Middleton, May 12th, 1814:

Dearest Diary,

I have always known that society is fickle and even capricious. With whimsical indifference it can toast a maiden as a Diamond of the First Water upon one evening and the next proclaim her unbearably insipid. It will insist that Kemble is all the rage and then condemn him as being utterly inferior to Kean. It will have the entire Ton scrambling to procure Chinese furnishings then blithely declare only Egyptian will do.

It is all quite foolish.

And a testament to the sheer shallowness of human vanity.

Why a maiden who was once considered a near fright and stinking of the shop could even be suddenly cheered as an Original.

Ah, yes.

The ridiculous absurdity of society.

* * *

It was all marvelously amusing.

After weeks of being thrust into the darkest corners and seated at the far end of the table, Jane was suddenly in demand. No longer was she the forgotten wallflower. Indeed, all those who once condemned her as a drab, ill-bred maiden now rushed to claim she was all that charming. She could not enter a room without being surrounded by hopeful hostesses and eager gentlemen. Her foyer overflowed with invitations. And her afternoons were suddenly filled with various callers.

She was an Original. The latest interest of Hellion.

Which, of course, made all the difference.

Ah, yes. It was all vastly amusing.

Or at least it should be.

Jane absently nibbled her thumbnail as she studied the list she had just completed of the numerous gentlemen she had encountered over the past two weeks.

It was impossible to pinpoint the source of the unease that plagued her heart. She should be delighted. After all, her scandalous scheme had worked even better than she had dared hope. Upon the arm of Hellion she had been introduced to nearly a dozen eligible suitors. Not only eligible but charming, handsome, and even witty. Any one of them might prove to be a comfortable husband.

So why then did she suffer from this restless disquiet?

Was it the sudden, unwavering attention after being hidden in the shadows for so long? Or the fact that her decision to choose a husband was now no longer a vague dream, but a very real possibility?

Or was it . . .

"Shame on you, Jane. You promised me faithfully that you would devote today to rest."

Hellion.

Lifting her head Jane regarded the gentleman negligently leaning against the doorjamb with startled eyes.

That now familiar shiver raced through her body. It did not seem to matter how often they encountered one another, she always felt that same jolt of shock. That breathless, tingling sensation as if she had just been struck by lightning.

It was annoying, really.

Granted he was handsome. As handsome as Lucifer in his pearl gray coat and black breeches. And there was a dangerous charm in that lopsided smile. But, after a fortnight of being in his company, of having him shower her with his charm, and of enduring his far-too-intimate caresses, she should have been accustomed to his presence.

Instead she felt more nervous and ill at ease than ever.

"Mr. Caulfield," she murmured, rising awkwardly to her feet.

His smile widened as he slowly strolled across the carpet. With casual ease he leaned against the desk, close enough to her stiff form to cloud her in his warm, male scent.

"You also promised to recall my name is Hellion, not Mr. Caulfield," he gently teased.

"I . . . I did not hear you announced."

As if sensing her rattled reaction to his sudden arrival, the dark eyes smoldered with amusement.

"No doubt because I was not."

She forced herself to take a deep breath. Stop acting like an ass, Jane Middleton, she sternly chided herself. Of course her heart beat faster when he was near. And of course she tingled with delicious awareness. This gentleman was an expert at making women melt into giddy puddles. It was, indeed, his stock-in-trade. The only danger was ever forgetting that for him it was no more than a well-practiced game.

"I see that I shall have to speak with my butler," she retorted in determinedly light tones. "He seems to have forgotten who is in command of his salary."

"Do not be too hard on the poor man." Without warning he reached out to tap the end of her nose with his finger. "He naturally presumed you would desire to receive a call from the gentleman who has stolen your fancy."

She blinked beneath the full force of his charm. "Naturally."

The dark eyes shimmered with a positively wicked light as he allowed his gaze to roam over her slender frame currently attired in a plain gray gown.

"You are delighted to have me call, are you not?" he murmured.

Forbidding her knees to buckle beneath that potent survey, Jane forcibly shrouded herself in a brisk composure. This was business, she grimly reminded herself. Nothing more than business.

"Actually I am," she said in steady tones. "You can be of service to me."

Expecting a hint of pique that she was not

fluttering in confusion as most he encountered, Jane was unprepared for the manner in which he slowly pushed away from the desk and framed her face in his hands.

"Ah, now that sounds intriguing," he said in husky tones.

Jane licked her suddenly dry lips. "Hellion, what are you doing?"

He gave a low chuckle as he slowly lowered his head and brushed his lips over her own.

"Being of service, of course."

Her breath fled as a startling heat rushed through her blood. Blast this gentleman. It should be against the law to be so dangerously sensuous.

"I did not mean . . ."

Her protest died a swift death as his lips teased the corner of her mouth. "Relax, my dear."

Relax? She smothered a near hysterical laugh. How on earth was she supposed to relax when a fierce pleasure was clutching her stomach into knots?

"Hellion, you are being absurd," she breathed. "There is no need to pretend when no one is about."

He continued to nuzzle her lips in that distracting fashion, his hands softly stroking over the heated skin of her cheeks.

"Of course there is," he whispered, his tongue reaching out to trace the outline of her lower lip. "I must remain in practice."

"You no doubt have practiced enough for a lifetime."

"Mmm, then it must be that you are in need of practice."

She reached up to clutch at the lapels of his coat. It was that or melt at his feet.

"I do not believe you."

He slowly pulled back, the dark eyes glittering with an oddly hectic glow.

"Perhaps I simply cannot resist temptation," he said before his hands tightened upon her face and his mouth claimed her own in a kiss that was no longer teasing, but starkly demanding.

Jane gave a soft moan as his tongue slipped between her lips. This was different from the casual touches and occasional intimacies that he had offered over the past weeks. There was a hunger in his kiss. A compulsive need that awoke a shimmering response deep within her.

Over and over he plundered her mouth, his fingers spearing into her soft curls. A strange throbbing began to pulse inside her and without conscious thought she was arching her body to press against his steely length.

Restless and confused, she did not know what she was seeking until she felt the hard bulk pressing into her lower stomach. Yes, she thought dizzily. That hardness was what she desired. She needed to have it next to her, within her, filling that hollow ache.

She should have been shocked. Even horrified. Instead she battled the most indecent urge to rub herself against that straining bulge.

As if sensing her rising desire, Hellion gave a gasping moan, and lowering his hands he pressed them into the curve of her back.

"Jane," he husked, pressing his hips indecently against her. "Let me feel your lips upon me."

"What?"

"Kiss me . . . taste of me."

The seductive words swirled through her fogged

mind, and barely aware of what she did, Jane discovered herself allowing her mouth to drift from his lips to the chiseled line of his jaw. Her touch was featherlight, but a violent shudder abruptly shook his body. A shudder echoed within her.

"Gads, but you are a dangerous woman."

With an effort Jane sucked in a deep breath. What had begun as a game was swiftly turning into something perilous. Something that could easily lead to disaster if she did not have a care.

Pressing her hands against his chest she forced herself to clear her scattered thoughts.

"You are the dangerous one, not I," she corrected in a voice that was oddly thick.

Keeping his arms firmly about her, Hellion peered down at her flushed countenance with a hooded gaze.

"Are you frightened?"

Jane could not halt her wry smile. She should be frightened. Even as an innocent she knew that the passion he stirred within her posed a genuine threat. It would be so easy to forget all in his arms. To forsake sanity for the pleasure he could offer.

But while common sense warned her to beware, she could feel no fear. Instead she was filled with a wondering, thrilling sense of elation.

The dazzling pleasure that he provoked might be a sin, but it was too delicious to regret.

"No," she at last admitted.

A slow, soul-stirring smile curved his lips. "I believe that is what I admire the most about you, my dear."

Her brows lifted at his puzzling words. "What?"

"That unwavering courage," he continued softly.

"Have you ever faced anyone or anything you could not conquer?"

You.

The unwelcome thought came without warning, and Jane was abruptly pulling from his grasp and turning to hide her horrified expression.

What was wrong with her?

She did not want to conquer this man. He was a rake. A rogue. A gentleman who could never offer a woman more than a fleeting, meaningless pleasure.

He was in her life only because she had offered him a fortune to be there. The moment she forgot that was the moment she was in true danger.

Grasping ruthless control of her shaken nerves, she firmly turned back to meet his searching gaze with a brittle smile.

"There is London, to begin with," she retorted. "It terrifies me."

"But you have conquered London," he argued with a lift of his brows. "You are on the lips of all society."

Jane gave a shrug. "Only because of you. And only for the moment. By next week I might very well be forgotten."

"Then we shall simply have to ensure that does not occur." He folded his arms over the width of his chest. "If I possess one talent it is for giving the rattles plenty of fodder."

"Still, I must act swiftly."

"What do you mean?"

With a determined motion she reached to pluck the sheet of paper from the desk. She had hired

Hellion for one purpose. To find a husband. Not to seduce her out of her wits.

A pity, perhaps, a renegade voice whispered in the back of her mind. She possessed little hope that any other gentleman would ever manage to bring her such wicked bliss. But there it was.

And the sooner she found her prospective husband, the sooner she could return to Surrey and sanity. Something she was in dire need of at the moment.

"I have been making a list," she said in what she hoped were firm tones.

Hellion grimaced. "Egads, not another list?"

"I have told you that it is the manner that I keep my thoughts in order."

"What is it?"

"It is a list of the eligible bachelors that have been introduced over the past fortnight."

Oddly his ruthlessly beautiful features seemed to harden, and his large form stiffened at her explanation.

"Indeed."

"Unfortunately I know little more than their names. I hoped you would be able to tell me more of them."

"Me?"

"Well, you are considerably better acquainted with them than myself."

A golden brow arched, the dark eyes glittering like shards of ebony. "My dear Jane, while I may be considered worldly, I can assure you that my interests do not include worthy young gentlemen."

Her lips thinned at his drawling words, but she

gamely kept her determination intact. "You must know something of them."

"Nothing more than the fact that I find them tedious bores."

Her brows furrowed at his mocking tones. Really, he was not being very helpful.

"Will you not at least glance at the names? Perhaps . . ."

"No." Placing his hands upon his hips, Hellion regarded her with a sharp impatience. "It is too fine a day to waste upon your ridiculous lists."

Her own patience came to an abrupt end. Her list was not ridiculous. Blast it all, she was attempting to be sensible. Not an easy task when he was standing there looking like a fallen angel and making her body shiver with unruly awareness.

"Unlike you, I am not in London to fribble away my days," she retorted in sharp tones. "I have only a few weeks until the end of the Season. By then I intend to have a husband."

His nose flared with annoyance. "And you think to pick one randomly off a list as if you were choosing a lottery ticket? It is absurd."

Jane flinched at his harsh accusation. Did he think she would not have preferred a normal courtship? That she had not dreamed of a gentleman tumbling deeply into love with her and sweeping her off her feet?

Did he not think she was utterly embarrassed to know that she could never, ever attract a gentleman without dangling her fortune beneath his nose?

"What would you have me do?" she demanded. "Return to Surrey and wed a local farmer? Or perhaps you believe a merchant more suitable for a maiden who smells of the shop?"

His breath caught then, and slowly his expression softened. With a rueful smile he reached out to gently tuck a stray curl behind her ear.

"Of course I do not think such a thing."

"Then . . ."

"Jane, I did not come here to argue," he interrupted in low tones.

She regarded him warily. "Then why did you come?"

"I thought we should be seen together in the park. It will be expected."

It would be expected, of course. The knowledge did not, however, soothe the prickly unease that made her feel raw and on edge.

What was it about this gentleman? One moment he had stirred her passions to a fever pitch and the next he had her snapping like a fishwife.

It was all utterly unlike her calm, sensible nature.

"Actually, I fear that . . ."

His hand shifted to gently cup her chin, and he was once again standing far too close for comfort.

"Jane, do not sulk. I apologize if I wounded you. Bring your damnable list and we will discuss your prospective husbands if you desire."

She wisely stepped away from the enchanting feel of his fingers against her skin. She had already fallen for his role of practiced seducer once today.

Once was quite enough.

"Please do not patronize me, Mr. Caulfield."

"I am not patronizing you. And I did apologize. Rather nicely, I thought," he retorted with a boyish grin.

"And do not think to sway me with your charm."

He did not appear at all put out by her warning. Indeed, a decidedly devilish amusement returned to the dark eyes as he studied her stubborn expression.

"No? Shall I beg?" He caught her hand before she could react and lifted it to press a delicate kiss in the center of her palm. "Please, my dear, will you accompany me for a turn in the park? I pledge to be upon my best behavior."

Her heart flopped in her chest. Oh, he was good. He was very, very good.

"I . . . I do not believe your best behavior is anything to boast of," she weakly chided.

"Do not be cruel, my dear," he coaxed with that irresistible charm. "Let us enjoy the lovely day."

Jane momentarily wavered. Say no, a warning voice whispered in the back of her mind. Hellion was dangerous enough when they were safely surrounded by society. To spend the day in the relative privacy of his carriage did not bode well for her already strained nerves.

Especially not after that kiss, which had left her breathless and nearly panting with need.

But even as the knowledge flared through her mind, she was dismissing it as the reaction of a coward.

She had known Hellion was a practiced rake when she hired him. And that their charade would involve a certain level of intimacy between the two of them. She had even logically acknowledged that she would be as vulnerable as any other foolish woman to his potent sensuality.

Nothing had changed.

She was still in want of a husband. And her only hope was allowing this gentleman to lure potential suitors to her side.

Sucking in a steadying breath, she gave an abrupt nod of her head. "I must change."

Satisfaction flashed in the dark eyes as he brushed careless fingers over her cheek.

"Wear your new carriage gown. It brings out the blue in your eyes."

Hellion was hard.

Hard and aching.

It was an uncommon sensation for London's most notorious rake.

Tooling his matched grays through the crowded park, he shifted uncomfortably on the leather seat of his high-perch phaeton. At his side Jane remained blithely indifferent to his pain as she gazed in interest on the numerous gentlemen that bowed and smiled in her direction.

Bloody hell.

He had discovered at an early age to direct his burgeoning lust toward those women who were readily available. He could see nothing romantic in torturing himself with desire for an innocent, respectable woman who would deny him the pleasure he ached to fulfill. It was far better to have a ready relief for his passionate nature.

A wise strategy, he wryly conceded, except for the fact that he had not taken into account the managing, shrewish Miss Middleton.

It was, of course, absurd.

There was nothing particularly desirable about

the small, gamine-faced chit. Quite the opposite, in fact. She was too skinny, her features were too plain, and her tongue sharp enough to flay a gentleman at a hundred paces.

She was not at all his style. Even if she hadn't been an innocent.

But absurd or not, he had discovered almost from the very first a sharp, undeniable urge to bed this woman.

What was it? Against his will his gaze lingered upon the elfin countenance next to him.

Perhaps it was that vivid spirit that crackled about her. Or the hint of tender kindness in the soft curve of her lips. Certainly he had never noted such kindness in other women of his acquaintance. Or simply that warm, enticing scent of spring that enfolded him whenever she was near.

Or maybe it was the knowledge that she was the complete opposite of him. Where he was selfish she was generous, where he was passionate she was coolly driven, where he was confident she was oddly vulnerable.

Was it not said that opposites were irresistibly drawn to one another?

Whatever the cause it was making him damnably uncomfortable, he acknowledged grimly. And it was not helping to ponder the odd fascination that was shimmering through his body.

With an effort he squashed the urge to drive to some remote location and complete what he had started earlier. He had been a fool to kiss her. A fool to press her so close that he could still feel her soft form brushing his aching thighs. A fool to urge her to drive him mad by teasing him with that soft mouth.

Squaring his shoulders he attempted to conjure his usual negligent charm. It would never do to appear twisted into knots over a mere dab of a maiden.

"You see, my dear, is this not preferable to spending the afternoon in that stuffy library of yours?" he demanded in light tones.

She slowly turned to regard him with a lift of her brows. "My library is not at all stuffy. It is very lovely and remarkably spacious for a London town house. It was, in fact, the reason I chose that particular location."

A flare of amusement raced through him at her staunch retort. Society was right for once. She was an Original.

"Is it so difficult to admit that it is a fine day for a drive?"

She gave a shrug. "I only came because you promised to help with my list."

Hellion's amusement died a swift death.

Damn it all, he did not desire to speak of her future husband. Not when his body still ached with need.

"Are you always so persistent?" he demanded.

She met his dark gaze squarely. "I have had need to be."

He stilled. It was true. She had not only lost her parents at far too young an age but she had been burdened with the vast responsibility of her father's business. Add to that the necessity of charging straight into the teeth of convention; she was bound to be obstinate.

That did not, however, ease his odd reluctance to discuss the vast crowd of unworthy fribbles who had been flocking about her the past week.

"Very well. Let us turn our attention to your prospective suitors. Who is first upon this list?"

With those brisk movements she pulled her list from the reticule that she had set upon the seat.

"The first is Mr. Steen," she said brightly.

Hellion shuddered in revulsion at the thought of the pasty-faced twit. "Timid Thomas? Good heavens, no."

Her brows pleated at his appalled tones. "Why do you call him that?"

"Because he is a weak-willed fool who is utterly terrified of his own mother."

"Perhaps he is merely shy."

He gave a dismissive snort as he angled his restless pair toward a less crowded area of the park.

"He fainted during the fireworks at Vauxhall and fled White's screaming in terror when Lord Dunn jokingly claimed there was a rat beneath his chair. Believe me, if you were ridiculous enough to tie yourself to such a fool you would soon find yourself lodged in Newgate for throttling him."

"Very well," she grudgingly conceded. "What of Lord Breckmore?"

"A drunkard," he swiftly condemned.

Her eyes widened in dismay. "You are certain?"

Hellion briefly hesitated. In truth he had seen the nobleman foxed on only a few occasions. Hardly enough to brand him as a raving drunk. Still, it was surely better to err on the side of caution? This woman would be at the mercy of her husband. She should be utterly confident he was respectable and beyond reproach.

"Yes," he readily lied.

Her frown deepened as she glanced at her list. "Mr. DeVille?"

"A gambler," he once again skirted near the truth. He had, after all, once seen the man in a disreputable gambling den. "He would soon have your fortune laid to waste."

"Mr. Patrick?"

Hellion gave a choked cough. "No."

"Why?"

"Let us just say that he possesses unsavory habits."

"Unsavory?"

"Habits no young woman should be exposed to."

"Oh." The faintest hint of color touched her cheeks. "What of Mr. Tatham? He seemed quite pleasant."

His hands tightened upon the reins. How the devil did Tat's name get on her blasted list? The handsome reprobate was one of the worst rogues in London. Gads, he would have Jane in his bed before she could blink. Clearly he would have to have a word with the scoundrel. A word that would ensure the gentleman understood that his elegant countenance stood in risk of certain damage if he so much as laid a hand upon Miss Middleton.

Feeling her puzzled gaze upon his tight profile, Hellion forced himself to relax. He would deal with Tat. Soon.

"Oh, very pleasant," he drawled.

"Then you approve of him?"

"Why would I not?" He offered her a wry smile.

"But I thought you specifically claimed that you had no interest in a rake?"

"He is a rake?"

"Quite an accomplished rake."

She heaved an annoyed sigh, her gaze narrowing in suspicion. "And I suppose there is something utterly wrong with Mr. Russell?"

Hellion shrugged. "He does not bathe with any frequency and it is rumored that he cheats at cards."

There was a stiff pause before she abruptly flounced back in her seat, the list crumpled in her fingers.

"You, sir, are impossible."

Well away from the rest of the traffic Hellion slowed the carriage to a mere crawl as he turned to regard the woman at his side.

"What?"

"I would think you would be anxious for me to discover a suitable husband. After all, the sooner I have a suitor the sooner you will be finished with this charade."

"You would prefer that I lie and allow you to wed a gentleman entirely unsuitable?" he demanded, not giving himself the opportunity to consider her accusation.

Of course he was anxious to bring an end to their charade. He had far better things to do with his time than to attend dull *soirées* and dance attendance upon an innocent woman. Frivolous, delightful things that would certainly not leave him aching with unfulfilled need at the end of the day.

Still, he was not about to hand her over to the first bounder who paid her attention.

She deserved better than that.

"Of course not." Her expression remained suspicious. "But . . ."

"Yes?" he prompted.

"I cannot believe all these gentlemen are unsuitable."

Perhaps not unsuitable, he silently conceded, but certainly intolerable.

"I fear the search goes on," he retorted with a smile.

Her gaze narrowed. "So it seems."

"There is still ample time, my dear." His gaze aimlessly strayed over her small countenance framed by a simple bonnet. He discovered himself lingering upon the darkly fringed eyes that shimmered with a brilliant intelligence, and then slowly slipping down to the tiny rosebud of a mouth. His determination abruptly hardened. No. He would not hand her over to any gentleman who could not appreciate her rare gifts. "You would not wish to choose hastily and spend the rest of your life regretting your decision. Eventually you will find a decent gentleman. Until then our flirtation will simply have to continue. Now tell me, what delightful pastime do we have in store for this evening?"

CHAPTER SIX

From the diary of Miss Jane Middleton, May 14th, 1814:

Dearest Diary,
I fear that I have discovered a rather disturbing fault within myself.
Arrogance.
Oh, it is not the shallow vanity of a beautiful maiden. Nor the haughty superiority of those born in the privileged ranks of aristocracy.
But instead, a deeply held conviction of my superior intellect.
I have always been clever. As a child I was a precocious student who devoured books with astonishing gluttony. As I grew older I began my training in my father's business and was swiftly more competent than most gentlemen twice my age.
Such natural talent managed to instill a decidedly dangerous belief in my own abilities.
Surely there was no dilemma I could not solve?
No problem that I could not overcome?

No goal I could not achieve?
It never occurred to me that I might encounter another who would not be easily outwitted. Or that my own cleverness could lead me into waters that were better left undisturbed.
And then Hellion swaggered into my life . . .
Good heavens. What have I done?

The supper room was swarming with guests.

Pausing at the door Jane grimaced, not at all anxious to do battle with the elegant throng. Not without stouter armor than her satin ball gown and slippers. More than once since arriving in London she had nearly been trampled when she braved such a mob.

She needn't have worried, however. Not with Hellion at her side.

With an annoying lack of effort he blazed a path through the crowd, his long strides never slowing as he arrogantly expected those before him to melt aside. To add insult to injury he had only to lift one golden brow to have a table procured so that he could gently set her in a hastily retrieved padded seat.

A wry smile twisted her lips as he casually moved to gather a plate and fill it with the food from the long table. She could only imagine how wonderful it must be to feel such confidence within herself. To be able to sweep through a room with such utter assurance.

Then, noticing that her gaze was not the only one following the magnificent male form, Jane determinedly wrenched her attention to the hands folded neatly in her lap. She was not at this tedious ball to lust after Hellion, she sternly chided herself.

A pastime that was becoming all too frequent.

She was here to discover a husband. And despite Hellion's blighting condemnation of her various suitors, that was precisely what she was going to do.

Ignoring the decided flare of unease that raced through her heart, Jane managed a composed smile as Hellion took his seat at her side and placed his bounty before her.

At first she was far too busy battling the ever-present awareness of his warm, male scent to take note of the food placed before her. Then with a hint of surprise she lifted her head to meet the shimmering black gaze.

"Champagne, oysters, asparagus, and strawberries? A rather odd combination."

Ignoring all proper manners, Hellion leaned upon the table, his expression one of devilish amusement.

"The selection will not be lost upon those who are avidly keeping track of our flirtation."

Grasping the champagne she lifted it to her lips. Anything to distract her from the tempting proximity of his mouth. A mouth that could wreak havoc in the staunchest spinster's heart.

"Why would anyone possibly be interested in what food you chose for me?"

"Because they are all well-known aphrodisiacs."

Jane promptly choked upon the expensive wine. "Sir, I have warned you that I will not be taken for a trollop."

He chuckled softly, his finger reaching out to toy with a curl that brushed her temple.

"Sweet Jane. If you were indeed a trollop I would not be so desperate as to stuff you with aphrodisiacs." His lips twisted in a rueful smile at her shocked expression. "Do not fear, society will merely presume that I grow desperate to have you, not that you are willing to share your favors. After all, it is not often that a notorious rake is led by his nose by an innocent maiden."

Setting aside her champagne, Jane regarded him with a faint frown. Despite his light tone and teasing manner, she sensed an edge to his words.

"Does that trouble you?"

"To be led by the nose?"

"Of course not. We both know such an absurdity is impossible." She steadily met his gaze, attempting to ignore the slender fingers that were now lightly brushing her cheek. Such a casual caress had no right to make her heart flutter and her stomach clench with a pleasurable excitement. "I meant does it trouble you to have society believe you are a fortune hunter?"

He gave an indifferent lift of his shoulder. "I rarely trouble myself with gossip."

Jane grimaced. "It must be pleasant to remain so impervious."

"Pleasant?" The dark eyes lost a measure of their warmth. "It was more a matter of necessity. When one is born into scandal there is little choice but to learn to turn a deaf ear to the rattles."

"Born into scandal?" she quizzed in confusion.

"Do not tell me that no one has anxiously filled you in upon my sordid family connections?"

"I know that you are the nephew of an earl."

"Ah yes, my stiff-rumped, utterly proper uncle." There was a sardonic bite in his voice that startled Jane. "Unfortunately, or perhaps fortunately for me, my father was not nearly so prim. As the younger son he was always allowed to run wild. He gambled and whored and traveled the world. It was not, however, until he possessed the audacity to wed a French actress that he was actually banned from his family and society. We lived in blissful isolation until my parents were killed in a fire when I was just ten."

Instinctively Jane reached out to touch his arm. "Oh Hellion, I am so sorry. To lose your parents is always difficult."

"Yes."

"And to lose both together at such a young age . . ." Her voice became husky with remembered pain. "Your loneliness must have been near unbearable."

The handsome features hardened at her sympathy, visibly retreating behind a mask of aloof indifference. "It did not improve matters to be taken to my uncle, who never missed an opportunity to remind me that I was the offspring of a hedonistic, ill-bred mother and that I was destined to bring shame to the family's honorable name."

Her breath caught. Dear heavens, how he must have suffered. Not only to lose his parents at such a young age, but to be so heartlessly condemned by his own uncle. It was little wonder that he possessed such a notorious reputation, she sadly acknowledged. He simply lived up to the expectations that had been laid upon him when he was but a child.

"What a horrid man," she breathed.

"Fairly horrid, yes." His fingers abruptly dropped from her cheek as he grimly attempted to conceal the wounds that had clearly never healed. "Of course, I managed to endure his disdain with the knowledge that I would have the final revenge. I was, after all, his only male relative and destined to become the next Earl of Falsdale."

That inner restlessness that she had noted during their first encounter shimmered about his taut form. Suddenly she realized that his inner anger was not entirely due to the abrupt loss of his inheritance. He had also lost his one genuine form of retribution toward the man who had treated him with such callous disdain.

"Ah."

Watching the comprehension sweep over her expressive countenance, he gave a mocking dip of his head.

"Precisely. He quite successfully undercut me when he wed a young maiden half his age and capable of producing an heir. He not only stole my revenge, but managed to land me in a mountain of debt I had no hope of repaying."

An unexpected tenderness filled her heart as she regarded the handsome countenance. A tenderness that was far more dangerous than the rampant lust that he always inspired.

She could not afford to care that this gentleman had been so deeply betrayed when he was a youth. Or that he possessed no one in the world who truly loved him. Or that he had lost the driving force of his existence.

Soon he would walk out of her life without once looking back.

She could not allow him to take her heart when he left.

"But now luckily you can repay them," she said in determinedly light tones, rising to her feet. "And I must continue my search for a husband. Shall we return to the ballroom?"

Anna Halifax felt her heart racing in a peculiar fashion as she studied the narrow, unassuming house. There was nothing to indicate the tidy home was out of the ordinary. Like the other homes on the modest block it was a plain brick structure with no attempt at pretensions and a small, tidy garden in the back.

The only thing unusual was the fact that she had recently tracked Lord Bidwell from the elegant streets of Mayfair to this modest residence.

Frowning at the heavy shutters that prevented even the smallest glimpse within the house, Anna debated her options.

It had been pure impulse that had prompted her to follow the sly gentleman when he had covertly slipped from Lady Standwell's ball. Of course he had been behaving suspiciously the entire evening, she had conceded. First he had relentlessly shadowed Jane as she struggled not to be overcome by her latest bevy of admirers, and then he had secluded Hellion for a long, private conversation in the corner of the room. Only moments later he had warily glanced about before disappearing toward the back of the large house.

Anna had been in swift pursuit.

She did not know what the devious gentleman was up to, but she did not doubt for a moment that it was no good.

And if it was somehow connected to her friend

then she was determined to do whatever was necessary to put an end to his plot.

Of course, she had not bothered to consider what she would do once she managed to follow Lord Bidwell. It had been difficult enough to keep him in sight as he had darted down the darkened streets without alerting him to her presence.

It was only now that she realized she had no specific plan in mind.

Did she return to the ball and alert Jane that the gentleman had been lurking about her? Or did she steady her sudden bout of nerves and dare to discover precisely what Lord Bidwell was about?

The intelligent choice was of course to return to the ball. What did she know of sneaking about like a thief? Or spying upon a gentleman, no matter how suspicious he might be?

She was more likely to stumble straight into disaster than to discover Lord Bidwell's dark secrets.

But the intelligent choice was far too staid and dull for Anna's current mood. Had she not been determined to step out of her tedious routine, just as Jane had done?

Now that the opportunity had arrived she could not simply turn away in fear. Adventure beckoned, and if she did not accept it she would spend the rest of the night cursing her cowardice.

Squaring her shoulders Anna forced her damp, reluctant feet to move toward the narrow door. She would not think of the scandal if she were caught sneaking into a gentleman's home. Or even the greater peril of walking into a secret meeting between Lord Bidwell and his shady acquaintances.

Instead she firmly concentrated on keeping her

full ivory silk gown from tripping her upon her nose. A worthy task and one that kept her fully occupied as she quietly slipped into the house and carefully made her way down a short, dark hall.

She paused briefly as the hall ended at a closed door. This was it. This was the moment she would discover if she were indeed the daring, courageous woman of her dreams.

Allowing herself only one deep breath she reached out and pushed open the door.

At first she could see nothing in the darkness. She sensed a larger chamber ahead of her, but it was shrouded in heavy shadows.

She took one hesitant step forward, then another. Where the devil was Lord Bidwell? She was certain he had entered only moments ahead of her.

Then there was a faint scratch that echoed in the darkness, and without warning a candle flared to life. Anna froze in shock as she turned to discover Lord Bidwell standing beside a marble fireplace across the room.

"Ah, at last, my dear," he drawled with a mocking grin. "I began to fear you would catch a chill standing in that damp garden. Perhaps a brandy will warm you."

Anna felt her throat close in horror as the gentleman urbanely crossed what appeared to be a sitting room to pour a small shot of amber spirit. Without pausing he turned to walk to her side and pressed the crystal glass into her numb fingers.

"My lord . . . I . . ."

"First finish your brandy," he interrupted her stumbled words, his lips twitching at her obvious distress.

"A fine spirit, if I do say so myself. Smuggled, of course, but what is a poor gentleman to do?"

Desperately she gulped down the smoky spirit, allowing the fiery heat to spread through her chilled body. She had to think. She had to . . . to what?

Her famed wits had deserted her completely.

"This is quite a surprise," she at last managed to choke out.

A sardonic brow arched. "A surprise?"

"Yes, I . . . I thought you had a home in Mayfair."

"I do."

"Oh." She nervously glanced about the small room. It was furnished in a plain style with heavy mahogany furnishings and crimson wall coverings. There was nothing to indicate that it was a secret den of devious spies or even the lair of a desperate blackmailer. In truth it appeared rather disappointingly ordinary. "Then what is this place?"

He reached out to pluck the glass from her fingers, lingering far too close for comfort.

"Oh come, my naughty minx, do not pretend that you did not know," he purred in silky tones. "This is my love nest."

Her eyes widened in startled shock. Well, that was one explanation she had not considered.

"Love nest?"

Setting the glass upon a nearby table, Lord Bidwell lifted a hand to lightly toy with a curl that rested against her cheek.

"It is where I enjoy the company of lovely women, as you very well know. Why else would you have so eagerly followed me?"

Anna stiffened in disbelief. Not only at the knowledge that the aggravating man had known all along

that she was following him, but at his outrageous arrogance in believing she was interested in a tawdry
flirtation.

Did he think her so desperate that she must sink
to trailing after gentlemen like a lost puppy?

Her soft features abruptly hardened. "You are
mistaken, my lord. I was not following you."

He appeared oddly fascinated by the curl he had
currently wrapped about his finger.

"No?"

"No, I . . ." She hesitated, not at all ready to confess the truth of her reasons for being at the house.
"I had become lost in the fog and I must have taken
a wrong turn."

His soft chuckle filled the shadowed room. "You
must have taken several wrong turns to have ended
up in this particular neighborhood."

"As you say."

He gave a gentle tug on the curl, sending the
oddest sensation inching down her spine.

"And what were you doing in my garden?"

"I told you, I was lost."

Astonishingly he stepped even closer. Close
enough to send a rash of prickles over her skin.

"Possible, I suppose, but hardly likely," he murmured softly. "Shall I tell you what I believe
occurred?"

She regarded him warily. "Do I have a choice?"

"I believe that you were at last overcome by the
passion that fills your innocent soul." The pale eyes
glittered with potent danger. "A passion that even
now rages within you."

Anna's heart jolted. Where was the frivolous
buffoon? The harmless dandy of fashion? This

determined seducer was entirely unexpected. And rather alarmingly exciting.

"You must be daft," she forced herself to breathe.

His finger shifted to outline the sensitive shell of her ear.

"There was no need to be so coy, my dear. You had only to whisper in my ear for me to oblige your needs. I am always anxious to please a lady. Especially a beautiful, enticing young lady."

Beautiful? Enticing? Surely he could not be speaking of her? Anna gave a bemused shake of her head. She should be frightened. Or at least furious. He was deliberately attempting to confuse her.

Unfortunately his efforts were proving all too successful.

"Sir."

"Yes?" he murmured, audaciously leaning down to place his lips against the bare curve of her neck.

Anna was jolted onto the tips of her toes. Oh my. Who would have known such a simple caress could do such naughty things to a woman's body? Sharp, poignant heat flared through her, making the oddest places warm.

Placing her hands against his chest she strained backward. "Sir . . . you must halt."

That long nose twitched, as if he were a predator on the hunt. Anna very much feared that she was the prey.

"But I have just begun."

"No."

He regarded her for a long moment before an unexpectedly tender smile curved his lips.

"Perhaps you are right. Such matters should not

be rushed." Before Anna could guess his intentions he had wrapped a solicitous arm about her shoulders and began ruthlessly steering her toward a small table hidden in the shadows. "First we will enjoy dinner and a particularly delightful champagne before continuing our fascinating game. I do hope you are fond of roasted pheasant?"

Already flustered by the intimate caresses, Anna regarded the elegant table already laden with platters of food in bafflement.

Her normally quick wits seemed sluggish and not at all capable of keeping up with the dizzying gentleman at her side.

"Oh."

"What is it?"

Her eyes continued to survey the table, passing over the delicate pheasants, the buttered mushrooms, the potatoes, and the fluffy soufflé. At last she pinpointed the source of her unease.

"There are two plates," she accused.

"Of course."

"But . . ." She reluctantly turned to regard his devious smile, the hair upon her neck stirring in alarm. "Who were you expecting?"

His smile widened. "Why, I was expecting you, my dear."

To all observers Hellion appeared his nonchalant, utterly elegant self. With a feigned expression of insufferable boredom he leaned against the wall of the ballroom, his powerful form shown to advantage in the black formal attire.

He had, of course, sought out Jane the moment

he had arrived. He had even strained the bounds of propriety by demanding a waltz and then the supper dance, so that he would have claim to lead her to the lavish buffet.

Now, however, he realized that he dared not impose himself on her further. His reputation as a rake might be all well and good for actresses and courtesans, but it was deucedly inconvenient when it came to proper maidens. The vile, shrill-tongued matrons would soon have Jane's reputation in shreds if he appeared interested in more than a mild flirtation.

And so he was stuck to the wall, his temper smoldering as he watched a swarm of ridiculous swains press their attention upon her.

His temper was not improved by the realization that the annoying minx was actually encouraging the adoring puppies.

Bloody hell, she was allowing Lord Stillwell to stand far too close, while Mr. Thomas was waving her fan before her smiling countenance. Even worse, that devil Tat had arrogantly ignored his dark warning and was currently dazzling the poor woman with his indecent charm.

Hellion discovered his teeth grinding in frustration.

It was not that he did not respect her desire to discover a suitable husband, he told himself. It was what all maidens desired when they traveled to London for the Season.

Nor did he entirely blame her for finding delight in having a string of admirers after her dismal weeks spent as a wallflower. There had to be a certain satisfaction in besting the Ton at its own game.

But . . .

But what?

But you desire her, an aggravating voice whispered in the back of his mind. And you cannot bear to consider the notion that some other gentleman might steal that innocence before you can do so.

His brooding gaze lingered on the gamine countenance currently flushed with excitement.

He supposed that he should be ashamed of himself. Whatever his faults he had never deliberately seduced a virgin. In truth, he had always condemned those men who enjoyed debauching innocents before tossing them aside.

But shame was not what was currently clenching his muscles and twisting his stomach.

Instead it was a fierce, possessive need to stalk across the room and toss Miss Middleton over his shoulder.

Gads, what a devilish coil.

"Hellion. I would have a word with you."

The sharp, petulant tones sent a chill of distaste through Hellion. With slow, deliberate reluctance he turned to confront his only surviving relative.

For a brief moment he considered giving the short, pudgy gentleman the cut direct. He did not enjoy the company of Lord Falsdale under the best of circumstances. Now he only wished to damn him to the netherworld so that he could return his attention to the aggravating minx across the crowded room.

Unfortunately his uncle was as tenacious as he was dull witted, and Hellion knew that he would not be dislodged until he had vented his latest complaint. It was the only reason he ever sought him out.

Folding his arms across his chest, Hellion regarded the unwelcome intruder with a mocking smile.

"Falsdale, what an unexpected honor," he drawled. "I presumed that it would take a French invasion to lure you from the bed of your child bride. But then I suppose at your age you must have a care not to overexert yourself."

The portly countenance became tinged with an interesting shade of purple as the nobleman battled to maintain his brittle dignity.

"Do not be clever with me, Hellion. I do not find it in the least amusing."

Hellion shrugged. "Hardly surprising. You find nothing amusing."

"Well certainly not the latest scandal you have brought to our family," he snapped.

A golden brow arched in a manner designed to annoy the elder gentleman. "Scandal?"

Falsdale clenched his hands into tight fists. "Do not pretend you do not know of what I speak."

"I haven't the least notion. Nor, I must confess, the least interest."

"Of course not," Falsdale sneered, the purple becoming more pronounced. "What do you care if your family is shrouded in ugly gossip? You positively delight in bringing shame upon us all. I suppose it is only to be expected. Your father possessed the same blithe arrogance."

With an effort Hellion contained his surge of anger. His father had paid dearly for his scandal. As had Hellion. He was not about to give the self-conceited twit the pleasure of knowing that his words had struck a raw nerve.

"You are either very brave or very stupid, Falsdale,"

he murmured with a deadly calm. "Shall I hazard a guess as to which it is?"

Not entirely suicidal, the earl briefly faltered. He might bluster and threaten, but both gentlemen understood he was no true match for Hellion. It was a knowledge that only fueled the older gentleman's resentment.

He swallowed heavily. "Do you deny that you have linked your name to that of Miss Middleton?" he at last managed to accuse.

Hellion smiled coldly. Of course. He should have expected this encounter. His uncle was an insufferable snob.

"Why should I deny it? I find the woman fascinating."

The heavy features tightened with repugnance. "Have you no shame?"

"And what precisely is shameful in enjoying the companionship of a lovely, proper maiden?" he demanded in even tones. "I would have thought you would be rejoicing. You have, after all, devoted enough of your time to condemning my choice in courtesans."

Falsdale gave a loud sniff. "All of society knows that your interest is in nothing more than her fortune."

Despite his best intentions, Hellion discovered his body stiffening in building fury. "I have discovered that only fools listen to the endless gossip that runs rampant through London. And only the most gullible fools actually believe such nonsense."

"You claim a genuine regard for a wench who is without beauty and possesses the blood of a merchant?"

"She is also intelligent, courageous, and utterly without artifice," he said between his teeth.

"She is common."

Hellion's dark gaze slowly narrowed with a lethal threat. This pretentious, tiny-minded dolt was not worthy of speaking the name of Miss Middleton. He would personally deliver him to the devil before he would allow him to treat her with disrespect.

"Have a care, Uncle," he said in tones that warned retribution.

Falsdale blinked at the prickling danger that suddenly filled the air. "What?"

"No one is allowed to condemn Miss Middleton in my presence. Especially not you."

"Fah." The earl shifted with obvious unease. "Do not pretend a fondness for the chit."

"There is no pretense," he corrected. "Not only do I greatly admire Miss Middleton, but I am honored to be considered her friend."

"Impossible. Why, the chit is a fright. What other interest could you possibly have but her fortune?"

Hellion knew that it would only take one hit to that weak chin to send his uncle sprawling onto the floor. It would not even have to be a particularly hard hit. He had even judged the distance when he realized that it would accomplish nothing more than an ugly scene.

There were better means of besting his irritating relative.

The mocking smile slowly returned.

"And you would, of course, know all there is to know of fortune hunters, would you not, dear Uncle?"

The round face became wary. "What the devil are you inferring?"

Hellion flicked his dark gaze dismissively over the earl's portly body. "What do you suppose a female half your age found the most charming about you, Uncle? Your paunchy form or dull wit?"

The thrust slid home easily and the older man quivered in offended rage. He clearly did not like to be reminded that he had been foolish enough to tie himself to a rank fortune hunter.

"One day you will go too far, Hellion," he gritted.

A sardonic smile curved his lips. "And then?"

"And then I shall deal with you once and for all," the earl blustered in vague warning.

Hellion would have laughed at the ridiculous notion of Lord Falsdale presuming that he could best him upon any level, but a movement near the door abruptly caught his attention.

Sharply turning he watched in disbelief as Jane boldly left the room on the arm of Mr. Barnett.

"Bloody hell," he muttered.

"What is it?" his uncle demanded in petulant tones.

Fed up with the blustering idiot, Hellion grasped the man's arm and drew him close enough so that he could not fail to realize his gathering annoyance.

"Return to your child bride, Uncle, and do not presume to interfere in my affairs again," he snarled softly. "On the next occasion I will not be so forgiving."

The purple faded to be replaced by a pasty white. "Dammit, Hellion . . ."

Whatever he was about to say was abruptly broken off as Hellion shoved him to the side and ruthlessly pushed his way through the thick throng.

What the devil was the matter with the woman? He seethed in disbelief.

Surely she realized it was not done to be alone with a gentleman? Not even if the gentleman in question was a rather stodgy, serious scholar.

For God's sake, what man would not take advantage of a moment of privacy? Which of them would not hope to taste of her innocence?

His gut was burning with an odd fear as he burst out of the ballroom and hurried down the hall. The two had disappeared but he never halted as he thrust open door after door to inspect the rooms within. He had reached the very end of the hall when he at last burst into a large library to discover Jane standing in the center of the chamber.

That burning became a flame of searing anger as he watched Mr. Barnett carefully fold the maiden in his arms and drop his head for a kiss.

Blinded by his flood of outrage, Hellion did not even realize he was moving until he had the young gentleman firmly by the throat and had soundly punched him in the nose. With a squawk of dismay Mr. Barnett flopped to the floor, his hand rising to cover his bludgeoned snout.

"Hellion, for God's sakes," Jane gasped in startled tones. "Halt this at once."

Hellion did not even bother to turn, his black gaze locked upon the scoundrel who dared to lay his hands upon this woman.

His woman.

"Return to the ballroom," he gritted.

Mr. Barnett awkwardly scrambled to his feet, still holding his wounded nose.

"Now see here. You cannot . . ."

"Return to the ballroom or be prepared to meet me at dawn."

The younger gentleman swayed in horror, nearly returning to the carpet as fear spread across his pale features.

"There is no need for violence," he sputtered, regarding Hellion's grim countenance with dismay.

"I fear I am a rather violent sort of chap."

"Really, Hellion," Jane protested from behind.

His gaze did not waver from the pasty countenance. "The next occasion you attempt to lure Miss Middleton alone I will lodge a bullet in your arse. Do you understand?"

"I . . . yes, yes. Quite." Backing toward the door, the gentleman performed a wary bow. "Miss Middleton."

He disappeared with gratifying haste, and Hellion slowly turned to ensure that Jane had not swooned or keeled over from her horrid tribulation. She was bound to be distressed by the entire ordeal.

Rather surprisingly she seemed her perfectly composed self. Unless one counted the faint hint of color in her cheeks and the decided glint in her eyes.

"Would you kindly explain what that was about?" she demanded.

"Are you harmed?" he growled, quite prepared to follow Mr. Barnett and punish him for any injury to this woman.

"Of course I am not harmed. It was merely a kiss."

His brows drew together as he stepped toward her slender form. Merely a kiss? Merely a kiss?

Had she lost her wits entirely?

"That lecher is fortunate I did not wring his scrawny neck."

"Mr. Barnett is not a lecher," she ridiculously argued. "He happens to be a very respectable gentleman."

Hellion clenched his fists. Damn it all. Why was she taking this so calmly? Did she not realize that the gentleman had been intent upon seducing her?

"He lured you to this room, did he not? Hardly the behavior of a respectable gentleman."

Her chin tilted in a manner that boded ill. "If you must know, I asked him to show me the library."

A bolt of shock raced through Hellion. "What?"

"He spoke of an Egyptian mummy that Lord Standwell had recently acquired and I told him that I wished to view it."

He manfully resisted the urge to reach out and give her a sharp shake. Gads, he had thought this woman intelligent. By far the most intelligent female he had ever encountered. Now the depths of her stupidity stunned him.

What if he had not noted her leaving the ballroom?

What if she had been left to the mercy of the scoundrel?

"That was very foolish, Jane," he chastised in sharp tones. "To be alone with a gentleman is an invitation for intimacy. I hope you have learned your lesson."

Far from appreciating his timely warning, the contrary woman abruptly placed her hands upon her hips and regarded him with a forbidding frown. Almost as if she were angry with him. Which was ridiculous, of course.

"I am not stupid, Hellion. I knew precisely what would occur when I requested Mr. Barnett to escort me to this room."

"You knew?"

"At least I hoped."

Hellion gave a slow shake of his head, not at all prepared to accept that Jane had deliberately allowed that man to handle her in such an intimate fashion.

"You desired that buffoon to maul you?"

At least she possessed the grace to blush. "I wanted him to kiss me, yes."

The anger that still simmered in his blood became dangerously overheated. "Why?"

"I should think it was obvious."

Obvious? The only thing obvious to Hellion was the fact that he would throttle any male stupid enough to poach upon his territory.

"Humor me," he gritted.

As if sensing the brittle danger that filled the shadowed library Jane reached out the tip of her tongue to wet her dry lips.

The unwitting motion only fueled the heat attacking Hellion. A heat that was edged with a pure, unrelenting male possession.

"I cannot choose a husband if I do not know if we will suit in all aspects of our marriage."

He reached out before he could halt himself, grasping her shoulders in a tight grip.

"You have chosen Mr. Barnett?" he rasped.

Her expression hardened. "Not as yet."

"But you wished to kiss him?"

"Yes."

His fingers instinctively tightened. Walk away,

Hellion, he silently told himself. His emotions were too tightly wound. First from his ugly encounter with his uncle followed by the shock of witnessing Jane in the arms of another man. He was not at all his rational self.

But, of course, it was the very fact that he was not his rational self that made him step close enough to feel the warmth of her seep into his chilled heart.

"And did he please you?" he demanded in soft tones.

She faced him with that extraordinary courage, but not even she could entirely disguise her hint of unease beneath his brooding intensity.

"It was . . . pleasant."

A shocking stab of relief raced through him. "Pleasant? A rather damning assessment."

She pulled against his hold. "Hellion."

"Did he make your heart race and your knees weak?" he murmured, shifting his hands to her back so that he could pull her against his already aroused body.

Her eyes widened at the determined desire etched onto his features. "Hellion, stop this."

He growled deep in his throat. "Did he make you ache to feel him deep within you? Did you plead with him to press you to the ground and end your torment?"

"Mr. Barnett is a very respectable and kind gentleman," she muttered.

He held her wide gaze with ease, noting the manner in which her eyes darkened with troubled awareness. Good, he thought in satisfaction. Barnett's kiss may have been all that was pleasant, but

it had not made her tremble with breathless anticipation. It had not stirred her darkest needs.

"He is not for you, Jane."

"That is my decision to make."

His lips twisted. "Do you think so?"

She swallowed heavily. "Hellion, what is the
matter with you?"

He sucked in a sharp breath, needing desperately to brand this woman as his own.

"This . . ." he murmured, lowering his head to
claim her lips in a kiss that could leave no doubt.

CHAPTER SEVEN

From the diary of Miss Jane Middleton, May 17th, 1814:

Dearest Diary,
   Desire.
   Such a simple word for such a complicated emotion.
   Lives have been destroyed by desire. Families broken.
   Wars have been fought and kingdoms have crumbled.
   Men have killed and women have sacrificed all for desire.
   Desire has at times altered history.
   It is one of the most powerful forces upon earth.
   So why am I so troubled by the knowledge that I have been afflicted by the prevalent disease?
   I had known, after all, that Hellion was a polished rake when I approached him. And a gentleman cannot logically become a rake without great expertise in stirring a woman's passions. It was only

to be expected that I would be a victim of his enchantment.

But logically knowing that I risked my first taste of lust and actually experiencing the sensations are two separate things entirely.

What a terrible bother it all is.

How am I to conduct my business when my thoughts are intruded upon by the memory of his kiss? Or enjoy a decent night's rest when I toss and turn with the oddest ache?

Even worse, how am I to discover a husband when they all pale in comparison to Hellion?

Desire.

As far as I am concerned, it should be banned from decent society.

Seated at her desk, Jane absently rubbed her temple that was throbbing in a painful manner.

It was a pain she had endured for several days.

Ever since her confrontation with Hellion at Lady Standwell's ball.

Blast the annoying man, she silently seethed. He was ruining everything. Not only by his untimely intrusion into the library just when she had managed to convince Mr. Barnett to kiss her, but now every gentleman in the Ton was terrified to even come near her.

How the devil was she to discover a husband when every eligible male feared they would be hauled onto the field of honor by the deadliest shot in England?

It was all vastly annoying.

Jane abruptly grimaced.

Of course, if she were being perfectly truthful with herself, she would acknowledge that her throbbing temple was not entirely caused by her sudden lack of suitors.

Against her will the memory of that shadowed library seared through her mind.

She had not lied when she said that Mr. Barnett's kiss had been pleasant enough. The world had not stopped spinning, but she had not been repulsed. It seemed quite enough at the time.

And then Hellion had pulled her into his arms and she had melted like a mindless fool.

All thoughts of eligible gentlemen and the need to marry were seared from her mind as she had allowed herself to drown in the dazzling pleasure. She wanted him to press her closer, to put an end to that dreadful need that was clutching deep within her.

It was not until she had realized that he had managed to slip his warm hands beneath her bodice and was caressing her in a shockingly intimate manner that she had been thrust back into reality.

Wrenching herself from his grasp she had fled the library and returned to her home. But even as she had fled she had realized that she could deny the truth no longer.

She would never discover a gentleman while Hellion remained in her life, she had grimly accepted.

How could she when every suitor paled in comparison? And when his kisses inflamed her to the point that she could barely tolerate the touch of another?

It was obvious she would have to put an end to their ridiculous bargain. As long as he was near she would never choose another.

And the sooner he was gone the better.

A heavy sigh broke into her brooding thoughts, and lifting her head Jane watched as Anna paced from the window back to the heavy bookcase.

The woman had arrived nearly half an hour ago, but beyond attempting to wear a hole in the carpet she had made no effort to claim Jane's attention. Instead she appeared lost in her own brooding thoughts.

"Anna, I do wish you would have a seat," she said wryly. "You are making me nauseous."

Coming to an abrupt halt Anna grimaced as she perched upon the edge of a nearby chair.

"Sorry."

"Is something troubling you?"

"You could say that. I . . . it is Lord Bidwell."

Jane felt a jolt of shock. She had been so distracted by her troubles with Hellion that she had entirely forgotten the thin-faced gentleman and the threat he posed to her reputation.

"Dear heavens. Have you discovered anything of his intentions?"

Anna clenched her hands upon her lap. "Not a blasted thing."

"But surely if he intended to blackmail me he would have done so by now?" Jane demanded, not at all eager to add further troubles to dwell upon.

"Who is to say what is brewing in his devious mind?" Anna retorted in dark tones. "He might very well be waiting until you believe you are safe. Or even hoping to discover even more discreditable evidence before approaching you."

Jane conjured a weak smile. "You are not very comforting."

"Do not fear. I shall deal with Lord Bidwell."

There was a dangerous edge in Anna's voice that had Jane regarding her with a worried frown. It was unlike the sweet-tempered young woman to be anything but cheerful and ready to laugh at whatever might come. She did not like to think that she had unwittingly placed the poor girl into a situation that might cause her distress.

"Anna."

The woman gave a vague blink. "Yes?"

"I do not wish you to take any risk to yourself or your reputation for me," she said slowly. "I would never forgive myself if you were harmed."

Surprisingly Anna appeared more offended than relieved by her words. "I am not a child, Jane. I am perfectly capable of making the decision of what risks I shall take and being fully responsible for any consequences."

"Of course." Jane's frown deepened. "Forgive me."

There was a moment of silence before Anna heaved a deep sigh. "No, it is I who should be apologizing. I am in a foul mood. It is that . . ."

"What?"

"That man."

Jane regarded her in puzzlement. Really, Anna was not at all herself. "Lord Bidwell?"

"Yes."

"What has he done?"

An astonishing blush abruptly flared beneath Anna's pale skin. "Nothing."

Jane slowly stood and walked toward her friend. There was something going on between Anna and Lord Bidwell. Something that was decidedly intriguing.

"Anna?"

The woman reluctantly lifted her head to meet Jane's probing gaze.

"He is just so annoyingly smug," she at last blurted out, her blue eyes dark with an emotion that Jane did not think was mere annoyance. "How I would love to outwit him."

"Are you certain that is all you desire?" she asked softly.

"What do you mean?"

Jane paused, debating whether to probe into Anna's troubles or not. Heaven knew that she had made enough of a mess with her own life lately. She was hardly the one to offer out advice to anyone.

At last the shadows that her friend could not entirely hide forced Jane to speak. She could not allow Anna to be miserable without at least attempting to offer her assistance.

"Are you attracted to him?" she asked cautiously.

The blush became a fiery red at the direct question. "I . . . gads. Yes. I do not know how it occurred. One moment he was the enemy and the next . . . I was in his arms and I thought I might swoon. It is humiliating."

Jane smiled ruefully at the grudging confession.

Less than a month ago she would have scoffed at the absurd notion that a woman of sense could be swept off her feet by something so illogical as desire. Surely only susceptible nitwits believed in such nonsense?

Now her heart swelled with sympathy.

"You are too hard upon yourself," she said kindly. The sweetly rounded countenance hardened with self-disgust. "No, I am not. Only silly widgeons allow themselves to be gulled by a rake. A sensible woman should be capable of keeping her wits, no matter how delightful a gentleman's kiss might be."

Jane gave a sharp laugh, her hands pressing to her churning stomach. "I have discovered that the most sensible maiden is not immune to the power of a rake."

Anna widened her eyes in dismay at the obvious bitterness in Jane's voice. "Oh dear, not you too?"

Jane gave a vague shrug. "I suppose it was inevitable. Still, I do not intend to allow myself to brood upon the matter. I have far more important matters to occupy my attention."

As if anxious to grasp an opportunity to change the rather depressing conversation, Anna peered upward with an expectant expression.

"How does the search go?"

Jane briefly thought of the numerous gentlemen who had crowded about her since Hellion had brought her into fashion.

Oddly she found the thought just as depressing as brooding upon her absurd desire for a rake's seduction.

"Slowly."

Anna appeared genuinely surprised. "But you have been nearly mobbed by eligible gentlemen."

"Yes, I know."

The woman leaned forward. "Jane, what is it?"

She grimaced. "Perhaps I am being too exacting in my standards, but . . ."

"But what?"

Jane took a moment to consider her response. Against her will she had forced herself to concede that Hellion had managed to wane her desire for other gentlemen. But why? It was not just the undoubted passion he stirred within her. Nor his practiced charm. She was not that shallow.

No. It was more his manner of speaking to her as if she were an equal rather than a slow-witted child, and his sincere approval of her habit of flouting the rigid strictures that bound women in roles of submissive weakness.

"I suppose I should like to discover a husband who possesses a modicum of intelligence who does not also presume that because I wear skirts I must be wholly without wits."

A rather wistful expression rippled over Anna's countenance. "Yes."

Jane abruptly wrapped her arms about her waist, feeling a cold chill inch down her spine. "There must be one gentleman among the Ton who will suit me. I must simply be patient."

Anna rose from the chair and gently reached out to touch her arm. "You will find him, Jane," she said with a faint smile. "Now, I must be on my way. I promised my aunt that I would accompany her to a poetry reading. I must have been out of my wits."

Jane chuckled, determinedly shaking off the cloud of doom that threatened to take permanent residence about her.

"Perhaps it will not be so horrid."

Anna tugged on her gloves with a grimace. "The poems are entitled, 'An Ode to the Prince, Our Glorious Leader into Battle.'"

Jane could not prevent a revealing shudder. "Ugh."

"Precisely." Anna heaved a tragic sigh. "I shall see you this evening."

Hellion paced.

He fumed.

He growled deep in his throat.

He even glared so fiercely at a mincing dandy that the poor buffoon tumbled into a passing servant and sent a tray of champagne cascading over a gaggle of unfortunate matrons.

Hellion never noticed.

Instead his dark, smoldering gaze continued to sweep over the growing crowd in search of a slender woman with a gamine countenance and enough contrariness to drive a reasonable gentleman batty.

Where the devil was she?

For three days he had attended one tedious function after another with the thought that Jane was certain to be present. He had even called at her town house on several occasions, only to be told that Miss Middleton was cloistered with her man of business.

At first he had been concerned.

He worried that his rather demanding kisses in the library might have frightened her. She was, after all, an innocent and not at all accustomed to the overwhelming force of raw desire.

He should never have allowed his frustrated passions to gain control of him.

As she had continued to avoid him, however, his concern had faded and an unexpected, wholly unexplainable fury had seized him.

His kisses may have been heated, but she had not been entirely submissive. In fact, for a brief, heart-stirring moment she had been with him all the way.

Even now he could still feel the ready response of her satin lips and the press of her slender body arching against him.

It was maidenly panic that had forced her hasty flight.

So why did she presume to treat him as if he were carrying the latest plague?

Nearly snarling in his seething frustration Hellion prowled the edges of the Marlow's dance floor, his forbidding expression keeping even the most determined encroacher at bay.

And then, across the room, he caught sight of the familiar dark curls and ghastly ball gown.

At last.

He stilled as his instincts came into full alert. A predator who had just spotted his prey.

She stood alone for the moment, but he did not allow himself to give into impulse and pounce at once. He had learned his lesson during his last heated confrontation with the minx. Instead he forced himself to regard her rigid expression and the manner in which she clutched the ivory fan.

It was obvious that she was not her usual calm self. There was an air of nervous tension in her slender form and a wariness in her sharp glances about the room.

He would have to approach with care, he grudgingly acknowledged. One wrong word and she might bolt into the night.

Not an easy task when all he desired was to

bundle her into his arms and ensure that she never dare to hide from him again.

Taking a moment to compose his features into something other than a snarl, Hellion sucked in a deep breath and slowly made his way toward the distant shadows.

Thankfully Jane appeared distracted by the passing dancers and she did not sense his approach until he had managed to step directly before her.

"Ah, Jane," he murmured, drinking in the vivid features and soft lips that had haunted his dreams for too long. "How very elusive you have been, my dear."

She blinked in surprise at his sudden appearance, before her countenance stiffened and her chin was tilting in a manner that warned of impending danger.

"Mr. Caulfield."

He arched a golden brow. "I believe we have agreed that you will call me Hellion."

"No," she denied in steady tones. "You made the decision that I was to call you Hellion and then you expected me to concede to your demands."

His gaze swiftly narrowed. So much for his determination to approach her with care, he acknowledged dryly. She was clearly determined to provoke him.

"Very well, Jane." He firmly took her arm and steered her deeper into the shadows. "You are clearly stewing for an argument. Let us be done with it."

"You are quite mistaken. I have nothing I wish to say to you."

Hellion frowned with a growing wariness. He had never seen this woman so rigid, so determined to hide her emotions from him. He found her measured control far more unnerving than any amount of anger.

"That should prove rather awkward considering that we are suppose to be in the midst of a glorious flirtation," he retorted in measured tones.

There was a short silence before she sucked in a deep breath. "No longer."

"And what precisely is that supposed to mean?"

She backed away from the narrowed black gaze, halting only when she came up against the wall.

"This afternoon I requested a bank draft for five thousand pounds to be delivered to your home on the morrow."

Hellion was momentarily stunned. Five thousands pounds . . . his for the taking. It seemed incredible.

No more creditors hounding him whenever he was at home. No more fear that all of society would learn of his embarrassing situation. No more worries that he might be forced to swallow his pride and turn to his uncle for charity.

And all he had to do was turn and walk away from this woman, and the dull duty attached to her, forever.

He should be delighted.

Instead he was battling a surge of fury.

Did she believe that he could be so easily dismissed? That he could be turned off as if he were a mere servant that was interested only in her money?

Placing his hand upon the wall next to her ear, he glared into the small countenance.

"Is that so?"

"Yes." She swallowed heavily, managing to keep her brittle composure in place. "We have accomplished what we set out to do. I now have ample suitors to choose from. There is no longer any need to continue our charade."

His nose flared at her ridiculous explanation. "This has nothing to do with those pathetic suitors of yours. We both know that none of them are worthy to become your husband, even if you are too stubborn to admit it. You want to end this charade because I kissed you and you kissed me back."

She fought a losing battle with a fiery blush that stained her cheeks. "Of course not. As I said, there is no longer any need . . ."

"I was mistaken in you, Miss Middleton," he growled.

"Pardon me?"

"I thought you were a maiden of courage. One of the rare few who could face whatever you encountered with your chin held high." His lips thinned. "Now I discover you are, in truth, no more than a coward."

The blue eyes flashed with a dangerous fire, but with sheer will she managed to keep her temper under firm rein. Which was a damn sight more than he could do.

"You are entitled to your opinion, of course."

"Tell me, my dear," he drawled. "What do you fear? That I might seduce you or that you are uncertain of your will to halt me?"

"Neither," she hissed in low tones.

"You have no talent for telling untruths. You are terrified of what has sparked between us."

"Your arrogance never fails to astonish me, Mr. Caulfield."

Indifferent to the vast crowd that swept past the shadowed alcove, Hellion audaciously lifted his hand to trail his fingers along the curve of her neck. Like any proper rake, he had already discovered where she was the most sensitive.

"Because I know when a woman desires my kisses?"

"My only desire is to find a proper husband."

He slowly smiled as he felt her pulse flutter beneath the slow, seductive sweep of his thumb. Ah yes, that was the spot.

"Liar."

She pressed herself against the wall, her tongue peeking out in a revealing motion. "This is absurd. You have the money I promised. Our bargain is at an end."

Hellion narrowed his gaze. Oh no. This bargain was far from over. Did she truly believe that he would allow her to blithely hand herself over to some buffoon who only desired her fortune? That he would watch her vibrant innocence tarnished by a thick-witted, heavy-handed poppycock? Perhaps even witness her spirited nature being ground into the dull obedience that most husbands expected from their wives?

He would be damned before he would meekly allow such a crime.

What she needed was a husband who could truly appreciate her unique qualities. A gentleman who would treat her with respect and admiration. A man who would fulfill that passionate nature until those gamine features were drenched in sated satisfaction.

A gentleman . . . like himself.

The thought came like a lightning bolt, and shocked him with the same intensity.

Him? Married? To this ill-tempered shrew of a woman who treated him more like a lowly flunky than a superior gentleman of society?

The mere notion should have sent him bolting out the nearest door and locking himself in his chambers until the obvious madness had passed. He did not want to marry. He did not want to bind his life irrevocably to a wife who would demand an intimacy he was incapable of offering. Certainly he did not want to wed a chit who did not even possess the good sense to tumble into love with him.

So why then was a slow, self-satisfied smile curving his lips?

CHAPTER EIGHT

From the diary of Miss Jane Middleton, May 17th, 1814:

P.S. Diary,
   Men.
   Was there ever a more incomprehensible creature?
   They possess all the power and freedom in the world. They are offered the finest in education and given positions that could alter the world. They are allowed to become artists, poets, and explorers. Their paths are unimpeded by a thousand tedious boundaries and yet, for all their glorious opportunities, they readily prefer the gaming hells to Parliament. They haunt brothels rather than the wonders of the vast world and more highly respect a man of sport than a man of intellect.
   Most unsettling of all, of course, is their thoroughly bewildering behavior toward women. How is it possible for a man to be seductively charming one moment, and the next an arrogant bully? How

could he appear almost sensible in one breath and in the next rave like a lunatic?

How could he pretend to be a friend and then without warning become an enemy?

Traitors.

Turncoats. Defectors. Lousy, rotten . . . men.

Standing in the shadows that she had thought she had put behind her for the Season, Jane glared about the crowded dance floor with a jaundiced frown.

How had she fallen from grace so swiftly? It had been less than a week since she had given Hellion his *conge*. Only five short days since he had silently turned and abandoned her at the elegant ball. She had suspected that society could be fickle, but this was ridiculous.

What had happened to all those anxious suitors who had claimed such an undying affection? The ones who had sworn they would expire if she did not save them at least one waltz? The ones who had promised the world if only she would offer them a smile?

Suddenly they could barely seem to recall her name. And certainly they had no interest in attempting to claim her attention. She had returned to being plain, ill-favored Jane Middleton. A wallflower. An unfortunate plague to society.

She angrily flipped open her ivory fan. The devil take the lot of them, she seethed.

"Ah Jane, how perfect. I see that you were as fortunate as myself to be politely steered to this dismal corner," Anna muttered as she abruptly appeared at Jane's side, already yanking at the fashionable plunge of her neckline. She seemed to think her full bosom a source of embarrassment no matter how often Jane proclaimed her envy. "Did Lady Vallace assure you that this was absolutely the perfect location to view the festivities, and of course, so conveniently out of the crush?"

Jane frowned in a sour fashion, not desiring to recall how efficiently she had been thrust into the shadows.

"I will give you ample warning that my mood is decidedly foul, Anna."

A wry smile touched the round countenance. "I had already hazarded as much from the intriguing shade of puce that is currently staining your cheeks."

In spite of herself, Jane felt her lips twitch. "Surely not puce?"

"Mauve? Crimson?" Anna tilted her head to one side. "Prinny pink?"

"Prinny pink?" Jane rolled her eyes heavenward. "That is not even a color."

"But of course it is. Our beloved prince has declared it so."

"Ridiculous." Jane returned her jaundiced glance to the laughing crowd that blithely swept past. "'Tis no wonder I find London such a bore. It is filled with empty-headed buffoons."

There was a brief silence before Anna stepped close enough to avoid being overheard.

"Are you ever going to confess what occurred between you and Hellion?"

The ivory fan abruptly cracked in half. With a hiss of annoyance Jane turned to toss the remains into a particularly ugly potted palm.

Blast it all. What was the matter with her? It was not as if she missed Hellion. Or, heaven forbid, that she longed to hear the honey rasp of his voice. Or watch those black eyes flash with wickedness.

She was far too practical for such nonsense.

She was merely disgusted at the fickleness of men, she grimly assured herself. The sharp pang in her heart had nothing to do with Hellion. Nothing at all.

"Nothing occurred," she staunchly retorted. "I simply felt that the time was proper and brought an end to our charade."

Anna regarded her with bland disbelief. "No."

"What?"

"You said that your . . . arrangement with Hellion was purely a business proposition."

"It was."

"That is impossible."

Jane gave a snort of exasperation. There were moments when her dear friend could use a good shake.

"What the devil are you attempting to say?"

"I know you, Jane." Anna planted her hands upon her waist. "You would never, ever make such a complete hash of a business deal."

A choked laugh was torn from her lips. Good Lord. It was true. If she fumbled as badly with all her business propositions she would be a pauper by now.

"I fear I miscalculated," she retorted with a grimace. In more ways than one. "I did not realize that gentlemen were such cads. Why any female of sense would chose to bind herself to such weak-spirited, unpredictable creatures is beyond my comprehension."

"No doubt because we are fools," Anna retorted dryly.

"True."

Anna's eyes abruptly widened as she glanced over Jane's shoulder. "Oh no."

"What is it?"

"The dim-witted duet."

Jane felt her heart sink as she reluctantly turned to view Miss Fairfax and the inevitable Miss Tully making a determined path in her direction. Even from a distance she could detect the smug malice that shimmered in the air about them.

"No doubt they intend to crow at my return to the corner. They have been seething with envy since Hellion first began his flirtation."

Anna muttered a curse worthy of a sailor. "Someday I am going to plant the pair of them a facer."

Jane smiled grimly, thoroughly enjoying the image of the maidens sporting bloody noses and blackened eyes. She even felt her hands curl into fists. Oh yes, someday.

"If only it were possible," she muttered.

Without warning her friend stepped beside her to lay a hand upon her arm. "Well, I may not be allowed to take a poke at their condescending noses, but I can at least distract them while you make your escape."

Jane blinked in surprise. "That is not necessary. I do not fear them."

"I know," Anna said with wry emphasis. "And in your current temper I hardly think a confrontation with those horrid wenches is wise. I should hate to see you lodged in Newgate for murder, no matter how justified."

She opened her mouth to argue only to snap it shut as she realized the sense in her friend's words of warning. Frustration, annoyance, and something that might have been a pang of regret boiled within her. She was ripe for a low-brow, ugly brawl.

Not, perhaps, the best means of luring a potential suitor.

"Mayhap I should heed your warning," she ruefully agreed with one last glare toward the menacing duo. "I shall be in the garden."

"I will come and retrieve you when I have rid the corner of such unwelcome vermin."

With a nod Jane sank deeper in the shadows and edged her way toward the nearby French doors. At least she need have no fear of her hasty flight being blocked by endless calls of friends, or gentlemen anxious to claim her for a dance, she acknowledged with dark amusement. Being a wallflower meant that she could move through the crowd without once ever being noticed. To be brutally honest, she could strip naked and play the cello without being noticed.

At least now that Hellion had lost all interest in her.

A bud of misery threatened to bloom in her heart, but with her usual sensible nature, Jane squashed it with a firm determination. Pity was a useless emotion. And not at all productive to her plans.

Besides which, she would dance the waltz through the netherworld before she would allow the fribbles of society to realize they possessed the ability to wound her.

With that brave thought in the forefront of her mind, Jane slipped through the door and stepped into the soothing darkness of the garden.

Or at least what passed for a garden.

She wrinkled her nose as she moved down the

narrow paths that were edged by a handful of piti-
ful roses and small fountains that determinedly
sprayed a thin stream of water. Nothing at all like
her own pleasure grounds in Surrey, she regretfully
acknowledged. Her mother had taken great pride
in creating the elegant sweep of terraced flowers,
winding pathways, and Grecian statues that framed
the large manor house. There had even been an
impish folly that had been her private sanctuary
when she had been but a child. It had not been created to impress others, or even to attempt to disguise the stench of the shop that clung to her
father. Her mother quite simply adored beauty and
devoted herself to achieving a perfect setting for
her family.

And that, of course, was what she truly missed,
she thought with a sigh. The lingering love that her
parents had bestowed upon her that filled her
home and gardens.

With aimless movements she drifted deeper into
the garden, heading toward the dainty grotto that
would offer a few moments of blessed quiet.

It was, in truth, a rare evening in London. For
once the sky was clear of the ever-threatening rain
clouds and even the fog was held at bay. She
breathed in deeply as she came to a halt and
glanced up at the star-studded sky.

"'All days are nights 'til I see thee, and nights
bright days when dreams do show thee me . . .'"

The dark, rich voice drifted softly through the air,
bringing Jane's heart to a shuddering, painful halt.
With a faint hiss of shock she glanced over her
shoulder to discover Hellion negligently strolling
down the lane.

"Hellion."

Appearing very much the fallen angel in his black attire, with his hair shimmering like priceless silver in the moonlight, he ruthlessly stalked forward. Jane tensed as he neared, her nerves tingling with that horrid awareness. She might even have fled into the darkness if he had not easily sensed her flare of panic and, with the speed of a swooping hawk, managed to gather her into his arms.

"No, do not run away, Jane," he commanded in low, urgent tones. "I must speak with you."

Firmly trapped, she gritted her teeth. Every instinct made her long to surrender at his touch, to breathe deeply of his warm, male scent, to press ever closer to the potent strength of his body. Instead she held herself stiffly and willed herself to ignore the fuzzy excitement that fluttered in the pit of her stomach.

"I did not realize you were here," she muttered in a strained voice.

The dark eyes swept over her pale countenance, seeming to linger upon the unsteady fullness of her lips. "I had just arrived when I noted you slinking through the shadows. What could I do but follow?"

Jane grimaced in embarrassment. Trust this gentleman to have arrived just in time to watch her behave as a cowardly fool.

"Oh."

"What has occurred? Is something troubling you, my sweet?"

"I . . ." Her heart jolted as his hands ran a tender path down her back. "Of course not."

He smiled wryly at her stumbling words, his hands continuing to roam with audacious boldness.

A boldness that was setting off all sorts of unwelcome tingles through her body.

"Jane, you truly are a stunningly wretched liar," he murmured.

She gave a muffled squawk as his hands reached the curve of her hips and he abruptly tugged her against his hard thighs.

"Hellion."

His grasp only tightened at her protest, his head lowering until his forehead was leaning against her own. The warm, sweet breath brushed over her lips in soft temptation.

"God, but I have missed you this past week."

Her sluggish brain seemed unwilling to concentrate upon anything beyond the press of his muscles through the thin silk of her gown and the nearness of his distracting mouth.

"You . . . you have?"

"Unbearably." He rubbed her gently against his obviously stirring body. "I did not realize how I had come to enjoy your companionship until it was denied to me. Most cruel of you, my dear."

She swallowed heavily, her breath coming in short gasps. "That is absurd. I do not believe I ever entered your thoughts."

"I may concede you to be managing, my shrew, but not even you are allowed to tell me what are my feelings."

Jane clutched at his arms. His soft words were nearly as seductive as his bold embrace. More so, in fact. She wanted to believe that he had missed her. She wanted to believe that he had discovered in her something more than a plain, unsophisticated wallflower. She wanted to believe that he had suffered the same pangs of loneliness that had haunted her over the past few days.

She wanted to believe that he had no devious motive in seeking her out.

It was a pity that her father had taught her far too well. She never accepted unexpected gifts without first discovering the cost. And there was always a cost.

"What do you want from me?" she whispered.

He offered a low groan as his lips brushed down the line of her nose and then with exquisite tenderness touched her trembling mouth.

"I want to touch you. I want to kiss you. I want to hear you say that you have missed me as much as I have missed you."

"Hellion . . . do not." Her head instinctively arched back as a nearly unbearable sweetness pierced her heart. "I cannot think when you are kissing me."

Denied her lips, Hellion promptly turned his attention to the vulnerable curve of her neck. With unnerving care he explored ever downward, his fingers holding her hips firmly against his rising passion.

"What is there to think of?" he muttered.

Jane moaned in soft pleasure, a heat spreading through her body with startling swiftness.

"Our charade is over."

"Good." He nuzzled the frantic pulse at the base of her throat. "Now you know that I kiss you because it is what I desire, not because of our bargain."

She clutched him even tighter. Why did her knees suddenly want to buckle? For that matter, why did her stomach quiver each time those maddening lips found a new source of interest?

"This is wrong," she said more to herself than to Hellion.

His husky laugh sent a thrill sizzling down her spine. "Wrong? How can a mere kiss be wrong? I assure you that I intend to do a great deal more. Shall I tell you how I will soon suckle the sweetness of your breast? How my fingers will explore the satin smoothness of your thighs until you moan in pleasure?"

"No, Hellion. I am here to find a husband, not to . . ."

"Hush," he commanded, and then, as if her words had abruptly snapped the tight leash of his control, he lifted his head and blindly sought her lips in a kiss of sheer hunger.

"Good gads, my lord, what possible interest could you have in a mere merchant?"

Biddles offered a charming smile. There was no hint that he had tediously whiled away hours in the library of Lady Vallance's town house as he awaited the rotund gentleman with a nearly bald head and enormous beak of a nose to slip from the crowded ballroom. Or that he had deliberately used his intimate knowledge of the gentleman's fondness for brandy to realize that it was as inevitable as a bee seeking nectar for him to search out this particular room. Or that he was about to use the ingenuous gentleman as a necessary pawn.

Now he casually poured them both a healthy measure of Lady Vallance's brandy and crossed to hand it to his companion.

"I?" He offered a delicate shiver as he sipped of

the fiery spirit. "Why none whatsoever. There are others, however, who have mentioned the fellow's name upon occasion. I always like to keep track of such individuals in the fortunate event they may prove of some value."

It took some time for his subtle hint to be fully grasped. Newton was not always the sharpest of fellows. Indeed, he could be as dull witted as a cheap spoon upon most occasions. Still, he was precisely the sort of gentleman Biddles was in current need of. Not only because he was personally involved in trade, but because he was one of the shabby genteel who clung so tenaciously to the fringes of society. He would do whatever possible to curry the favor of such an illustrious personage as Lord Bidwell.

"Value?" Newton offered a knowing wink. "Right. You mean you desire to sell the information?"

Biddles winced at the brash lack of delicacy, although his smile did not falter as he set aside his glass and carefully pulled a lace handkerchief from his cuff.

"Knowledge is like any other commodity. Unfortunately its worth is entirely dependent upon what another is willing to pay."

"Ah. Of course. Yes, indeed." He nervously licked his pudgy lips. "What is it you wish to know of Mr. Emerson?"

The problem was that Biddles did not know himself what information was needed. He had nothing more than the bill of sale from a Mr. Emerson & Sons that he had discovered in Jane Middleton's desk. A bill of sale that was so vague and oddly written it had naturally captured his interest.

"I understand he is in the clothing trade," he at last murmured. "A most lucrative industry."

Newton wrinkled his brow. "I suppose he does well enough. He has a modest home in Cheapside and a large flock of children."

"Only modest?"

"Yes, well, he is no Midas, if that is what you are asking."

Biddles absently touched the handkerchief to the tip of his pointed nose. "Has he had any . . . difficulties?"

Newton appeared to stiffen in offense at the question. "Do you mean with the law, sir?"

"Or financial."

There was a moment's pause, as if the man struggled between his loyalty to a fellow merchant and his desire to please such a prominent member of society.

"There was a rumor a few years ago that he had been caught selling shoddy material for military uniforms," he at last grudgingly confessed. "It was all a hum, of course. Sort of vile rumor that gets started by a jealous rival."

Biddles pursed his lips. Well, well. It appeared that his suspicions were well founded after all. "You do not believe he would attempt such a rewarding arrangement?"

"No." Newton offered his companion a gathering frown. "He and George Middleton were always on the up and up. As I said, it was all a hum."

"Middleton." Biddles experienced a pleasant flare of surprise that the gentleman's name would be so easily brought into the conversation. "Now there is a merchant who has done well for himself.

His daughter is in London enjoying the Season, I believe?"

"A fine girl, Miss Middleton. Her mother was the daughter of an earl, you know."

"Indeed." Biddles attempted to look properly impressed while determined to turn the conversation back to its original purpose. "Were Emerson and Middleton partners?"

Newton lifted a thick shoulder. "More competitors, although I believe they were always close friends."

"I see."

Clearly uneasy at discussing those he considered friends, the older man gave a gruff cough. "Is that all? I promised Cornett a few hands of piquet. Shouldn't like to disappoint him."

"Certainly not." Biddles offered his most charming smile. "I thank you for your information. I shall not forget your assistance."

A hint of relief lightened the round face. "Yes, well I always consider myself a gentleman who can be depended upon to offer what help I can. A good night to you, sir."

With an awkward bow Newton set aside his glass and turned to hurry from the room. Biddles allowed him to flee without protest. For the moment he had enough to consider. Once he had sorted out his various thoughts and speculations he would determine what was to be done next.

For now he intended to leave the stifling boredom of the ball and seek out more pleasurable entertainments without further ado. No doubt Hellion was enjoying the delights of a willing woman. He would be damned if he would waste his entire night on procuring information for his friend.

It was time to seek a bit of fun.

As if on cue there was the faintest of noise just outside the open door. Biddles narrowed his gaze as he silently moved across the room and stood with his back to the wall. Then, using all the skills at his command, he slowly reached through the opening and grasped the intruder lurking in the hallway. There was a muffled squeak as he gave a sudden jerk to pull the eavesdropper into the room.

The familiar round face of Anna Halifax flushed with embarrassment as he offered a pleased smile.

"Well, well, what have we here?"

"My lord." She swallowed heavily. "You nearly frightened me out of my wits."

His brows lifted in mocking amusement. "Do you know, my dear, I was just hoping for a lovely female to relieve my boredom." With a deliberate motion he shifted so that he could firmly shut the door and at the same moment slip a firm arm about her waist. All thoughts of fleeing for more bawdy entertainments were seared away. What could possibly be more enjoyable than teasing this enchanting creature who not only stirred his passions, but was also rare enough to intrigue his mind? "Tell me, sweet Anna, did you follow me in hopes of overhearing my very private conversation?"

"I . . ." Flustered and clearly embarrassed at having been caught in the act, Anna pressed her hands against his chest. "No. Certainly not."

He smiled deeply into the wide, startled eyes. "Good. Then that can only mean you are here for one purpose."

Her tiny tongue peeked out to wet her lips in a most seductive manner. "What purpose do you mean?"

Biddles gave a low growl as he pulled her delicious warmth ever closer. "Obviously you followed me in the hopes of snatching a few stolen kisses. A notion that I approve of wholeheartedly." His breath caught in his throat as he watched a shimmer of heat enter her blue eyes. "Oh yes. Quite, quite wholeheartedly."

CHAPTER NINE

From the diary of Miss Jane Middleton, May 17th, 1814:

P.P.S. Diary,
In all good conscience I cannot allow my previous claim of gentlemen being the oddest of creatures to stand. Such a prestigious honor must surely belong to women.

It does not seem to matter how reasonable or how independent she may be, it appears she will always be prey to her foolish emotions.

Allow a gentleman of charm to show her a bit of attention and she begins to flutter like the veriest nitwit. And should the rogue be practiced in the arts of seduction, well all he need do is pull her into his arms for her to lose whatever sense she might claim to possess.

Oh yes. Women are certainly the oddest and the most foolish of creatures.

* * *

Hellion did nothing to hide the burning desire that had plagued him for days. He could not if he wanted to. Hellfire, he was no saint. Night after night he had been tortured by the memory of Jane's sweet lips and warm, creamy skin. He had precisely recalled the manner in which her slender curves molded to his body. And of course, the delicious way that she shuddered when he nibbled at the sensitive pulse at the base of her throat.

But perhaps more than anything he recalled the astonishing pleasure of her hesitant response to his caresses.

He was a gentleman accustomed to those females who were well versed in the arts of seduction. He had been made love to by practiced courtesans from the most exotic locations and those widows who knew all there was to know about enticing a jaded gentleman.

Who the devil would have suspected that it would be the uncertain, decidedly awkward touch of a pure innocent that would make him awake during the night, shaking with a burning need?

Breathing deeply of her sweet spring scent, Hellion cupped her soft backside and pressed her urgently to his aching arousal. Thank God he had already decided to wed this minx. Otherwise he might very well be on his way to Bedlam.

"Jane . . . my damnable shrew," he muttered rather roughly. "Let us go somewhere more private."

She shuddered as he suggestively rubbed against her. "What?"

He returned to his gentle assault upon her neck. "We can hardly continue this delicious encounter in the middle of the garden. While I do not care if someone were to stumble across us, I fear that you would not be nearly so indifferent." His tongue reached out to taste of her satin skin. "Besides which, I can imagine a setting more pleasing to our needs."

Ruefully he felt the slender, eager body stiffen at his bold words. It was not that he had actually expected her to readily allow herself to be tumbled into his bed. She was a woman who believed that affection and passion were one and the same. Nothing less would do. But while his mind might logically accept her maidenly withdrawal, his body rebelled with a shuddering protest. It only knew that it was destined for another long, unrewarding night of fevered dreams.

Pressing her hands flatly against his chest, Jane tilted back her head to regard him with a wary gaze. "Please let me go, Hellion."

With a stern reminder that he would first have to win her heart to win her chastity, Hellion reluctantly loosened his grip. He did, however, maintain enough caution to keep his arms about her. He was not yet prepared to have her flee back to the safety of the house.

"But, my sweet, it is just becoming interesting," he murmured softly. "Do you not think?"

She pressed her hands to his chest, her eyes wide and beautiful as they glittered with a delicious passion.

"No . . . I do not want this."

"I could make you change your mind, you know." His fingers lightly traced the curve of her spine, his gaze easily noting her responsive shudder. "This awareness that has grown between us possesses a power of its own."

She searched his countenance that was strained with the effort to control his smoldering hunger.

"But you will not."

He smiled wryly at her instinctive trust of his sense of chivalry. Odd, that. He had never considered himself particularly noble.

"No. I will not. Not until I am certain it is what you want . . ." Hellion shifted his hand to lightly stroke his fingers over the rapid beat of her heart. "Here." A jolt of need clenched his stomach at the feel of her satin-soft skin, but with uncommon restraint he managed to halt from exploring any further. Being a proper gentleman was a damnable business, he abruptly decided. Remarkably akin to torture. "However many nights I might be left to pace the floor in frustration, I do not wish for regrets when you become mine."

"I . . ." She visibly struggled to maintain control of her faltering will. "No. This is insanity. I will not be seduced. I will belong only to my husband."

Warmth flared through his heart. A startling and peculiar warmth considering that he had never considered himself a prude. Far from it, in fact. He was a gentleman of society. He was intimately familiar with the decided lack of fidelity among noble marriages. Good God, it was nearly mandatory to indulge in a series of discrete liaisons if one desired to be fashionable.

Who the devil would ever have suspected that he would find such a deep sense of satisfaction at the sincere knowledge this woman would never play her husband false?

He smiled tenderly. "I am well aware that you hold your honor dear, Jane. That is one of the things that I most admire about you. Believe me, a gentleman does not readily commit his destiny to a woman who offers her favors to every rake and rogue who happens by."

A tense silence descended at his revealing words. Hellion discovered himself watching with rueful amusement as her eyes slowly widened with a stunned wariness.

"Hellion?"

"Yes, my love?"

Her brows drew together. "Have you been drinking?"

He gave a sudden chuckle at her hesitant words. "Not as yet. However, I do fear that it shall come to that before the evening is done. I have discovered a profound dislike for frustrated desire. It not only makes my temperament uncertain, but it ensures a long, decidedly unpleasant night."

The moonlight revealed the various emotions that flittered over her expressive countenance. Bewilderment, suspicion, and a growing unease at his unexpected behavior.

"What do you want from me, Hellion?" she at last demanded in low tones.

"What do I want?" He deliberately paused as his gaze ran a slow, thorough survey over her slender form. "I want you, of course. Your slender, delectable body. Your tart tongue and shrewd intelligence. Your peculiar habits and amazing skills. I want all of you."

Without warning she was roughly wrenching herself from his light grasp and glaring at him with unexpected resentment.

"I suppose you are attempting to be amusing?"

Hellion lifted his brows. "I should be very much obliged if you would not discover me a figure of jest. No gentleman desires his beloved to consider him a buffoon."

Jane wrapped her arms about her waist, stepping back as if knowing he would not hesitate to pull her back into his arms if the urge should take him.

"I . . . I wish you would not tease me so, Hellion. It is not at all kind."

His smile faded as he slowly realized that he had unwittingly struck her most vulnerable wound. Despite her rare intelligence and independent spirit, she possessed an unrelenting lack of confidence in her ability to attract the attentions of a gentleman. A lack of confidence that had only been reinforced by the pathetic dandies she had encountered since arriving in London.

"For such a very clever woman you are being excessively dense, my lovely shrew," he said with a gentle smile. "I think it should be obvious by now that I am not teasing. Indeed, I am attempting to woo you in the prescribed manner. Clearly with a ghastly lack of talent."

Her frown only deepened. "That is absurd."

Unable to help himself, Hellion reached out to touch a soft curl that lay against her temple. He was deeply thankful that Jane was not a shallow flirt. The sort who was well aware of her beauty and used it as a means of manipulating those about them. The mere thought was enough to make him shudder in horror. Still, he was beginning to suspect her refusal to accept the depth of her own delightful charm was bound to try his patience to the fullest.

"I must say you are rather brutal upon a gentleman's pride, my sweet. I will admit to having little experience in the arts of courtship but surely I cannot be making such a hash of it?"

"This is absurd. Why would you court me? I have already given you the money I promised."

Hellion was caught off guard by the fierce flare of anger that raced through him. "Do not do that."

She blinked at his harsh tone. "I beg your pardon?"

He grasped her chin in firm fingers and sternly glared into her wide gaze. "I will readily accept any insults that you might decide to hurl in my direction. Most are no doubt well earned. I will not, however, allow you to insult yourself."

"Sir . . ."

"No," he ruthlessly overrode her instinctive protest. "I do not know what maggot you have gotten into your head to believe that your only allure is that of your fortune, but allow me to tell you that while many frivolous gentlemen might seek shallow beauty and brittle charm, there are a rare few of us with enough intelligence to prefer those maidens of genuine wit and steady temperament. We are also, surprisingly enough, wise enough to recognize genuine worth from amongst the dross."

That aggravating disbelief refused to be shaken. If anything her wariness only deepened as she fiercely studied his somber expression.

"You are saying that you wish to court me?" she demanded in abrupt tones.

"That is the traditional means of acquiring a bride, I believe."

"A . . . bride?"

"I desire to wed you. Is that so shocking?"

"Saints above, of course it is."

"Why?"

She sucked in an unsteady breath. "Well to begin with, you have no desire to wed. I heard the words from your lips. You said that you had no intention of becoming *leg-shackled* to any female."

Hellion swallowed a sigh. Damn it all. It was bad enough to have his rakish reputation hanging about his neck like a yoke without also having Jane acutely aware of his long-held distaste for marriage. His uphill battle to convince her of his sincerity became even more slippery.

"That was true enough until I encountered a stubborn, sharp-tongued, utterly desirable shrew," he murmured in seductive tones. With considerable care he allowed his fingers to leave the stubborn chin to stroke over the softness of her cheek. "Now it does not seem nearly so unbearable. Indeed, the notion holds such temptation I can no longer resist."

He thought that the blue eyes darkened with a hint of longing, but before he could take any hope from the brief glimpse into her heart, Jane was abruptly stepping from his light touch.

"No," she breathed in a harsh tone.

"What?"

"I do not believe you."

Hellion allowed a slow, wicked smile to curve his lips. About him the warm scent of roses and the enticing moonlight added the perfect atmosphere for romance. He took a step closer, his entire body humming with a smoldering excitement.

"Well, I am quite prepared to convince you of my sincerity, my sweet. In truth, I can think of little that will bring me more pleasure."

Easily sensing his barely leashed passions she took another hasty step backward, nearly tumbling over a nearby rosebush.

"Hellion. Stop this at once."

He smiled wryly. So much for a swift, painless seduction. Romance might be in the air, but Jane's reaction appeared closer to panic than delight.

Planting his hands upon his hips he regarded her with a stern expression. Whatever her reluctance she would not be allowed to leave this garden believing he was anything but fully determined to win her hand.

"You are going to be my wife, you know," he said in tones that revealed the depth of his conviction. "Oh, you might protest and attempt to deceive yourself that I am not the one gentleman in all of London that is perfectly suited to be your husband. After all, I am not a comfortable, easily swayed man. Nor will I settle for a relationship of mere friendship. I desire you too much for that. But in the end you will accept that I can bring you far greater happiness than any other."

She paled at his blunt honesty. Almost as if she feared his stark declaration.

"I . . . I must return to the ballroom," she at last muttered.

He instinctively opened his mouth to insist that she accept the truth of her inevitable future. She might be stubborn, but not even she could hope to resist his determination. But the air of restless tension that shimmered about her taut form held the impulsive words.

Perhaps it would be for the best to allow her time

to adjust to the knowledge she was to become his wife, he reluctantly concluded.

His body gave a sharp pang of protest at the thought. The decidedly male desire to conquer and possess had no comprehension of the virtues of patience.

"I will escort you."

"No." She gave a violent shake of her head as she stumbled farther down the path. "That is not necessary."

Hellion's brows snapped together. "I am well aware that it is not necessary. It is simply what I wish to do."

She swallowed heavily. "Hellion, please. I wish to be alone."

He muttered a curse as he leashed his darker desires. Soon enough she would be his. Heart, soul, and body. Then he would sate himself in her temptation until both of them were fully satisfied.

"Very well." He met her gaze squarely. "But do not believe that you can escape me for long, my sweet. Your fate was decided that first night you approached me with your wicked bargain. You are mine."

Her eyes widened, but with that staunch courage he could not help but admire, the woman forced herself to gather her badly rattled composure about her and with only the faintest tremble in her step turned to sweep up the path toward the ballroom.

With a small smile Hellion allowed her to escape. As he had warned, there was nowhere she could go that he would not follow. Not now. He had chosen her as his bride. The future was settled whether she was willing to accept the truth or not.

* * *

Anna choked back a small groan as the deceptively experienced Biddles nibbled his way down the arch of her throat.

This was not the reason she had followed Lord Bidwell, she fuzzily attempted to assure herself. She had known from the moment he had disappeared into the library that he was up to something nefarious. Not that he wasn't up to something nefarious almost every moment, she silently conceded. But this appeared more nefarious than usual.

And her suspicions had only been confirmed when she had witnessed the portly gentleman entering the library and remaining for several long moments.

What possible interest could a gentleman of Lord Bidwell's social standing have with a man who was well known to dabble in trade and barely clung to the fringes of society?

Was he simply slumming? Or had he cleverly ensured he would encounter the man because he was well known to have been acquainted with Mr. Middleton?

She knew she had to slip close enough to overhear what was being said. Even at the risk of being caught by the unnervingly clever rogue.

It had all seemed quite reasonable. Quite necessary, in fact.

Until the moment that she had been gathered in strong, demanding arms and knowing lips had covered her mouth in a kiss that threatened to steal every wit she claimed to possess.

It was then, when pleasure was coursing through her and her knees were trembling, that she had to reluctantly confront the notion that it might not have been entirely selfless motives that had led her to stalk the flamboyant gentleman. Or why she had remained when it was obvious the impromptu meeting was at an end.

Some sneaking, weasely part of her had hoped that this was precisely what would occur when she had snuck down the hall and lingered in the shadows. A part that had slyly remained hidden until too late.

Now she desperately battled the fierce urge to simply close her eyes and allow this gentleman to continue with his delightful seduction.

"No," she whispered softly. "No."

Ever so gently he nibbled the line of her collarbone. "Yes, yes."

"Lord Bidwell . . ."

"Biddles," he breathed against her sensitive skin. "Or Horatio, if you prefer."

A warm tension was building deep within her. A distracting, delicious tension that seemed directly connected to the lips that relentlessly explored down to the curve of her breast.

"What I prefer is that you release me," she forced herself to mutter.

"No, that is perhaps what you *should* prefer," he mocked softly, his breath sending a rash of excitement over her prickling skin. "But I hear the beat of your heart and feel the heat of passion that flushes your satin skin. You cannot hide the truth from me."

Nor could she hide it from herself.

She was drowning in sensations she was incapable of controlling. All too soon she would be beyond sense. Her only hope was a cowardly retreat. And the sooner the better.

Unfortunately she did not believe that Biddles

would readily allow her to flee. Not when he must be aware how very close she was to surrender.

Clearly a distraction was in order.

"What were you doing in this library?" she asked, at last managing to launch an attack. "Waiting for Mr. Newton so you could question him about Jane?"

Anna sensed her seducer stiffen with a mixture of relief and unmistakable regret. The ploy had worked. Her virtue appeared to be saved.

Damn.

Pulling back, Biddles regarded her with an oddly tender smile. "Very clever, my sweet Anna, but one of these days you are going to forget to halt me."

Anna sucked in a sharp breath. Blast but it would be lovely to toss the smug claim back into his face. She was no silly widgeon who could have her head turned by every gentleman who revealed the slightest interest in her. Oh no. She was wise and clever and all too aware of the dangerous games such rakes enjoyed playing.

Unfortunately she was also far too honest to even consider such a ridiculous ploy.

They both knew she was playing with fire. And that it would take only one moment of weakness for disaster to occur.

More shaken than she cared to admit, she silently slipped from the warmth of his arms and forced her heavy feet to carry her to the waiting ballroom.

CHAPTER TEN

From the diary of Miss Jane Middleton, May 18th, 1814:

Dear Diary,

I suppose every maiden dreams of the moment when a gentleman might fulfill her fantasy and propose marriage to her.

Even dull, practical wallflowers who should be too sensible for such nonsense.

In my daydreams I imagined a rather small, kindly suitor much like my father. Bending on one knee he would offer a lovely bouquet of violets. He would be nervous, perhaps even stumble and stammer as he spoke of his wish to have me as his bride, but his eyes . . . oh, his sweet eyes would glow with the love he sheltered in his heart.

Never in all my life would I have ever imagined my first, and perhaps last, proposal would come more as a command than a request. Certainly I could never have guessed that the gentleman in question would be a large, sinfully handsome rake who

*could have his pick of women. Nor that the glow in
his eyes would have nothing to do with love and yet
would send dark demons and wicked need racing
through my blood.*

"Marry you? Hellion?" Anna sputtered out the
tea she had just sipped and regarded Jane with blatant disbelief.

"Yes."

"Hellion desires to marry you?"

Standing beside the window of the library Jane
smiled wryly. She could not blame her friend for
appearing shocked. Even dumbfounded. After all,
only a loon would ever suspect the Ton's most elusive, most sought-after bachelor would propose
marriage to a plain, eccentric wallflower. And Anna
most certainly was not a loon.

Still, she could not deny a small prick of wounded
pride.

It was not as if she were entirely repulsive, she
told herself. Or witless. Or upon her last prayer.
Indeed, some might say she was intelligent, well
tempered, and tidy. She even possessed all her own
teeth.

What more could a gentleman desire?

Jane gave a sudden chuckle. She knew very well
that most gentlemen desired a great deal more.
Beauty, breeding, and of course, luscious curves.
Her charms were unfortunately meager when compared with other maidens. Regardless of whether
she possessed all her own teeth or not.

"'Tis shocking, is it not?"

"It is . . . unbelievable." Setting aside her teacup,

Anna gave a slow shake of her head. "Truly, utterly unbelievable."

"Yes . . ."

"Hellion?"

"Hellion."

"Married to you?"

"Married to me."

"Good heavens."

"I believe that we have adequately determined that his offer of marriage to an aging wallflower is a shocking thing."

As if suddenly realizing she was being less than complimentary to her friend, Anna offered a rueful grimace.

"Oh, it is not his offer of marriage to *you* I find so amazing. I mean any gentleman of sense would far prefer you to those horrid, simpering chits that fill the ballrooms. It is his offer of marriage to any woman," she hurriedly explained. "I would have wagered my aunt's ruby tiara that the man was a confirmed rake and rogue."

Jane absently leaned against the window, recalling her brief encounter with Hellion in the garden. It was a memory that had haunted and plagued her throughout the long, sleepless night.

"He is a rake and rogue." She folded her arms about her waist. "No doubt the most accomplished in all of England."

"And yet . . . he desires to make you his wife."

Wife. A terrible thrill of pleasure raced through Jane before she was sternly squashing the sensation. It was precisely those unfamiliar tingles, flutters, and palpitations that made her so wary of Hellion, she reminded herself. No woman could think in a sensible manner when her nerves were quivering and her heart thumping about with excitement.

"That is what he claims," she murmured.

"Claims?" Anna slowly rose to her feet. "What do you mean? Do you believe his proposal a jest?"

"In truth, I do not know what to believe, Anna."

"Well, what did he say?"

Jane paused only for a moment before relating the baffling, disturbing encounter in the garden. Oh, not the bit about the drugging kisses and skillful caresses. Some intimacies were too private to share even with her best friend.

When at last she fell silent Anna gave a disbelieving laugh.

"Well, it does not seem as if he were jesting. Indeed I would say he is quite determined to have you as his wife."

Jane was not at all comforted by her friend's words. In some ways it would be easier to presume that Hellion had merely been playing a poor jest than to consider the notion that he intended to press a courtship upon her.

"But why?"

Anna gave a small lift of her hands. "Could it not be because he cares for you and knows that you will bring him happiness?"

With a sigh Jane wrapped her arms about her waist. "That is the trouble, is it not?"

"What do you mean?"

"How does a woman ever know what is in a gentleman's heart? How does she know if his regard is sincere or if he seeks to deceive her?"

A startling dry smile abruptly twisted her friend's soft lips. "You ask your questions of the wrong woman, Jane. All I know of gentlemen is that they were placed on this earth to vex and plague poor females."

Jane wrinkled her nose in rueful agreement. "True enough."

There was a short pause before Anna slowly walked to stand before Jane with a somber expression.

"What is it you fear, Jane?"

Jane took a moment before she gave a restless shrug. "I do not understand Hellion's motives. He could possess any woman he desired. Why would he wish to marry me?"

"Does it matter?" Anna reached out to gently touch her arm. "You came to London to discover a husband, and now you have managed to interest the most elusive catch of the town. Why quibble over motives?"

The quiet words took Jane by surprise and she discovered herself regarding her friend with wide eyes.

"That should be obvious."

"You are not attracted to him?"

Jane gave a sharp, humorless laugh. "A woman would have to be in her grave not to be attracted to Hellion. Which is precisely the point."

"What?"

"Only a fool would desire a rake as a husband," she retorted in what she could only hope were firm tones. "I came to London to discover a gentleman who can share my life in Surrey. Someone who is interested in handling the estate and sharing my love for business. Most of all I desire someone who will care for me enough to begin a family."

Anna offered a distinctly mysterious smile. "And

how can you be so certain that Hellion cannot offer these things?"

"Hellion?" Jane briefly wondered if Anna had been sneaking into the brandy. Or perhaps she had simply been spending too much time in the company of Lord Bidwell. Something had certainly turned her shrewd wits to mush. "The man is a creature of London. He would be miserable stuck in the midst of the country with nothing more to tempt his fancy than a handful of dull assemblies, or worse, remaining home with his plain, tedious wife and children. How long do you think it would be before he became bored beyond bearing? Before he returned to town and his more pleasing entertainments?"

"Jane." Anna squeezed her arm once again. "You have judged him without allowing him to reveal what he desires in a marriage with you. How can you not be certain he has not wearied of his life as a rake and rogue? Or that he might inwardly long for a family? Should you not at least give him the opportunity to prove whether he is his willing to be the sort of husband you wish?"

A sharp, poignant memory of Hellion speaking of his parents rose to mind. There had been no mistaking the aching loss he had experienced. And the pain of being forced to reside with an uncle who shamed him. For that moment she had sensed the deep loneliness within him. A loneliness that was echoed within her own heart.

Was it possible that he did seek to discover someone he could share his life with? That he could put aside his enjoyment of exotic mistresses and gambling clubs to settle into a mundane existence as husband and father?

It seemed utterly nonsensical. Rather like expecting a dangerous, predatory panther to be trained as a house cat.

A shiver raced down her spine.

She had told the truth. She had come to London for a safe, comfortable, quietly dependable husband. How foolish would it be to instead return home with a dashing, restless, utterly gorgeous rogue?

Foolish. Very, very foolish, a dark voice warned in the back of her mind.

But . . . ah, so tempting.

Realizing that her friend was regarding her with growing concern, Jane gave a faint shake of her head.

"It is not so simple, Anna."

"Nothing ever is." She offered a faint smile. "All I am suggesting is that you offer him the opportunity to court you. What can be the harm? If you decide you do not suit then you can decline his proposal. In the meantime why not enjoy being wooed by a true expert?"

Jane discovered herself without an answer.

She was quite certain that there was a great deal of harm that Hellion could wreak in her quiet, sensible life. But annoyingly it was impossible to pinpoint the exact source of her vague fears.

Instead she once again recalled the guarded vulnerability she had glimpsed within those wicked eyes.

"I do not know, Anna," she murmured uncertainly, her heart whispering with unease.

"Just give it some thought before you do anything you might later regret."

* * *

"You intend to wed the chit?"

Hellion could not hide his grin as he watched the end of Biddles's nose twitch in unmistakable shock. He had known when he had decided to seek his friend's help that his announcement would cause something of a scandal. He was after all renowned for his allergy to intimate relationships. Especially those that might be permanent.

But after watching his intended flee from his marriage proposal as if the devil were upon her heels last evening, he had known that he needed advice.

Advice . . . he heaved a rueful sigh.

It was ridiculous, of course.

Gads, he had seduced a countless number of women over the years. He knew precisely the intricate steps of the delicious waltz.

The first knowing glances. The casual brush of fingers. The deliberate encounters. The kiss. The intimate caress. And at last the fulfillment of the passions that had been stirred to aching life.

Even more importantly he understood the small details demanded by such a seduction.

Sending flowers in her favorite color. Indulging her love for pretty baubles. Remembering the first moment they met or her birthday. And of course, showering her with the unwavering attention that assured the woman that his entire soul was focused upon her alone.

Thus he was the consummate rake.

But for once in his life, Hellion was forced to acknowledge that all his well-honed skills were going to be tested to the limit when dealing with a young woman.

Jane . . .

His stubborn, independent, stoically practical Jane had no interest in the frivolous games of romance. She might accept his flowers, but she preferred to view them in the garden. She disdained baubles. And as for his unwavering attention . . . well, he could not deny that she would just as soon be closeted with her damnable man of business as to be receiving compliments from him.

And while he was confident that she desired him, she was not about to allow her passions to rule her heart.

It was enough to make a hardened rogue take to the bottle.

"Yes, I intend to wed her," he retorted in firm tones, leaning back in the comfortable sofa with his legs stretched before him.

"Good Lord." With swift motions Biddles was at the heavy sideboard to pour a large measure of brandy. Only when he had swallowed the lot in one gulp did he turn back to regard Hellion with a glittering gaze. "Why?"

"Why what?"

"Dammit, man. Why has the most notorious bachelor in all of England suddenly decided to toss aside his joyous existence to join the dull ranks of pathetic drudges?"

Expecting a pang of regret at the accusation, Hellion was startled to discover nothing more than vague amusement at his friend's obvious disbelief.

"Because I met Miss Jane Middleton," he answered simply.

"That is your reason?"

"Yes."

"Is she with child?"

Hellion's smile abruptly vanished. Perhaps it was because of the scowl that darkened his countenance.

"No, she is damn well not with child," Hellion growled, unreasonably annoyed by the question. "And I warn you that the next slur you make upon my intended bride will be the last you make with a full set of teeth."

There was a moment of silence as Biddles carefully scrutinized his forbidding frown, and then quite inexplicably the sly rascal tilted back his head to laugh with a rich enjoyment.

"Yes, I see," he at last murmured, moving to settle upon a plush velvet chair, his amusement still visible upon the thin countenance.

"What do you see?"

"Either a miracle or a tragedy. Time will tell." He leaned back with a faint smile. "Now, tell me why you came to see me this morning. Surely it was not merely to receive my best wishes for your upcoming nuptials?"

Hellion forced his stiff muscles to relax. Perhaps it was understandable that his friend was somewhat rattled, he told himself. Hell, he was rattled. And he did need assistance, as much as it rubbed his pride to admit it.

"Actually your best wishes would be rather premature," he grudgingly conceded. "She has not yet agreed."

"Fah." Biddles lifted an elegant hand. "A mere technicality. You cannot suppose she would be daft enough to refuse your suit, do you?"

Hellion gave a humorless chuckle. "Without hesitation. Miss Middleton has a mind of her own and is not at all impressed by the knowledge I am considered an enviable catch among the Ton. Indeed, I believe that it is one of the reasons that she hesitates to accept the sincerity of my offer. She cannot accept that I would truly desire her as my wife."

"A mind of her own, eh? That could prove a problem," Biddles acknowledged wryly. "I have lately discovered women with their own minds can be shockingly difficult to train to the leash."

Hellion gave a lift of one brow. "*You* have discovered? My dear Biddles, whatever do you mean?"

Startled, the sly gentleman gave a discomfited cough at the blunt question. "Nothing more than a passing acquaintance with such a female. Thankfully we are discussing you and your troubles this morning. Tell me of your plans to win Miss Middleton's agreement to your proposal."

Hellion resisted the urge to torment his friend. It would be a delight to discover precisely who this mystery woman was who had put him in such a twit. That would have to wait until later, however. When he could fully enjoy the pleasure of watching Biddles squirm.

"I haven't a plan," he admitted with a hint of frustration. "Unfortunately, I am discovering that there is a considerable difference between seducing a woman and courting an innocent maiden. Especially a maiden who has no interest in the usual flirtations."

Biddles templed his fingers beneath his chin. "You are certain she is so opposed to flirtations?"

Hellion smiled dryly. "Well, she certainly is in no danger of being overwhelmed by my brilliantly pathetic attempts."

"That was when she thought your attentions were merely a ruse that she had bought and paid for. She would have been a fool to be swayed by your charm before you announced your intention to wed."

Hellion was not so easily convinced. "She did not seem any more amenable to my charms even after I proposed. In truth she fled from me as if she feared I might carry the plague."

"Well, you can hardly blame her. No doubt she was somewhat caught off guard by your offer," Biddles soothed, his lips twisting. "God knows I was."

Hellion frowned as he pondered the explanation. It was true enough that he had taken Jane by surprise. Hell's fire, she had been shocked to the tips of her tiny toes.

"Perhaps." His fingers tapped an impatient tattoo upon the arm of the sofa. He did not like this feeling of uncertainty. It was not at all what he was accustomed to. "So you believe she will welcome my attentions once she accepts that I am in earnest?"

Biddles offered a faint shrug. "Unfortunately that is impossible to say. Miss Middleton does not seem to be the type to give her heart lightly. Especially not to a seasoned rake."

"Well, that is a bloody lot of help," Hellion muttered in exasperation. "Do you suppose I should toss her over my shoulder and haul her to Gretna Green?"

A decided amusement tugged at his companion's lips. "I do not believe such a drastic action is called for. At least not yet."

"Then what the hell am I to do?"

"Romance her."

Hellion blinked in bewilderment. "What?"

"Every young woman dreams of romance," Biddles patiently explained.

"Not Jane," Hellion retorted in stubborn tones. "She is far too wary to allow herself to be seduced. I will have to win her trust before I can bed her."

Biddles gave a click of his tongue. "I did not mean to seduce her. Or at least, not exactly."

"Then what the devil do you mean?"

"I mean that you must offer her romance, not the shallow flirtations that the more sophisticated women enjoy."

Hellion abruptly grimaced. "Gads, you cannot mean spouting hideous poetry and kneeling at her feet like a besotted fool? I could not bear it. Not to mention the fact that Jane would have me committed to Bedlam."

"I mean considering how best to please her. Discover what she enjoys, what makes her laugh or stirs her emotions. And of course you must be unpredictable. Shower her with surprises until she does not know what to expect from one moment to the other." A sudden gleam entered the pale eyes. "If nothing else such things will keep her off guard until you can lure her into your bed."

Despite his uncertainty that such tactics would sway his utterly sensible Jane, Hellion gave a slow nod. He supposed it was worth a try.

And if it didn't work, then he would reconsider the notion of Gretna Green.

Or perhaps taking her to his bed and not letting her out until she admitted he was the only gentleman who could bring her happiness.

"Very well. Let us decide precisely how I am to romance Miss Middleton into my arms and up the nearest aisle."

It was three days later when Hellion was at last prepared to approach his reluctant bride. Attired in a striking blue coat and pale breeches he called for his tilbury and matching grays. From there it was only a short drive to Jane's tidy town house.

Leaving his groom to walk the restless horses, Hellion vaulted up the steps and offered a ready smile for the butler who held open the door.

"Good day, Reeves. I presume Miss Middleton is at home?"

The elderly servant offered a regretful shake of his head. "I fear not, sir. She left quite early to take a stroll through the nearby park. She should be returning at any moment if you would care to wait."

A sudden smile curved Hellion's lips. He had realized that the most difficult part of his scheme would be luring Jane from the protection of her home. She could be extraordinarily stubborn when she desired. And while he was quite willing to simply toss her over his shoulder and carry her out, if worse came to worse, he preferred not to start off their journey with her temper in full fury. He was, after all, intent on romance.

Thankfully it appeared such pirate tactics would not be needed. She had readily left herself available to be swept off her feet.

Now, he just had to track her down so he could start his sweeping.

With an impatient lift of his hand he had his groom hurrying back to the curb and within moments Hellion was bowling down the road toward the small park. He had just reached the gates when he spied the familiar slender form in a plain gray gown and straw bonnet walking briskly in his direction. With a pleasurable tingle of anticipation he pulled the carriage to a halt and watched her approach.

Not yet aware of his arrival Jane continued down the path with her head lowered as if in deep thought. Hellion leaned back upon the leather seat with a flare of amusement.

Gads, but she appeared a dowd, he acknowledged with a low chuckle. The dull gray of her gown did nothing to compliment the dusky skin or the lovely blue eyes. And no lady of style would be caught dead in a bonnet that would have been more fitting for a milkmaid.

Still, he could not deny the intense pleasure that filled him at the sight of her. Not just a sensual awareness, although he ached for her with a desperation that was nearly frightening, but more an odd warmth that seemed to ease the restlessness that constantly plagued him.

This woman offered what no other woman had ever offered.

A peace and deep sense of security that he had not even realized he longed for.

Unaware of the glow of contentment that smoldered in his dark eyes, Hellion waited for his soon-to-be-wife to reach the gates. Then, with the swift grace of a hunting panther he was leaping from the carriage and moving silently to place his large form directly in her path.

With her head still lowered Jane had no warning

of his sudden approach. Not until she was within touching distance did she abruptly come to a halt. Then, as if already sensing who stood before her, she slowly lifted her head.

"Good day, my sweet," he murmured.

"Hellion." An expression of sweet longing, or at least what he convinced himself was sweet longing, briefly rippled over the gamine countenance before the staunch composure was wrestled back into place. "What are you doing here?"

His lips twitched at the question. From any other woman he would presume she was being deliberately coy. Jane, however, was never coy.

"Seeking you, of course."

"Oh." She folded her hands together, as if to hide her unease. "Why?"

Instinctively his hand lifted to gently touch the amazing softness of her cheek. At the same moment he leaned just close enough to catch the intoxicating scent of sweet spring that clung to her skin.

"It seems to have become rather a habit lately," he murmured, his gaze drifting toward those soft lips that had become a nightly torment in his dreams. Soon, he told his frustrated body. Soon those lips would be performing every erotic fantasy he had ever harbored. "I do hope you are not so elusive once we are wed. I prefer the thought of us comfortably settled in each others' arms before a warm fire to dashing through the neighborhood in pursuit of my wife."

He heard her breath catch before she was forcing herself to regard him with a stern gaze of disapproval.

"I have said nothing to indicate that I am willing to be your wife, sir."

Hellion merely shrugged. "But you will. It is inevitable."

"Nothing is inevitable." The finely arched brows rose in a silent reprimand. "Especially when it comes to my future husband."

He countered the stern words with a deliberately bland smile. "If it comforts you to believe so, my sweet."

An exasperated sigh hissed through her clenched teeth. "Saints give me patience. You truly are . . ."

"Arrogant? Impossible? Utterly enchanting?" he helpfully supplied.

The blue eyes flashed, but the irrepressible sense of humor that was such a part of her charm curved her lips in a reluctant smile.

"Utterly daft."

"Perhaps." He lowered his gaze as his fingers lightly drifted to stroke over the maddening lips. A foolish mistake. His randy passions were instantly stirred as he easily imagined those lips pressed beneath his own. Or better yet, feeling them stroking down his throat and nibbling softly over his chest. Perhaps they would tease at his nipples before straying downward over the tense muscles of his stomach and then . . . damn, damn, damn. He abruptly cut off the persistent image before he became completely aroused. Why the devil did he continue to fantasize about those damnable lips? With an effort he returned his wicked thoughts to less dangerous terrain. "They claim that all gentlemen become incomprehensibly daft once in their life and that the only cure is marriage. You hold the return of my sanity in your delicate hands, my dear."

Jane appeared oddly flustered by his soft words. "I . . . Why did you wish to see me?"

"Ah." He regarded her with a mysterious smile. "I have a surprise for you."

He felt her stiffen beneath his fingers. "A surprise? For me?"

He did not expect the squeals of delight and excitement that he had come to expect from his mistresses at the mention of a surprise. Or even the impassioned kisses that they readily bestowed.

Still, there was no call for the guarded wariness that shrouded her.

"Do not regard me with such suspicion," he said dryly. "I do not have a special license tucked in my pocket, nor do I intend to haul you off to Gretna Green, as tempting as the thought might be."

"What is it?"

"It would hardly be a surprise if I tell you."

She unwittingly gnawed upon her lower lip as she searched his countenance for some hint of his intentions.

"Then where is it?"

"Ah, that is part of the surprise."

"You truly expect me to simply allow you to take me off heaven knows where for heaven knows how long without the least concern?"

His smile faded as he shifted to take her small hands firmly in his own, waiting until he had firmly captured her gaze with his own.

"I hope you will trust me."

Her eyes darkened as her teeth continued to worry her poor lip. "I do not know if I can."

A sharp stab pierced Hellion's heart at her hesitant words. He had always avoided the sort of entanglements that would demand another's trust. Such close relationships came with responsibilities that he did not desire. Now he found himself struggling to find the means of proving he was worthy to command her confidence.

"Jane, all I am asking for is your faith in this one moment," he urged in husky tones. "How else will you ever learn that you can believe in me?"

"I . . ."

"Please, my sweet."

Hellion held his breath as Jane silently battled within herself. No doubt her common sense was urging her to flatly refuse to spend a moment in his company. As she was well aware he was a rake and rogue who could easily take advantage of the slightest vulnerability. But at the same time there was a hint of curiosity that she could not completely deny. And a renegade desire to be in his company.

At last she sucked in a steadying breath and lifted her chin to a defiant angle.

"Very well, Hellion. But I warn you, if this is a trick I shall make you regret your deception."

A flare of relief rushed through him as Hellion gave a low chuckle. He had won the first skirmish. And without the least amount of bloodshed.

Surely that boded well for the future battle?

"Consider me properly warned, my sweet. Shall we go?"

CHAPTER ELEVEN

From the diary of Miss Jane Middleton, May 21st, 1814:

Dear Diary,

After three and twenty years I am intimately familiar with my earthly body. I realize that it is too slender and lacking the more feminine curves. It also moves with a brisk impatience no matter how often I practice a more graceful sway. All in all it is far more functional than beautiful, but I have learned to accept what cannot be changed and at least appreciate the sound health and strong constitution that I have been blessed with.

It was not until Hellion blazed his way into my life that I realized a body could become a fickle traitor that refused to obey the commands of the more rational brain.

He has only to be near for my heart to thunder with uncontrollable excitement, my palms to sweat in the most embarrassing fashion, and my stomach to quiver with the strangest longing. There are even moments when I must remind myself to breathe.

Jane perched upon the edge of the carriage seat in stiff silence.

It was not that she feared the swift pace as they rumbled toward the outskirts of London, she acknowledged with a faint shiver. Heaven knew that Hellion was far too notable a whip to put them into danger.

Nor did she fear the mysterious destination he had chosen. If he truly desired to marry her, he would never dare to create a scandal that might ruin her reputation.

The truth was that she could not be at ease when seated so close to the dratted man.

A grim smile curved her lips. She might as well attempt to be at ease as a bolt of lightning struck her.

It felt remarkably similar.

With every sway of the carriage she was lurched against the granite-hard muscles of his thighs. Each breath she took was laced with the warm, male scent of his skin. And even with her eyes trained firmly forward she could feel the searing brush of his gaze as it lingered upon her profile.

Heat and awareness crackled about her, making her muscles tense and her heart leap and jump with peculiar unpredictability.

Dash it all. She must have been crazed when she allowed Anna to convince her to allow Hellion the opportunity to court her.

Perhaps she did enjoy his companionship and his clever wit. Certainly she appreciated his rare ability to treat her as a woman of intelligence and independence. And she would not be human if she did not take a measure of pleasure from the knowledge that she had managed to attract the interest of a gentleman desired by every damsel in England.

The sophisticated, utterly fascinating Hellion desired to wed her. Her. Jane Middleton. The woman who was always overlooked and sentenced to molder in the shadows. The woman who was never asked to dance or to stroll upon the veranda. The woman all others pitied. It was bound to tempt her vanity.

But considering the notion of Hellion as a suitor from an intellectual fashion was one thing. It was decidedly different when she was perched at his side and her entire body was tingling with fierce awareness.

How the devil was she to logically assess him as a potential mate when her thoughts kept straying along pathways that were not at all productive? Paths that were positively wicked.

She already knew she wanted him as a lover.

What she needed to know was if he could be a dependable companion and friend.

It was time to make a passing bid for sanity.

"How far do you intend to travel?" she demanded in tones deliberately serene.

She sensed his quirk of amusement at her pretense of calm. No doubt the rat was well aware that her pulse was racing and her stomach clutched in a tight ball of nerves.

"Not far," he evaded, skillfully keeping the powerful grays under control as he weaved through the heavy traffic. "And the trip will take us through some lovely countryside. I thought it might be nice for you to be away from the city."

She suppressed a dry smile. He was attempting to maneuver her as effortlessly as he did the willful stallions. Still, she could not deny that it was rather nice that he recalled her love for the fresh air and rolling fields.

"It is always nice to be away from London."

"Oh, surely it is not so bad?"

Jane grimaced. "It smells."

Hellion tilted back his head to offer a sudden laugh. "Well, I cannot argue with that. Then why do you not tell me of your estate in Surrey? Does it smell more inviting?"

"Of course. In the summer it smells of flowers and in the winter the air carries the scent of the sea."

"It sounds quite enticing. I can hardly wait to view it for myself."

Jane abruptly stiffened, wondering if he thought that marrying her would bring him some lavish, elegant estate.

"I fear that most would consider it a small estate. It is not nearly as grand or large as you might expect. Indeed, we have only a handful of tenants and the house is not at all what you have become accustomed to . . ."

"Enough, Jane." He tossed her a stern glance. "You will not frighten me off with such foolishness."

She blinked with seeming innocence. "What foolishness?"

"Your attempts to convince me that your estate is some cramped, shabby affair," he retorted. "You will not alter my determination to wed you and it surely is an insult to your home."

She wrinkled her nose at his shrewd perception. Why did she continue to underestimate him? For all his rakish ways he had proven to be astonishingly intelligent.

"I did speak truly, it is not large," she retorted, unwittingly allowing her expression to soften as she thought of her beloved home. "Still the parklands are well tended with gardens that are so lovely they will steal your breath. My father claimed that my mother must be part fey to create such beauty."

"Do you work in the gardens?"

"No." She gave a soft chuckle. "I do not possess my mother's magic. Indeed, I have only to brush past a plant to have it wither and die. But I do have several talented gardeners who keep the grounds as my mother left them."

He offered a gentle smile before returning his attention to the road leading out of London. "What of the manor house?"

A mellowed brick struck with two sweeping wings and a columned portico rose within Jane's mind.

"It is not vast but it possesses an aging charm. My father used to tease my mother that it might tumble beneath a strong breeze and that he intended to replace it with a more elegant Italian villa. Of course, he would never dare. They both loved the rambling old place despite the smoking chimneys and roofs that tend to leak during a heavy rain."

Feeling his gaze upon her Jane turned to meet his penetrating survey.

"Your eyes have a lovely glow when you speak of your father," he murmured.

The familiar pang of loss clenched her heart. "My father was a very special man. Not only did he create a financial empire with nothing more than his wits and hard work, but he always ensured that my mother and I were the most important things in his life. He was never too busy to assist me with my studies, or teach me to ride. He claimed that a man who neglected his family to amass a fortune lost the true worth in life."

His expression seemed to become oddly guarded at her soft words. "A most admirable gentleman."

"Yes."

Abruptly returning his attention to the thinning traffic he urged his horses to a brisk pace.

"And your mother?"

Uncertain what thoughts were hidden by his determined mask of interest Jane gave a faint shrug.

"She was very kind with a tender heart." Her features tightened with remembered regret. "Much too tender a heart."

"What do you mean?"

"She never truly reconciled herself to the knowledge that her parents could command her to marry my father for his wealth and then cut her out of their lives because he was a Cit." Jane allowed her gaze to aimlessly watch the passing fields that had replaced the narrow town houses of London. "And then to make matters worse my father's family could not be at ease in the company of an aristocrat. For a woman who had once enjoyed endless days among society it was difficult to be so isolated."

"And you?" he demanded. "Did you feel isolated?"

She briefly considered her childhood. There had certainly been moments of disappointment. And perhaps even disillusionment. But overall her most lasting memory was that of a young girl secure in the knowledge that she was well loved.

"I suppose I occasionally wondered why I did not have cousins to visit like other children, or why I was not invited to the finer homes in the neighborhood," she replied with simple honesty. "But as a child it is not quite so obvious that you are being excluded. As long as I had my mother and father I was content."

"You must have been devastated when they died."

"Yes. For the first time I truly understood what it was to be alone." Her hands clenched in her lap as the darkness that always hovered in the depths of her heart threatened to rise. "So alone that there were nights when I lay in my bed aching and unable to sleep for the silence. I just wanted . . . someone who could hold me."

She heard his breath catch, as if her words had somehow brushed a vulnerable nerve.

"Is that when you determined to come to London to choose a husband?" he asked huskily.

"In part, although my promise to my father would have ensured that I eventually wed."

A silence descended, broken only by the steady thud of horseshoes upon the road and an occasional call of a bird. Jane resisted the urge to fidget. It was not a simple matter to reveal her most hidden wounds. Still, it seemed necessary to share such thoughts with a gentleman who desired to be her husband.

At last he pulled upon the reins until they traveled at a sedate pace and turned to regard her with strangely darkened eyes.

"You are quite an amazing woman, Miss Middleton."

She battled the most ridiculous urge to blush at his startling words. "What?"

His expression was uncommonly somber as he allowed his gaze to sweep her pale features.

"I know no other maiden who would have dared to organize her own Season in London. From hiring her own establishment to discovering her own companion. It reveals a great deal of courage."

A dangerous flare of warmth surged through her heart. He was so very good at this. When she looked into those impossibly dark eyes she did feel courageous, and bold, and wondrously special.

Everything she had wanted to feel all her life.

Oh . . . blast.

"More stupidity than courage, in truth," she muttered in embarrassment. "I did not have the least notion of the difficulties I would face or I assure you that Napoleon's entire army could not have dragged me from my home."

"I do not believe that for a moment. It would have been a simple matter to leave London at any moment, but you refused to cry craven. Instead you remained and battled to establish your place among society."

Jane could not prevent a shudder at the thought of her awful first days in London. She had not lied. She would never have stepped foot in the city had she known what was awaiting her.

"I would hardly call my efforts a success. The moment you turned your interest from me, I was shoved back into the shadows."

He shrugged aside her logic. "A momentary setback. I do not doubt you could overcome any obstacle." Without warning that wicked glitter returned to his midnight eyes. "Thankfully you have no more need to concern yourself with shadows. As my wife you will be one of the leaders of society."

Their gazes clashed, then locked. Breathe, Jane, breathe, she anxiously reminded herself. It was difficult enough to think in this gentleman's presence without her brain lacking the proper ingredients to make it function.

"You are very persistent, sir," she managed to choke out.

His smile was slow and perfectly designed to send a searing jolt of heat down her spine.

"Persistent enough to win even the most elusive heart, as you will learn soon enough, my sweet."

Wisely realizing they were treading toward waters too deep for her to swim, Jane reluctantly untangled her gaze to view the passing meadows. It was far safer to count the dancing butterflies or delight in the antics of frolicking ponies than to seriously ponder the notion that this gentleman was determined to become her husband.

Expecting Hellion to press his obvious advantage, Jane was relieved when he instead allowed a silence to descend. It offered a welcome opportunity to collect her thoughts and force her tautly clenched muscles to ease. A task that was all too commonplace when in the company of this gentleman.

Several miles passed before she felt suitably calm to slowly turn her head and regard the fiercely beautiful profile outlined by the slanting sun.

"Do we have much farther to go?" she demanded.

"Actually, our destination is just ahead."

Glancing toward the only building that was near, Jane gave a lift of her brows at the large stables and bustle of carriages that were pulling to a halt before the large stone building.

"A posting inn?"

Turning the grays through the gate with an elegant tug of the reins, Hellion headed toward the back of the wide yard.

"Ah, not just a posting inn," he corrected as they came to a smooth halt. "One of the most elegant posting inns in all of England. You have not truly lived until you have sampled the Fox and Grapes beef pie."

Jane did not doubt the boast. Despite the numerous people scurrying about the stable yard, there was an organized pattern to the chaos and a well-tended tidiness about the structures that spoke of an owner with the sort of capital and concern to keep a first-rate establishment.

Still, that did not explain why Hellion would desire to bring her here. Unless . . .

Her heart gave a sudden, tender leap of excitement. Of course. The Fox and Grapes. She had heard of the establishment during the exhaustive research she had done over the past few weeks. As Hellion had stated, it was by far the most famous inn for miles around. And now she clearly recalled telling him that she wished she could have the opportunity to study the establishment firsthand. How better to learn precisely why it had earned its enviable reputation? And perhaps model her own posting inn in the same style.

"Oh, Hellion," she breathed.

He smiled at her obvious glow of excitement. "Are you pleased?"

"I . . ." She struggled to clear her throat of the odd

lump that threatened to form. "I cannot believe that you thought to arrange this."

He appeared faintly puzzled by her open delight. "It was not so very difficult, my love," he assured her softly.

"It is not that." Jane lifted a helpless hand. "It is the fact that you would realize how much it would mean to me to be allowed to examine such a fine establishment. And, of course, that you bothered to recall my interest in posting inns at all. Most gentlemen prefer to overlook my odd fascination with such matters. If they don't outright condemn them."

He seemed to stiffen at her husky words. "Examine?"

Realizing that he had misunderstood her meaning and was now visualizing her crawling about the floor and poking through cellars, Jane impetuously reached out to lay her hand upon his forearm.

"Well, at least viewing a successful inn firsthand," she said softly, her eyes unconsciously gentle as she gazed into the handsome features. "As you obviously realized it will greatly assist me when it comes time to make my decisions for my own inn."

"Oh yes . . . quite." He gave a sudden cough. "I do know how important your business dealings are to you."

Her heart melted a little more.

"No gentleman beyond my father would have ever thought of such a thing."

His smile returned, although it was faintly strained. "I consider myself in fine company then. I cannot imagine anyone I would be more proud to be compared to than your father."

Jane gave a soft gasp at the sweet words, and then

barely aware of what she was doing, she shifted forward to press her lips to the smooth skin of his cheek.

Perhaps there was more to this gentleman than she had been willing to give him credit for.

"Thank you, Hellion," she whispered softly.

It had been a spontaneous gesture, without thought to the fierce chaos the merest touch could create within her. She was duly reminded of the danger when a swift, shocking jolt raced from her lips to the center of her stomach. Caught off guard she was hurriedly pulling away, only to be halted when a pair of steely arms wrapped about her to hold her firmly against the unyielding male form.

"Oh no," he murmured close to her ear. "I have waited too long to have you kiss me of your own accord to allow you to shy away so swiftly."

Jane could not halt the shudder of pleasure that raced through her at his touch.

"Hellion."

His mouth gently brushed her temple. "You have no notion, do you?"

"No notion of what?" she whispered.

"How desperately I long to feel your lips upon me."

Her fingers instinctively grasped the lapel of his moss green coat. It would take very little effort to imagine the warm silk of his skin as she slid her mouth over the strong jaw that was faintly rasped with his dark whiskers. And down the column of his neck to linger upon the beat of his pulse . . .

Oh my. She shifted uneasily, aware of a heat beginning to simmer where no heat should ever be.

"You are being absurd."

"That is what I tell myself," he murmured in distracted tones. "A gentleman of my age and experience should not be aching in his bed at night like a schoolboy in his first flush of passion. Nor should he harbor such wicked thoughts of what he would do if he should chance to have your slender, delectable body beneath him . . ."

"Are you wanting your horses stabled, sir?"

The male voice intruded into the magical moment, sharply reminding Jane that she was seated in full view of dozens of passing servants and guests. A fact she had astonishingly forgotten.

At the same moment Hellion pulled back with a surprising heat flaring upon his high cheekbones.

"Damn." He gave a faint shake of his head. "Absurd, indeed. I fear we shall have to continue this . . . delicious conversation later."

Later? Jane licked her desperately dry lips. That, she was quite certain, was a very bad notion.

Hellion smiled with wry amusement.

Gads, what had happened?

It had all started out well enough. Jane had proven to be a willing companion as he had whisked her from London. Not only willing, but unusually vulnerable as she had spoken of her family and home.

And even when he had pulled to a halt at the Fox and Grapes she had not balked. Instead she had regarded him with such a bemused and delighted expression he had felt his heart swell with hope.

At that moment he was confident that he had schemed the perfect romantic afternoon.

A ride through the charming countryside. A private parlor at a lovely inn, where they could share an intimate luncheon. And in his pocket a golden locket with a golden curl he had cut from his hair.

What could possibly be more romantic? Surely Jane was utterly bewitched?

But of course, despite all his careful planning and scheming, the minx had managed to confound him.

She always managed to confound him.

Thank goodness he had enough wits about him to prevent a disaster, he told himself wryly. With a swift skill he had left Jane in the foyer and demanded that the innkeep be brought to him. The proprietor was well enough acquainted with nobles and their peculiar habits, and with a few low words, and a discrete bribe, he managed to ensure a quick tour before they were led upstairs to the private rooms he had requested.

Or at least what was intended to be a quick tour.

Trailing behind a vivacious Jane and as equally animated innkeep, Hellion realized that he had been thoroughly forgotten.

Not an easy admission for a gentleman accustomed to creating a stir of excitement and interest by merely walking into a room. Gads, he could not recall a moment when he felt as if he were no more than shadow without substance. And never in the company of a young, unwed chit.

How often had he bemoaned the hordes of *débutantes* who tossed themselves in his path? Or the numerous widows who schemed to entrap him into marriage?

Now he realized that he had always taken his un-

doubted effect upon the opposite sex for granted.
Perhaps he had even felt it his due.

And thank goodness for such arrogance, he wryly
acknowledged. Were he a gentleman of lesser self-
assurance he might have been offended by his fiancée's seeming indifference. As it was, Hellion
determinedly thrust aside his wounded male pride.

This moment was for Jane, he sternly reminded
himself. He would soon enough have ample opportunity to claim her undivided attention. An
entire lifetime.

Besides which, he could not deny a measure of
enjoyment in simply watching her as she scurried
about the crowded inn.

Gone was the stiff, rather awkward female that
clung to the edges of the ballrooms. And even the
uncertain lover who fluttered at every compliment.

In her stead was a commanding, nearly overwhelming force who moved through her surroundings with the encompassing absorption of a
general surveying his battlefield.

This was a vision of Jane he had never been privileged to share before and Hellion discovered himself watching her in fascination.

There was a brisk competency to her manner that
demanded the respect of all, from the innkeep to
the chambermaids. And a smooth charm that eased
any awkwardness in speaking with a woman of what
were essentially considered male interests.

Even more fascinating was the undoubted glow
of enthusiasm that added a sparkling beauty to her
frail features.

Studying her countenance as she shrewdly questioned the cook on everything from the cost of

potatoes to the best means of storing flour, he covertly noted the shimmer in her wide eyes and faint color upon her cheeks.

A startling flare of heat seared through his body.

This was how she would look when she was laid beneath him, the voice of the devil whispered. Her face would be flushed with passion and her eyes would darken with a much more enticing excitement than mere business. And that slender form would be taut with need as he slowly, carefully sheathed himself in her sweetness.

With a shuddering breath he stepped forward and grasped her hand to lay it upon his arm. He had shared Jane enough for one day. Now he desired her undivided attention. Alone. Together. With ample opportunity to quench at least a portion of his sharp hunger.

"Mr. Parker, I believe I requested a luncheon?" he smoothly took command.

The round, rapidly balding proprietor gave a startled blink as he shifted his attention to the looming nobleman. "Oh yes . . . forgive me." He gave a lift of his pudgy hands. "I fear I had nearly forgotten. It is not often that I encounter such a shrewd investor who possesses an interest in my modest inn. I must thank Miss Middleton for a most pleasant day."

"Yes, she is quite unique." Hellion possessively tugged the blushing damsel closer to his side. "And no doubt famished after her busy day."

Taking the less-than-subtle hint, the innkeep assumed a businesslike demeanor as he motioned for two waiting maids to lift their covered trays and disappear through a side door. Then with a faint nod toward Hellion he turned to lead them out of the kitchen and up the steps that led to the private parlors.

Hellion remained silent as they weaved through the crowd entering the public rooms, his gaze straying toward the woman at his side. He had half-expected her to balk at the realization that they would soon be secluded in the parlor, but the happy distraction upon the countenance assured him that she was still consumed with her fascinating thoughts of posting inns, bank ledgers, and escalating profits.

He heaved a rueful sigh. No doubt he should be grateful that he did not have to toss her over his shoulder and carry her kicking and screaming to their luncheon. But in truth, he was beginning to discover that her ability to cut him so easily from her thoughts was more than a bit annoying.

Surely most virginal females would be hesitant at being swept off to a private room by a notorious rake? Or wary? Or even frightened?

Or, better yet, breathless with bewildered excitement?

Anything would be preferable to blatant lack of interest.

Feeling very much like a predator stalking a prey that refused to obey the rules of the hunt, Hellion firmly steered Jane through the door held open by Mr. Parker.

"I believe you will find everything in order," the proprietor murmured, his eyes swiftly sweeping over the tidy furnishings that included a small table and chairs as well as a stuffed sofa settled near the bay window. "If you have need just ring the bell."

Hellion offered a faint nod as he waited for the

man to discretely back from the room and close the door behind him.

Alone at last. A shudder of anticipation raced through his large form before he was firmly quelling the renegade lust. First luncheon and then seduction, he told himself.

As long as they ate swiftly.

Very swiftly.

With elegant ease Hellion led his companion to the table and settled her onto one of the seats before taking his own. Then leaning forward he began to whisk the covers off the numerous dishes that had been placed on the linen tablecloth.

"Ah, let me see. How can I tempt you? Trout in cream sauce? Roast beef with mushrooms? Soufflé? Carrots with a tempting honey glaze?"

Coming out of her deep thoughts Jane glanced about the laden table with a hint of surprise.

"Goodness, it all looks delicious."

"Then some of each," he murmured, taking a plate to fill it with the various treats. He settled it before her and then reached for the waiting bottle of wine to pour her a healthy measure. "I would imagine you have managed to stir up quite an appetite."

"Actually I did not even notice until this moment." She offered a sweet smile, not at all conscious of the fact she had not bothered to notice him until this moment either. A fact that was about to change. "Now I must admit that I am famished."

His gaze drifted over her gamine features. "As am I."

She blinked, as if suddenly sensing the smoldering desire that shrouded him. "Oh . . . then I suppose it is fortunate that Mr. Parker so thoughtfully provided us with a feast."

"I did not say that I was famished for roast beef or trout," he corrected in low tones. "What I hunger for Mr. Parker cannot provide."

She hesitantly licked her lips, no longer protected by her intense preoccupation. "Hellion . . ."

"Eat your luncheon, my sweet," he interrupted, leaning back in his chair as he sipped the delicate wine. "We have the entire afternoon to satisfy my appetite."

CHAPTER TWELVE

From the diary of Miss Jane Middleton, May 21st,
1814:

P.S. Diary,
    Crossroads . . .
    *They seem so terribly romantic. The meeting of
two destinies. A sudden choice that will change a life
forever. An opportunity to forge a new path.*
    In truth crossroads are quite fraught with peril.
    *One can awake in the morning perfectly con-
vinced that it is just another day to enjoy and then,
without warning, a crossroad appears and the entire
future hangs in the balance.*
    Crossroads . . .
    *They are surely best given to the daring and ad-
venturous, not to poor souls who only desire a safe,
predictable life.*

Despite the brooding male gaze that remained
unwaveringly upon her, Jane took full pleasure in

the delectable luncheon. Indeed, as she polished off the last of an apple tart she was already considering the various means she possessed to lure the cook away from the Fox and Grapes. Such an artist would be invaluable to her own posting inn once it opened. And would no doubt ensure a steady trade.

Perhaps a small cottage would tempt the older woman, she silently mused. Or the promise of a position for her eldest son, whom she had confessed was currently without work.

The sound of a low chuckle broke into her thoughts and with a blink Jane regarded her companion, who leaned back in his chair sipping his wine with negligent ease.

Her distraction was seared away and the familiar tension returned as she noted the wicked amusement in the dark eyes and the deceptive nonchalance that did not entirely cloak his coiled power. She was sharply reminded of a slumbering predator who was prepared to pounce without warning.

And much to her dismay she was uncertain she was entirely opposed to a good pounce.

Hoping that her expression did not reveal her unexpected bout of insanity, Jane primly set aside her napkin and cleared her throat.

"May I inquire what you find so amusing?"

"I was just pondering how such a tiny thing could possibly tuck away so much food. It befuddles all logic."

That was not at all what she had expected him to say and Jane felt a heat of embarrassment rush to her cheeks.

"Oh, forgive me." She grimaced. "My governess was forever warning me that I should never reveal my appetite. She was quite convinced that a gentleman preferred to believe that a true lady subsists upon mere air, but my father insisted that there was little point in spending a fortune upon a French chef if his women were not allowed to enjoy the luxury."

Leaning forward Hellion set aside his wine and before she could guess his intention managed to capture her fingers in a firm grip.

"I am not complaining, my love," he murmured, bringing her bare fingers to his lips. "As a matter of fact I fully agree with your very wise father. Despite your governess's rather dubious notion of what a gentleman might or might not believe, most men deeply appreciate a woman with healthy appetites. It reveals an instinctive sensuality that is quite enticing."

Her heart gave a leap as he aimlessly nibbled upon her fingers. Rats. He was not playing at all fair.

"It does?"

"Oh yes. But then I already know of your passions." His dark gaze pinned her own with a smoldering intent. "They have left me burning until I can barely think of anything but my need for you."

"Hellion . . ."

"Are you finished?" he interrupted, his voice oddly rough.

"Yes, but . . ." Her words became a squawk of surprise as he abruptly rose to his feet and in one smooth motion scooped her out of her chair to cradle her against his chest. Glancing at the determined set of his expression she could not pretend she did not know what he was about. Frustrated desire was carved into every beautiful feature. "Hellion, the maids will soon be returning."

With a lift of his brows he carried her toward the door and slipped the latch before moving to the distant sofa and settling upon the cushions. Jane discovered herself perched upon his lap with his arms firmly about her.

"No one will intrude," he announced with a pleased smile at his cunning.

Fiercely aware of the hard muscles pressing into her thighs and the scent of warm male skin, Jane struggled to recall how to think.

"Obviously not without a battering ram," she managed to mutter.

His lips twitched as his hand ran a path up her stiff spine.

"Relax, my love. Beyond its excellent food the Fox and Grapes is renowned for its discretion. The servants are paid a generous wage to avoid petty gossip."

"I shall have to keep that in mind when it comes time to hire the staff for my own posting inn."

The dark eyes flashed with an unexpected annoyance. "No."

Jane blinked in surprise. "I beg your pardon?"

"There has been enough talk of business for one day. It is now time for pleasure."

Without warning Jane discovered herself being tilted backward onto the sofa. Hellion smoothly followed, half lying over her as he reached up to pluck off her bonnet and toss it impatiently aside.

A part of her knew that she should protest. It was obvious that Hellion had deliberately lured her to this private chamber with the intention of seduction.

A greater part of her, however, did not desire to protest. She wanted to be here with him. She wanted to lie beneath him and learn where these astonishing sensations would lead. She wanted his hands upon her bare skin and an end to the aching need that haunted her.

"Precisely what sort of pleasure do you have in mind?" she breathed.

Swiftly removing the pins from her hair he ran his fingers through her curls. "That is entirely in your hands."

"My hands?"

His expression became oddly somber as he studied her flushed countenance.

"You have claimed me a rake and a scoundrel. I cannot deny the charge. I have known many women and taken pleasure with them. Most would say too much pleasure. But with you . . ." He gave a slow shake of his head. "With you it is different."

Something in his tone made her heart skip a beat. "Why?"

"I truly cannot say. At first I presumed that it was your innocence." His lips twisted wryly. "I am unaccustomed to proper virgins, to say the least. But the more I am with you the more I suspect that it is something else."

Almost absently he trailed a silken curl over the curve of her breast, sending a shiver of excitement jolting through her body.

"And what would that be?" she whispered.

His gaze tangled with her own. "I care. I care that you desire me as much as I desire you. I care that I please you. I care that you find happiness when you are in my company. I care and it is oddly frightening."

Her eyes widened as his words struck directly at

her heart, and blinking back ridiculous tears she lifted her arms to wrap them about his neck.

"Oh, Hellion."

His eyes darkened as his gaze slowly lowered to her mouth. "Dear God, Jane, if I do not kiss you soon I shall surely go mad."

"Yes," she breathed, tangling her fingers in his hair to draw his head downward.

He needed no second urging. With exquisite care his mouth brushed over her trembling lips before returning to plunder their softness in a kiss of sheer possession.

Jane groaned, her head spinning as a blaze of heat raced through her blood. Oh heavens, he was so damnably good at this.

As if sensing her faint hint of panic, Hellion reluctantly eased back, his lips gently nuzzling the corner of her mouth.

"I have another confession to make," he husked.

Barely capable of coherent thought, Jane swallowed heavily. "And what is that?"

"Watching you today as you toured the inn made me wish to toss you upon the floor and have my mad way with you."

Jane stiffened, certain he was mocking her. No gentleman would ever find her love for bourgeoisie trade anything but repulsive.

"That is not amusing."

His gaze narrowed as his hand boldly moved to cup her breast. "I am perfectly serious. There was something incredibly erotic in watching you take command. Whoever claimed women the weaker sex have never seen you march into battle."

In spite of herself Jane felt her tension ease and a ridiculous pleasure warm her heart.

"You are being absurd."

Hellion gave a low growl as he pressed against her hip, revealing his hard erection.

"Does it feel as if I am being absurd?"

Her stomach clenched in response. "Oh."

"Once we are wed I shall insist upon a private chamber close to your office. I sense we shall have need of it with astonishing regularity."

"Hellion." She frowned in sudden warning. "Our future is far from decided."

His dangerous chuckle washed over her skin with unnerving intensity, raising a rash of goose bumps.

"On the contrary, my shrew, it most certainly is decided. From the moment you appeared from behind that urn our destiny has been firmly entwined. A believer in fate would claim our marriage was written in the stars."

Her breath caught in her throat despite the logical part of her mind that dismissed the ludicrous words.

Written in the stars?

It was all nonsense, of course. But as she watched his features harden with a stark hunger that was echoed deep within her, she could not deny that there was something about this man that ensnared her senses. Whether it was lust or love or sheer madness was impossible to say.

Perhaps it was all three.

"You feel it too, do you not, Jane?" he rasped, his fingers shifting to drift along the plunge of her bodice.

Refusing to be lured into a confession she was not yet prepared to make, she sucked in a deep breath.

"I do not believe in fate. Our future is decided by the decisions we make."

"How pragmatic you are." He smiled with wicked amusement. "But life is not all about what we can see or touch or taste. What of your heart? Do you decide how it will respond? Can you explain faith or hope or love?"

A finger slipped beneath the thin muslin of her gown, brushing her nipple and making her jump at the shocking pleasure.

"Hellion," she choked in protest. "I cannot contemplate philosophy when you are touching me in such a manner."

"Good, then contemplate this," he murmured, his lips brushing her temple as he efficiently tugged the sleeve of her gown and shift off her shoulder. Pulling back he regarded her with a glittering gaze. "I want to see you. I want you naked and trembling beneath me."

A convulsive shiver raced through her body, her heart lodged in her throat as the soft air prickled over her bared skin.

"I am already trembling."

Hesitantly Hellion stroked his hand gently over her face, his brow furrowed as if concentrating utterly upon that delicate contact between them.

"So fragile," he murmured. "You are always so bold and fiercely in command that I forget just how tiny you are. I do not want to accidentally hurt you."

A poignant sweetness swept through her, banishing the lingering doubt. She was poised upon the edge of destiny, a voice whispered. And while she could not yet determine what path the future might bring, she knew with absolute clarity that in this moment she wanted Hellion. If she never possessed anything else of him, she wanted this.

"You will not hurt me," she whispered, but even as she said the words she was not at all certain they weren't a lie.

His hand trembled, cupping her face while his thumb stroked a slow path over her bottom lip. "Are you certain, Jane? Is this what you desire?"

He was offering her escape from the rapidly mounting desire, his features tightening as if preparing for a crushing blow. In answer Jane lowered her hand to place it against the thunderous beat of his heart.

"I am certain."

He gave a low groan, burying his face in her hair. "Say it, my love. Say that you want me. I need to hear the words."

"I want you, Hellion."

She was as startled as Hellion by the calm certainty of her voice. With a broken moan he planted frenzied kisses over her face, his hands roughly pulling off his jacket and waistcoat. His cravat was swift to follow along with his shirt. Jane barely noticed his effort. She was intoxicated by the lips that were now exploring the curve of her neck, and nuzzling the tender pulse at the base of her throat.

But then he grasped her hands and placed them against the silken heat of his chest.

"Touch me," he pleaded in a dark rasp. "I have longed to feel your hands upon me."

Tentatively Jane allowed her hands to glide over the hard muscles, marveling when he sucked in a sharp breath of pleasure. The knowledge that he genuinely desired her was as heady as any aphrodisiac.

"Dear God," he muttered, his seeking lips claiming her mouth in a kiss filled with aching need.

Jane sighed, her hips instinctively arching to press against his swollen muscles. She was not certain what she sought but she needed more.

With restless urgency she moved her hands over his shoulders, moaning deep in her throat as his lips moved down her neck, his tongue stroking a white hot path of pleasure.

"Hellion . . ." she muttered, uncertain why he was prolonging her torment.

"No, my love, lie still," he commanded hoarsely. "It has been so long, and I want to make love to you as I have dreamed of night after night."

Even as he spoke his hands moved, slipping beneath her to tug the ribbons loose. With swift ease he was removing her gown and then the linen shift from her body.

"Bloody hell." Allowing his gaze to wander over her slender form he sucked in an unsteady breath. "You are beautiful."

Jane allowed her lids to slide shut, her straining breast already anticipating the touch of his mouth. Perhaps she was willfully fooling herself but in this moment she felt beautiful. Every tremble of his hard body, every rapid beat of his pounding heart convinced her that he desired her. This sensual, magnificent beast wanted her. Her. Miss Jane Middleton.

She smiled slowly, and then caught her bottom lip between sharp teeth as a moist warmth covered the tip of her nipple. Hellion teased the quivering peak, his tongue flicking softly until she gave an impatient moan, her fingers threading through his satin hair, silently demanding more.

Eagerly he satisfied her plea, sucking gently but insistently as she arched beneath him with a flare of pure pleasure.

She barely noted the hands smoothing her stockings and shoes out of his path, unconsciously kicking them aside to allow his searching fingers an unfettered freedom to explore her thighs, then, shockingly, the warmth between her legs.

Unprepared for the surge of sharp delight, Jane cried out in surprise, a hint of embarrassment touching her cheeks as she felt a wet heat moistening his fingers.

"Oh."

Lifting himself onto his elbow, Hellion made a soothing sound in his throat, relentlessly stroking that point of intense delight.

"You are so warm, so sweet," he murmured in soft tones.

"I . . ." It was oddly difficult to keep her eyes open as her entire body focused upon the building pressure deep within. "I do not know what to do."

His eyes smoldered with a midnight fire. "Shall I show you?"

"Yes."

With a gentle motion he took her hand and lowered it to the waistband of his breeches. Her breath caught at the feel of his straining bulge, but she did not hesitate as she fumbled to undo the buttons. His erection sprang free as the last button was opened and she gingerly allowed her fingers to test soft skin that sheathed the hardness.

Hellion's teeth snapped together as he heaved a strained groan, pressing himself against her touch. Then with an awkward motion he was moving to hastily tug off his boots and breeches before returning to cover her body with his own.

"My God . . . you are going to be the death of me," he muttered.

Jane stilled as she absorbed the sensation of bare skin brushing together, the hard urgency of his arousal pressing into her thigh.

Something deep inside her clamored in recognition, her body shifting to accommodate the unfamiliar weight, her legs spreading and encircling his poised hips.

A harsh breath teased her ear as Hellion readied himself, his voice uneven as he attempted to reassure her.

"I do not wish to hurt you, Jane . . ."

"Hellion, do not stop," she broke in anxiously, her body clenched tightly as if already searching for some unknown goal.

His hands grasped her hips, his lips urging her to relax as he slowly, carefully entered her willing body. There was a flare of discomfort and Jane stiffened as she felt him thrust his way past her maidenhead. Good gads. Just for a moment she was not at all certain that this was going to be possible. Oh the theory was sound enough, no doubt. It had to be for so many couples to procreate. Most more than once. But until this moment she had not precisely considered the vast differences in their respective sizes.

Easily sensing her tension Hellion stilled, then without warning he moved, withdrawing and sliding silently down her body. Jane gasped, her hands clenching in his hair as he kissed her stomach, and then stroked his lips along the inner length of her thighs.

Her breath was oddly labored as his tongue tasted of her skin and then disappeared altogether as he shifted once more and boldly claimed a kiss at the very heart of her pleasure.

Shocked by the sheer intimacy of his mouth, Jane wanted to protest. Or at least she wanted to protest for the merest fraction of a second.

After that she would have considered murder if he halted.

The sensations were so exquisite, so temptingly erotic, that she could only arch her back in mute approval. With a relentless expertise he coaxed her to the point of near insanity, seeming to sense precisely when she was prepared for him to once again cover her body, continuing the rhythmic stroke with firm thrusts that had her soaring to paradise.

She had occasionally thought of this moment, even assumed that she knew how it would feel, but nothing . . . nothing could have prepared her for the heart-stopping pause as she rode on the crest of a wave. A harsh cry wrenched from her throat as she tumbled over the edge and floated in the dark waters of complete satisfaction.

Above her she felt Hellion grow rigid, his countenance tensing with the same stunned wonderment she had experienced before he shuddered and sank onto her shoulder with a slow sigh.

"My shrew," he whispered against her damp skin, a possessive hand moving to cup her breast. "You are mine."

The town house in the aging, but once-elegant London square was the very essence of solid English tradition. The red brick was sturdy without undue pretensions; the wrought-iron fence framed a garden with the proper roses growing in proper rows and a well-polished doorknob that was a mandatory requirement for any establishment in a decent neighborhood.

To most, the home bespoke old money and respectability. To Lord Bidwell it bespoke a tedious predictability that was enough to make him break out in a rash.

Fortunately for his own delicate sensibilities, his business rarely took him among the ghastly prim and proper.

Not so fortunately, however, today he had need of information that only one intimate with the War Department could offer. Not an easy task considering that most of the stodgy lot readily accepted his invaluable services as a spy while thoroughly disdaining his dubious morals.

Wisely coming prepared with a tempting bribe Biddles squashed the urge to slip in through the cellar and properly waited on the porch for the elderly butler to pull open the door. Just as properly he handed the servant his calling card and watched him shuffle toward the back of the house.

He waited only a half a heartbeat before he was in pursuit. His sense of propriety had been strained to the limit and besides which, he was not about to have his morning wasted by being ignored and avoided by a pompous half-wit.

Remaining a step behind the servant Biddles paused in the doorway as the butler crossed the library to hand his card to the gentleman seated behind a large mahogany desk.

Like most of the blooded gentlemen in England, Lord Carson was a large, rawboned man with a paunch growing at the same steady pace that his hair was receding. His countenance was square with a reddish hue that spoke of his love for fine food and finer spirits. Unlike many, however, he did possess an occasional flash of intelligence that Biddles had found useful during his course of work.

Hidden in the shadows Biddles watched Carson briefly glance at the gilded card, his face taking on an additional layer of puce as he abruptly rose to his feet.

"Bidwell," he growled. "Bloody hell, not that rat-faced demon. Inform him that I am not at home, Potter. Better yet, tell him that I have died and am currently rotting in the family crypt."

With his lips twitching in amusement Biddles stepped through the doorway to regard his unwilling host with a raise of his brow.

"Ah, Carson, I must say you appear remarkably well for a rotting corpse. Perhaps a bit tattered about the edges, but that is only to be expected, I suppose," he drawled.

Flicking an annoyed glare over Biddles's lime-green coat and lemon breeches, Carson pointed a dramatic finger toward the nearby door.

"Out. Out, before I have you tossed out."

"Now, now, old chap, I come bearing gifts." Biddles held up a bottle of expensive spirits. "You see, your favorite brandy, aged to perfection."

Carson gave a loud snort, although he could not prevent his gaze lingering upon the bottle. He possessed a notorious weakness for French brandy.

"Your Trojan horse, I suppose. I am not that much a fool."

"I have only a few questions." Biddles smiled with the small bit of innocence he could conjure.

"And that is supposed to reassure me? On the last occasion that you desired to ask me a few questions, I awoke with a pistol pointed at my heart."

"I did manage to dispatch the villain, Carson, and you were personally thanked by the prince for your service to your country."

The older gentleman frowned at him in a sour fashion. He clearly still held a grudge over the minor squabble that they had endured with the son of an earl who had been selling troop movements to the French.

"After I spent a fortnight recovering from the shock. No. I am too old for your devious schemes."

"I assure you that on this occasion there will not be the slightest danger to you."

"Your notion of danger is considerably different than my own, Bidwell."

Biddles placed a hand to his heart, the hand that conveniently held the bottle of brandy.

"I swear upon my favorite Weston coat."

There was a prickling silence before the gentleman at last heaved a frustrated sigh and reached out to pluck the bottle from Biddles's fingers.

"Oh bloody hell, give me the brandy. I feel I shall have need of it." With practiced efficiency Carson pulled out the cork and poured himself a generous portion. "What do you desire to know?"

Pacing toward the valuable leather books that lined the room, Biddles shrugged with a seeming nonchalance.

"I need to know what you recall of a Mr. Middleton."

"Middleton? The name is familiar."

"He comes from Surrey and managed to marry the daughter of an earl."

"Ah yes." Carson frowned as he downed the brandy in one appreciative gulp. "There was something. Damn. It was several years ago."

"I believe it had to do with uniforms," Biddles prompted.

"That is it." Carson set down his glass to promptly refill it. "There were accusations of shoddy workmanship and even rumors of receiving payment for uniforms that were never delivered. Messy business."

Messy, indeed. Biddles slowly turned, his nose twitching with curiosity.

"And yet, any scandal seems to have been nicely hushed up."

"Yes." Carson tossed back another shot of the fiery spirit. "Rather odd."

"You do not recall how Mr. Middleton escaped justice?"

"I cannot say that I do." Carson shrugged. "No doubt the Earl managed to soothe over ruffled feathers. Or Middleton was wise enough to share his profits with those men in position to hide his crime."

They were both perfectly reasonable explanations. Those in power often preferred to cover over unpleasantness rather than seek justice. Especially if there happened to be a profit in it for them.

Unfortunately, such vague rumors and innuendos did nothing to help Biddles's cause. He needed proof, not gossip.

"Any notion of who those particular gentlemen might be?"

Carson set down his glass with a loud bang. "Absolutely not. You have asked your questions. Now it is time for you to be on your way."

"What if I were to offer you an entire crate of that most excellent spirit?"

Carson scowled in a fierce manner. "I would drown you in it. Now, toddle off before I recall just how much I dislike you."

Biddles briefly considered the possibility of ferreting out further information before offering a reluctant bow. Experience had taught him that there was no more stubborn beast than a titled Englishman.

"A pleasure as always, Carson."

"Do not feel the need to keep in touch, Bidwell," his host growled.

Straightening, Biddles flashed his most provoking smile. "Ah well, who can say what the future might hold, my lord? Until then."

With graceful silence Biddles slipped from the room and out the front door. Gathering his horse he set back toward his own house in Mayfair.

It had not been his most productive afternoon. In fact, he had learned precisely nothing he did not already suspect.

Still, he supposed that he had at least confirmed that he was upon the right track, which was something. He had chased enough shadows to possess a genuine dislike for false leads. And with a bit more probing he might very well discover precisely who would have been involved in purchasing uniforms.

Brooding upon whom he might approach next, Biddles paid little heed to the traffic crowding the

London streets, or even the passing houses. At least not until he realized that he had taken a wrong turn and had gone several blocks out of his way.

With a frown he slowed his mount to glance about the small square he had just entered. What the devil was the matter with him? He could find his way through London with a blindfold on. Not to mention Paris, Rome, and even Brussels. How could he have become lost less than a mile from his own home?

It was not until he noticed a narrow, shabbily dignified town house set behind high hedges that he suddenly became aware of his precise location.

A chill inched down his spine.

He knew that town house.

He should. He had spent more than one dark night watching it from the hedge, although he had refused to ponder the reason why.

And now it seemed even his subconscious was obsessed with the place.

A far-from-comforting realization, considering that Miss Anna Halifax was currently residing behind the thick walls.

"Blast you," he muttered, tugging on the reins with far more force than necessary.

He never mooned over well-bred young ladies. Never. They were a plague and a pestilence to confirmed bachelors.

Even if they did possess lips as sweet as summer honey and curves that a man would sell his soul to possess . . .

A shiver raced through his body. "Damn."

CHAPTER THIRTEEN

From the diary of Miss Jane Middleton, May 21st, 1814:

P.P.S. Diary,

I believe that every woman should be allowed to make one ghastly, foolish, utterly glorious mistake once in her life.

Oh, I do not mean tossing away an inheritance at the faro table. Or rushing off to Gretna Green with a blackguard who is destined to make her life a misery. Or shooting a bullet into a hellion's arse, no matter how much he might deserve it.

I speak of those brief moments of temptation that appear without warning and offer a dazzling opportunity to taste of a danger that so rarely enters a proper female's dull existence.

Drinking fine wine until your head spins in a pleasant haze.

Buying a ridiculously expensive painting simply because you like the pretty colors.

Eating an entire plate of apple tarts for breakfast.

Or being seduced by a handsome, delectable rake . . .

Hellion was decidedly . . . perturbed.

Oh, not because he had just taken a young lady's innocence, although he had never done so before. Or even the realization that the experience had been one of the most exquisitely pleasurable in his life.

It was more the warm sensations that had filled his heart as he had thrust to his release.

He was supposed to feel pleasure. And satisfaction. It was what every gentleman felt when he at last bedded a woman he desired.

But the profound sense of peace that had settled about him was not at all familiar.

How could holding a woman in his arms make him feel complete? As if a part of himself had been missing. A part that had been taken from him years ago.

It was little wonder that he was startled enough by the unexpected sensation to lift himself from Jane's delicious warmth to struggle into his breeches.

A man needed to pace about when his entire world had just been turned upside down.

Intent upon his own thoughts, Hellion took a moment before he realized that Jane was stirring upon the sofa.

Damn. What was the matter with him?

His only concern should be for this young woman who had just offered him her body, her trust, and her entire future. At a moment such as this Jane needed to be comforted. And more than that she needed to understand he would honor the gifts she had offered, not wonder what the devil he was doing pacing about like a lunatic.

With a pang of annoyance at his decided lack of gentlemanly behavior he hurriedly dampened a cloth from the washstand and returned to the sofa.

"No, do not move," he murmured softly, pressing the cloth to the faint smear of blood upon her thighs. He knew he should say something. Anything. But for once his glib charm and ready wit did not seem at all appropriate.

This was not a transitory mistress he would be rid of upon a whim. This was the woman he intended to make his wife. It seemed only fitting he should say something extraordinarily romantic. Something that she could hold dear to her heart for the rest of their lives together.

While he was still struggling to conjure the perfect words Jane unexpectedly pushed his hands aside.

"Please, Hellion, that is enough," she husked, reaching with not-quite-steady hands to retrieve her shift and pull it over her head. Hellion watched her struggle with the ribbons, deciding that she appeared astonishingly adorable with her curls tumbled about her shoulders and her skin still flushed with passion. Adorable enough to make him consider removing the ridiculous shift and reminding himself of just how sweet she tasted. Smiling at the thought Hellion was unprepared when she cleared her throat and abruptly stabbed him with a wary gaze. "It grows late. We should be returning to London."

He rocked back on his heels. Well. That was certainly not what he had expected from a lady who had just cried out her fulfillment in his arms.

"I beg your pardon?"

"I said . . ."

"I bloody well heard what you said," he growled, rising to his feet to glare down at her.

She frowned at his rough tone. "What is the matter?"

Hellion was not entirely certain.

He had not expected Jane to swoon into his arms, or to proclaim a sudden, undying love. Not precisely, anyway.

But he had expected something more than a bland request to be removed from their romantic interlude as if they had shared no more between them than a bit of trout and roast beef.

Gads, such blithe indifference was more insulting than if she had slapped his face.

"What do you suppose is the matter?" he demanded. A ridiculous question, of course. But at least it was a step above the outraged sputtering that had nearly flown from his lips.

"If I knew I would not be asking."

"In case you have forgotten you just gave your innocence to me."

Her cheeks heated at his blunt words. "I am not likely to forget, Hellion."

"And yet, all you have to say is that it is growing late?"

Jane sucked in a sharp breath as her brows drew together. "Forgive me, but as you have just pointed out I do not have a great deal of experience in these matters. What would you have me say?"

Her calm logic only fueled the flames of his own unreasonable annoyance. Shoving his hands through his hair, he struggled to contain his uncommonly ruffled emotions.

"It is traditional to at least make mention of the intimacy that has just occurred. To immediately demand to be returned to your home rather tarnishes the romance of the moment."

A stubborn expression settled on her delicate features. "You knew from the beginning that I am a prosaic woman not at all inclined to romance."

"My dear, you have far surpassed mere prosaic."

Without warning her lashes lowered to hide her eyes and her hands clenched in her lap.

"What do you want from me?"

His heart gave a sudden twitch of dismay as he realized just how ridiculously he was behaving. Blast, he was making a muck of this. Decidedly odd, and more than a little frustrating, for a gentleman renowned for his skills in seduction.

With a grimace he moved to kneel before her, taking her hands into his own.

"Jane, I merely desire you to tell me what you feel," he murmured softly. "Do you regret what occurred?"

Her gaze remained firmly veiled as she gave a slow shake of her head. "No."

"Please, Jane, look at me."

With obvious reluctance she at last lifted her head to meet his searching gaze.

"Hellion . . ."

Hellion pressed a finger to her lips. "We have just been as close as two people can be; why are you now attempting to hide from me?"

"I am not attempting to hide. It is only . . ." Her words trailed away as she caught her lower lip between her teeth.

"Yes?"

She gave a restless shrug. "I am not entirely comfortable discussing this."

"You are embarrassed?"

"Is that so shocking?" she demanded in tart tones.

A rush of intense relief flooded through Hellion, making him feel light-headed. So that was it. She was not horrified, nor convinced she had just made the greatest mistake of her life.

She was embarrassed.

Thank God.

"No, of course not." He lifted her hands to press them to his lips. "Forgive me, my love. I did not intend to be an insensitive brute. It is only that I am more than a bit unnerved and suddenly in need of reassurance."

She blinked at his sudden bout of honesty. "Whatever do you mean?"

He pressed her fingers to his cheek. "I have never before been with a complete innocent. I need to know that I did not hurt you, or God forbid, give you a disgust for me."

A flush crept beneath her skin. "You know you did not."

"How am I to know?" he demanded in low tones. "One moment you were sweet and willing in my arms, and the next you were avoiding my gaze and appearing as if you wished to be anywhere but here with me."

"Yes, well, you appeared rather distracted yourself," she accused.

He smiled wryly, unable to deny her allegation. "No, not distracted. Panicked."

"I beg your pardon?"

Hellion battled his instinctive desire to hide his emotions behind a flippant response.

"Unlike you I cannot claim such innocence," he admitted. "In truth, I would have claimed to know nearly all there is to know of the act of love. But as usual you managed to destroy my arrogant pretensions."

Her lips gave a grudging twitch of amusement. "A worthy goal even if I do not comprehend what you speak of."

He turned his head to lightly nip her finger. "I am supposed to be a well-versed rake, not an overeager school lad. I wished to ensure that you found pleasure, but the moment I touched you I was lost. That has never happened to me before."

As was only to be expected of his imminently practical Jane, she did not flutter or preen at his confession. Instead she regarded him with open suspicion.

"I find that difficult to believe."

"Why?"

"Because I am hardly the sort of female to inspire passion in a gentleman."

Hellion gave a slow shake of his head, his gaze sweeping over her slender curves barely concealed beneath the thin linen shift.

It would no doubt be far preferable to prove his claim with deeds rather than words, but he sensed that at the moment it was best to keep his wits unclouded with passion. Goodness knew he had managed to make enough of a muddle as it was.

"You are wrong, you know," he said firmly.

Her lips thinned. "Hellion, I know perfectly well . . ."

"Will you please just listen for once?" he interrupted.

The lips thinned even further. "Well?"

"I am beginning to discover that there is a vast difference between lust and passion." He held her gaze with the sheer force of his will. "A pretty countenance or well-endowed form might turn a gentleman's thoughts to a pleasurable interlude, but it is a transitory lust that is easily forgotten."

"And passion?"

He paused for a moment to consider his words. "It has nothing to do with the color of hair or the curve of an ankle. It is a deeper sense of need that makes a gentleman desire to be with a particular woman and no other will do."

He sensed more than felt her tense at his words. "And yet, it is just as transitory."

Less than an hour ago Hellion would have secretly agreed with her conclusion. Desire was desire. And like any craving it could be satisfied and then forgotten.

Now he suspected that he had somehow miscalculated badly.

He could not even conceive of his life without this woman at his side. The mere thought was enough to make his chest tighten and his heart feel oddly heavy.

"Who is to say?" he demanded.

"My father, for one."

Hellion gave a choked cough. "Your father spoke to you of passion?"

Her chin tilted to a defensive angle. "My father spoke to me of many things."

"Obviously." Hellion briefly considered the man who had treated his daughter like more of a son.

He wondered if Mr. Middleton realized just how rare and unique his efforts had made Jane. "And what did he tell you?"

Without warning she tugged her hands from his grasp, folding them in her lap like a prim governess. Hellion gritted his teeth as he battled not to reclaim his possessive hold.

"He warned me that passion is much like any other force of nature, such as a thunderstorm or flood. It will sweep into a life without warning and cause great excitement, but when it inevitably moves on it leaves behind only destruction. He said that companionship and genuine respect for one another is the foundation of a steady relationship."

Hellion inwardly cursed. Had Mr. Middleton desired to condemn his poor daughter to a cold, passionless marriage?

Surely she deserved better?

"Rather melodramatic," he cautiously murmured. If nothing else he had learned that Jane would never concede her beloved father had been mistaken. Not upon any matter. "Although it is hardly surprising. Most fathers do not wish to think of their daughters in regards to passion."

Jane offered a firm shake of her head. "No, it was not that. He sincerely believed that friendship and caring for one another's happiness was far more important than . . ."

Her words abruptly trailed away and Hellion gave a lift of his brows.

"Yes?"

She cleared her throat. "Physical pleasure."

His lips twitched at her obvious difficulty in even mentioning their passionate lovemaking.

"And two people cannot possibly enjoy both physical pleasure and friendship?" he demanded.

There was a long silence before she at last sucked in a deep breath.

"I am not yet certain."

A stab of fear clenched at Hellion's heart. Bloody hell. He had been so certain that if he managed to seduce her that all his troubles would be solved. He had taken her innocence; she should be desperate to ensure that they wed with all possible haste. That was the way with most women.

Now he sensed that it might not be quite so simple.

Whatever her feelings for him, Jane was clearly wary of placing her faith in him. A knowledge that he discovered sharply painful.

"I will make you certain," he said fiercely. "You belong with me."

"Hellion . . ." With an abrupt motion she was on her feet and scrambling for her gown. "We must return to London."

His hand reached out to halt her fumbled movements, only to fall when he noted the grim set of her features.

It was obvious that his well-practiced proposal would not be received with the delight he had imagined. In fact, he was not at all certain he desired to hear what she might have to say to a demand that they wed. As much as he cared for this delightful shrew, he knew that her tongue could flay at a hundred paces.

Damn. Once again he had managed to win the skirmish while losing the battle.

He would have to once again consider his strategies.

And for that he needed the devious mind of Biddles.

"Very well, my love. I shall return you to London." He reached for his shirt, his own features hard with determination. "But do not for a moment believe that this is over."

Standing with Anna in the shadows of the ballroom, on this occasion seeking the darkness by choice rather than obligation, Jane watched as Hellion dazzled the eager young bucks that crowded about him.

Even from a distance she could feel the magnetic pull of his glittering charm. And she was far from alone. It seemed that every gaze in the room lingered upon the golden-haired scoundrel. Some with longing, some with envy, and some with simple admiration at his undoubted allure.

Hellion, of course, took little notice of the attention that fluttered about him. He was at perfect ease, like an actor upon the stage performing for his audience.

Jane felt a pang as she watched him tilt back his head to laugh at some jest. Oh, not out of jealousy. Or even some childish need to have him to herself, although she could not deny that a part of her longed to whisk him from the room and have her way with him. It was the mere fact that he appeared so utterly comfortable.

This was why she continued to waver, she acknowledged grimly.

For three days she had fought back the urge to simply give in to her fierce desire and toss all sense aside. Why should she not wed Hellion, her heart had whispered? He was handsome, charming, and intelligent. He treated her with a genuine respect that was all too rare and made her feel as if she were a fascinating and beautiful woman. That did not even take into account the fact that he could make her melt with one wicked glance.

It was far more than any woman could hope to have in a husband. Certainly it was more than she had ever dreamed possible.

But yet she continued to waver.

This was not just another business arrangement that could be sold off if it proved too costly, her common sense warned. This was her entire future, and the future of her children.

At the moment Hellion could consider nothing beyond the thought that she could provide for him the lifestyle that he had grown accustomed to. And no doubt he had every intention of making her happy.

But what would happen a year from now? Five years? Or ten?

How long would it be before he became bored with his role as the doting husband? How long before he returned to London and the beautiful women who would toss themselves at his feet?

How long before he broke her heart and she allowed herself to become one of those bitter old women who were a plague to their children?

Of course, her heart continued to whisper, was she not destined to possess a broken heart regardless of what decision she made?

She could no longer deny that she loved Hellion. Their afternoon at the posting inn had proved that beyond doubt. And the mere thought of giving herself to another man was enough to make her stomach clench in dread.

What if she discovered she could not bear to wed another?

What of her promise to her father? And her own need to have a family?

Dear Lord, it was all such a tangle that it was no wonder her head ached and her eyes were scratchy from lack of sleep.

Intent upon her survey of Hellion, Jane did not notice when her friend shifted to stand just behind her shoulder.

"He is quite handsome," Anna murmured directly in her ear.

Smiling wryly, Jane did not even pretend she did not know to whom Anna referred.

"Undoubtedly."

"And there is a rakish manner about him that makes a woman long to tame him."

"Definitely rakish."

"And any woman who managed to capture him would be forever the envy of society."

Jane's smile widened. "She would be a near legend."

Anna gave a soft chuckle as she leaned even closer. "And of course, he is scoundrel enough to ensure that a woman would be well pleased in his bed. My God, the way he looks at you is positively wicked."

Jane abruptly turned her head in bewilderment. "What?"

Anna waggled her brows in a ridiculous fashion. "He looks as if he longs to devour you."

"Anna," Jane breathed, her cheeks warming with something that was suspiciously close to pleasure.

Anna batted her arm with her ivory fan. "Do not pretend to be so shocked, Jane. When a lady is contemplating marriage there is nothing the matter with considering a gentleman's more intimate skills. It would not be at all wise to wed a man who was incapable of pleasuring you."

All sorts of tantalizing shivers raced through Jane's body. Pleasure, excitement, and a measure of wicked anticipation. The very last thing that she need worry about was Hellion's ability to please, she acknowledged. If he pleased her any more she would soon be six feet under.

"Pleasure is all well and good. Well, perhaps better than good," she murmured, her gaze covertly straying back to the man who had taught her the meaning of passion. "Still, it is not the most important thing."

"And what is that?"

Jane considered a moment before giving a small shrug. "Contentment. Respect. Friendship. Mutual affection."

Anna gave a choked laugh. "Ah well, as long as you are not overly particular."

"You did ask."

"What happened to the desperate spinster who was determined to wed the first decent gentleman who offered?"

Jane smiled wryly. "She has discovered that a decent gentleman is considerably less dangerous than one who can break your heart."

She felt Anna stiffen in shock. "Jane?"

Cursing herself for allowing the unguarded words to slip past her lips Jane gave a sharp shake of her head. As much as she cared for her dear friend she was not yet prepared to discuss her feelings for Hellion. Not when she had yet to decide what she was to do about them.

"Excuse me, Anna, I must find the withdrawing room."

CHAPTER FOURTEEN

From the diary of Miss Jane Middleton, May 24th, 1814:

Dear Diary,

I have discovered that being a woman of logic is a bothersome thing.

If I were a silly romantic or simply still naïve enough to believe that love could cure any troubles then I would not be so plagued with indecision. Indeed, I would be anxious to toss my heart at any scoundrel's feet and assume that the future would take care of itself.

Unfortunately, I am incapable of such blithe dreams.

My heart might whisper that true happiness is within my grasp, but my common sense refuses to ignore the unmistakable warnings.

Can a rake and rogue truly be domesticated?

Or is he like any wild beast who will eventually grow to hate his prison and more so the spinster who put the chains upon him?

* * *

Hellion was aware the moment Jane entered the room.

Bloody hell, who was he fooling, he wryly conceded. He was aware of the smoky heat of the room. And the fact that the champagne had been unpleasantly watered. He was aware his boots were beginning to show a hint of wear and that Lady Grantwood had just grabbed his backside as she passed behind him.

But with Jane it was far more than simple awareness.

The moment she had stepped through the door his entire body had tingled with a charged excitement, as if he were standing in the midst of a thunderstorm. And even more unnerving was the sense he could actually feel her presence. Every blink of her lashes, her every breath, every beat of her heart. As if they were a part of one another.

Ridiculous, of course. Unless Jane had indeed driven him to madness.

Resisting the urge to thrust his way through the crowd and sweep her into his arms, Hellion instead continued his amusing story for the crowd of young bucks who had gathered about him. Over the past three days he had played a cautious game with Jane, knowing that to press her in any manner might be fatal. Instead he had remained close enough for her to know he was near but never directly approaching her.

Biddles assured him that such a tactic was bound to succeed where outright pursuit would fail. Jane was a woman who preferred to feel she was in control of every situation, he had warned Hellion. Even when it came to matters of the heart. It would be best to allow her to decide when she was prepared to speak of their inevitable future together.

A wise scheme no doubt, but Hellion could not deny that he was growing impatient with the plan.

Dammit all, surely he had waited long enough?

What if she were actually awaiting him to approach her? What if she were still shy of their passion and felt too awkward to seek him out?

What if . . .

Abruptly Hellion stiffened as he watched Jane hurry away from her friend toward the nearby door. Even though a hundred guests separated them he could tell that something was the matter.

It was in the stiff set of her shoulders and the manner in which she kept her head turned as if she were hiding the urge to cry.

He did not even hesitate as he offered a hasty bow and pressed his way through the group of dandies. He took no note of their demands that he finish his rather highly embroidered tale, or even of Lady Grantwood, who attempted to block his path with her well-endowed form.

Enough. He was done with waiting. If Jane were upset, or even if she were not, he wanted to be with her.

Battling his way through the surging crowd Hellion at last slipped out of the ballroom and entered the darkened hall. It was too late, however, to catch Jane before she slipped out of sight.

Hesitating in the shadows Hellion was reluctant to return to the ballroom. He had come this far. He could not bear to allow another night to pass without speaking with Jane. Without hearing her voice. Without catching a whiff of her spring scent. Without tasting of her lips . . .

His expression hardened as he pushed open the door to an empty study and slipped into the dark silence. She had to return to the ballroom eventually. He would be waiting for her.

It took less than a quarter of an hour before he heard the rustle of silk and caught that light, tantalizing aroma that could only belong to Jane.

With a motion too swift to alert his approaching prey he reached out and grasped her by the arm. Then with a sharp tug he had her in the room and was closing the door.

He heard her give a small gasp before her eyes adjusted enough to recognize her captor.

"Hellion."

Stepping close enough to be enveloped in her warmth, Hellion placed his hands upon her shoulders.

"Ssh. We do not wish to attract unwanted attention," he murmured.

He thought a faint shiver raced through her body at his touch, but her voice was steady.

"Whatever are you doing?"

"You seemed upset when you left the ballroom. I was concerned."

"I . . . what made you think that I was upset?"

It had been a mistake to bring her into this dark, isolated room, Hellion acknowledged too late. Already his blood was warming and his thoughts were turning in directions that were distinctly dangerous.

Far better to have remained in the hall where

the chance of being seen would have at least tempered his surge of awareness.

"I know you well enough to sense when something is troubling you." Of their own will his fingers lightly skated over the satin skin of her neck. "Tell me what it is."

"There is nothing." Her breath caught as his fingers moved to trace the modest line of her bodice. "Good heavens, Hellion, you must halt that."

He smiled ruefully. She was still clearly naïve when it came to gentlemen. At the moment he could more easily halt his heart from beating than to keep his greedy touch from worshipping the ivory heat of her body.

"Must I?" he husked, bending down to stroke his cheek over her scented curls. "This is what I desired to do for the past three days. You cannot know how difficult it has been to keep myself from charging across the room this evening and tossing you over my shoulder."

In the tumble of moonlight that was muted by the inevitable fog, her features were softened and shrouded with mystery.

"Do you make a habit of tossing women over your shoulder?"

"I have never before desired to," he retorted with perfect honesty. "You, Miss Middleton, have stirred to life demons within me that I did not even know I possessed."

"That sounds distinctly uncomfortable."

He offered a humorless laugh. "You can have no notion."

There was a short pause before she heaved a sigh. "Actually, I believe I might have a very good notion."

Hellion gritted his teeth at the unexpected confession. Oh yes, this had all been a terrible mistake, he grimly acknowledged. He was already hot and randy just having her near. To actually have her confess her own needs was like tossing a match onto dry kindling.

Growing uncomfortably hard, he barely resisted the urge to tug her against his aching erection.

"Good Lord, do not say such things, my sweet," he groaned, a sweat breaking out on his forehead. "I brought you in here so that we can have a moment alone to speak. A remarkably difficult task when you are so near."

If she had possessed the slightest sense of self-preservation she would have stomped upon his toes, or better yet, thrust her knee where no knee should be thrust.

Obviously, however, she was currently plagued with the same reckless need and just as incapable of summoning the least amount of common sense, he decided as her hands crept upward to stroke over his chest.

"I suppose I could stand across the room if you prefer," she offered in a breathless voice.

Allowing his arms to slip about her slender form Hellion discovered his head lowering so that he could softly nibble at the lobe of her ear.

"That might be for the best," he conceded.

She shivered as she arched against his straining muscles. "Or I could go to the gardens and you could shout down at me from the window."

He trailed his lips down the curve of her neck, savoring the taste of her as he reached the curve of her breast.

"Far more sensible," he muttered. "Although much less pleasurable."

She sucked in a shaky breath. "There is that."

Reaching the barrier of her silk bodice Hellion impatiently tugged at the devil-spawned sleeve to allow him greater access. Damn and blast, it was a sin against nature the manner in which women draped themselves in endless layers of foolishness. How the hell was a gentleman to properly seduce them when he was battling against silk and linen and ribbons and any other number of falderals?

"And in truth, whenever I seek to talk with you I always manage to make a muck of it," he confessed, at last able to hone in on a hardened nipple.

With a low moan Jane roughly rammed her fingers into his hair, eagerly encouraging his moist caress.

"True," she breathed.

Hellion gave a low chuckle as he gave a tug on the nipple. "You did not have to agree with such enthusiasm."

Determinedly guiding him to her other breast Jane moaned in pleasure.

"It does not matter," she assured him. "At the moment I have no wish to speak."

"Thank God." With one fluid motion he pressed himself against the wall, reaching out to slip the bolt on the lock. "I can think of much better ways to employ those maddening lips of yours."

Not even bothering to hide his hunger he took her lips in a devouring kiss, his hands cupping her breasts to rub his thumbs over her aching tips. Her arms encircled his neck, her nails biting into his nape with an unabashed need. A searing jolt of excitement nearly sent him to his knees. It seemed like weeks, months even since he had held her in his arms, and his jaded senses were shocked by the fierce desire that clutched at his stomach.

Dear God, he wanted her. Every last satin curve of her.

"Hellion . . ." she whispered, pressing even closer.

Across the darkened room was a convenient sofa, but Hellion was far too impatient to seek the relative comfort. Instead his hands reached down to grasp the skirts of her gown and slide them upward.

"I need you, Jane," he muttered, at last discovering the warm skin of thighs. "I need you now."

She gave a small gasp as his fingers explored ever higher, at last reaching the sensitive cleft that was already damp. Her nails nearly drew blood as he slid a finger deep within her, using his thumb to stroke her point of pleasure.

"Yes," she husked, her hips moving in concert with his slow strokes. "Oh lord, I did not know . . ."

Hellion gave a rasping groan, shifting so that he could hastily unfasten his breeches. His smooth expertise was distinctly absent as his fingers trembled and he nearly pulled off the buttons before he at last managed to tug them open.

Hellfire, this was not at all like him. Seducing young women during the midst of a ball. Panting and fumbling about as if he were a raw greenhorn rather than a seasoned rake. Feeling as if he might burst any moment.

His fully aroused shaft sprang free and he shifted his hand to the back of her thigh to pull her leg over his own. Astonishingly, however, he felt her stiffen as if not yet prepared for his entry.

"Jane?" he whispered in a tortured voice, unable to believe she would halt him at this late stage.

Pulling back she met his gaze in the muted shadows. "I want to touch you," she murmured.

Hellion sucked in a sharp breath at her hesitant request. Oh yes. To have her touch him would be a fantasy come true. If only he could bear it without embarrassing himself utterly.

"Allow me," he rasped, reaching up to take her hand and lower it to his straining manhood.

With his gentle direction her fingers closed about him, at first so tentative that his hips instinctively thrust forward to plead for more. Then, as if sensing her feminine power she began to explore with greater enthusiasm, stroking him from the very root to the tip.

Hellion battled back a primal growl as a flood of exquisite pleasure raced through his body. Ah . . . it was paradise. Flopping back against the wall he allowed her to work her magic, grimly battling back the rising orgasm. He wanted this to last an eternity. Or until his knees buckled with unbearable delight.

Clearly curious Jane explored him thoroughly, tracing the throbbing veins and cupping him with a tender squeeze. Hellion gave a low cry of joy as he reached out his hands to grasp her face and pulled her close for a ravaging kiss.

"No more," he muttered against her lips. "I want to be in you."

"Yes."

Her whisper barely stirred the thick air but it was enough for Hellion to grasp her hips and tug her off the floor. Holding her against his chest he positioned her above his shaft and slowly slid her down, the tight heat sheathing about him.

"Dear God, Jane," he moaned, his hips already thrusting as he struggled for control. "I cannot be gentle."

Her breath was coming in short bursts as she pressed her lips to his jaw. "Just do not stop," she commanded.

As if he could, Hellion wryly conceded, his fingers digging into her hips as her legs wrapped about him. He could as easily stab a dagger in his heart as to halt the fierce thrusts deep within her.

Clenching his jaw he listened carefully to her soft moans, determined to await her pleasure before giving release to his building climax. Her legs tightened about him, allowing him to sink ever deeper. He increased his pace, his hips rolling upward. A keening cry was wrenched from Jane's throat as she shook with her fierce release and her teeth shockingly sank into his throat.

Feeling himself clenched by her contractions Hellion gave a low shout of triumph, his thrusts becoming frenzied as his climax hit him with stunning force. Pumping his seed inside her, he was struck by the notion that they might very well be creating a child during this erotic interlude.

A thought that should have made him shudder in horror, but instead sent a fierce satisfaction soaring through his heart.

There was no woman he would rather have as the mother of his children.

"Sweet, so sweet," he choked out, holding her tight as they slowly floated back to earth together.

Pressing her face into his shoulder Jane slowly

struggled to regain her composure. Then, with obvious reluctance she leaned back to regard him with a somber expression.

"Hellion . . ."

"I know, I know," he wryly interrupted, pressing a brief kiss upon her lips. On this occasion he was prepared for his practical, always logical shrew. "We must return before we are missed."

"Yes."

Heaving a deep sigh, Hellion pulled himself from her warmth and lowered her feet to the floor. Damn and blast, he wished they were already wed. That way he could easily sweep her away from the tedious ball and off to the privacy of their bed. As sated as he might feel at this moment, he knew it would only take a kiss from those maddening lips to have him aroused and ready once again.

Covertly watching her fumble with her clothing as he straightened his own, Hellion smiled with an unwitting tenderness.

He was uncertain when this tiny, unpredictable creature had become an essential part of his life. He only knew that she was.

And the sooner he had a ring upon her finger the better.

Fussing with her hair she sent him a rather nervous glance. "I think it best that I return alone."

He gave a lift of his shoulder. He was quite prepared to let everyone in the ballroom know what they had been up to; indeed, it would suit him to perfection. But the thought of embarrassing Jane kept his possessive urges at bay.

"As you wish."

"Hellion . . ."

"Yes, my love?"

She regarded him for a long moment before giving a slow shake of her head. "'Tis nothing."

The faintest trickle of unease tarnished his glow of deep satisfaction.

"You are certain?" he demanded, not at all caring for the thought she might be hiding something from him.

"I am certain." Patting her hair to make certain it was all in place, she caught him off guard by stepping forward and touching her lips softly to his own.

Instinctively he reached out to tug her close, but already she was moving away. In silence he watched her unlock the door and then with a last glance slip out of the room.

For a moment Hellion wavered, his thoughts dwelling on her brief hesitation. What had she been about to say? Was she still uncertain? Did she still question him? Did she still believe that she could possibly live without him?

Giving a shake of his head Hellion sternly dismissed the unnerving questions. After tonight Jane could not possibly possess doubts. They were perfect for one another. Not only in the physical sense, but upon a deeper level that he could not even explain.

Besides which, she might very well be carrying his child, he acknowledged rather smugly.

She could have no option but to become his wife.

Feeling his earlier good will returning, Hellion carefully tugged his cravat high enough to hide the marks Jane had left upon his neck.

Ah yes, the future was most definitely written in stone.

And what a delicious future it promised to be.

* * *

Not far from Charing Cross Road the aged brick building stood with molding dignity. The mullioned windows reflected the gray sky in sullen reproach, while the baronial stateliness maintained a snobbish distance from its more flamboyant neighbors.

Allowing her agent to open the door, Jane was not surprised to discover herself greeted by a cloud of dust and cobwebs. It had been over a year since the once-grand coffeehouse had closed its doors for the last time.

Although it was a historic treasure, the owner, Mr. Christian, was incapable of holding back the tide of change.

It was not his fault.

He could not compete against the flourishing gentlemen's clubs that lured away customers with the promise of aristocratic seclusion. Nor the cheaper gin houses that catered to the poor and desperate. Even worse, the entire neighborhood had been ravaged by the flight of the wealthy toward the West End of London.

The few buildings that had remained intact now housed brothels or, worse, opium dens that had put paid to Mr. Christian's few loyal customers.

What respectable person would even enter such a neighborhood?

Wrinkling her nose at the musty scent, Jane paused to allow her eyes to adjust to the gloom within. At her side the slender, silver-haired land agent pulled out his notebook and pencil as he prepared to meticulously inventory the various contents left behind.

"As you can see the former tenant left most of the furnishings." He pointed toward the small tables and chairs set about the outer room. "I would suggest we sell them at auction."

Jane pushed off her bothersome bonnet and settled her thoughts to the business at hand. It was usually an easy task, but this morning she found it astonishingly difficult.

No, not so astonishing, she wryly conceded.

What woman could possibly concentrate upon a dusty old building when her body still ached from Hellion's fierce seduction? It would be far more astonishing if she weren't forced to battle the urge to grin like a looby. Or to have her thoughts drift back to the delicious sensations that had made her bones melt.

Still, she had no desire to worry her agent that she had completely taken leave of her senses. And in truth, she simply desired to be done with her morning work so she could return to her home and consider her future.

A future that was still too uncertain for a woman who had always known precisely her path in life.

Giving a shake of her head she peeled off her gloves. "You do not believe we shall increase the value of the building by leaving the furnishings intact?"

"To be honest, Miss Middleton, I do not believe it would make a farthing of difference. The place is worthless except for the land it stands upon. And even that is declining with every passing year."

"A pity." Jane cast a sad glance toward the open-timbered roof that was nearly black with layers of soot. "This once was a landmark of London. My father told me that Sir Walter Raleigh and even

Shakespeare could be found seated near the window."

The agent gave a sympathetic sigh, his gaze flicking over the worn planks to linger upon the heavy pewter plates that were placed with pride above the enormous fireplace.

"The price of progress, I suppose," he murmured.

"Yes." Jane shrugged. "And rather shameful profit. At the moment this building is a worthless waste of my resources."

"Far better to sell before all hopes of a buyer are lost."

Jane had to agree. Whatever her fondness for the coffeehouse, it was absurd to hang on to the place out of mere sentimentality.

In silent agreement the two wandered toward the heavy mahogany counter at the back of the long room, occasionally pausing to study the names, many of them of famous actors, painters, and politicians of a distant age, that had been scratched onto the wooden tabletops.

They were sifting through the numerous etchings that had been piled near the fireplace when the door to the building was unexpectedly thrust open.

With a startled blink Jane turned about, her heart coming to a sharp halt at the large, gloriously familiar male form that stepped over the threshold.

Hellion.

Unable to help herself, Jane discovered her gaze hungrily sweeping over the black breeches, his ivory waistcoat, and the crisp perfection of his dove-gray coat. Simple attire that emphasized rather than detracted from the graceful lines of his hard body.

Her gaze skimmed higher, lingering upon the

elegant beauty of his male features and the wicked temptation of his dark eyes that smoldered with a restless power even in the dim shadows.

He was the undoubted fantasy of every woman. Was it any wonder that she felt the urge to babble and swoon like a goosecap when he was near?

The silence stretched as they regarded one another, a slow devilish smile at last curving his lips as a hint of color touched her cheeks.

Blast the arrogant man. He knew precisely how his appearance was making her heart race and her stomach quiver with awareness.

Still holding her gaze he performed a small bow. "Good morning, Jane."

"Hellion." Sharply aware of the agent's curiosity at the unexpected intrusion, Jane moved across the floor to stand before him. "Whatever are you doing here?"

Turning he reached behind him to lift the basket he had left outside the door.

"I am attempting to save you from your own foolishness."

She frowned, finding it difficult to adjust to Hellion's sudden arrival. Since coming to London she had attempted to keep her role as a powerful financier carefully separate from that of her role as *débutante*. Not only because most of society found her business connections so distasteful, but also to be able to keep her thoughts focused when she was making decisions that were worth a vast fortune.

It was distinctly unsettling to have Hellion enter this separate part of her life.

"I beg your pardon?"

"I spoke with your housekeeper, who assured me that you had left this morning without so much as a nibble of toast."

She shrugged. "I overslept and was late for my appointment with Mr. Steinman."

"Indeed." He leaned close enough for her to catch the scent of freshly scrubbed male skin. "Whyever would you have overslept?"

His murmured innuendo sent a rash of prickles through her body. Oh my. This was precisely why it was not wise to have him near. Not, at least, while she was in the process of conducting business. Or walking. Or eating. Or attempting to breathe . . .

"Hellion, I think it best if you . . ."

Her words were cut off as he laid a finger across her lips. "I promise to be upon my very best behavior."

She arched her brows at his soft words. "I believe we have already concluded that your best behavior is nothing to console me."

"Ah, but I have brought with me a delicious luncheon." He lifted the lid of the basket to allow a most tempting aroma to fill the air. "Thinly sliced ham, lobster in butter, bread warm from the oven, and apple tarts."

"A blatant bribe," she chided, even as her stomach loudly growled and her mouth watered. It had been hours since she had last eaten.

His lips twitched at her traitorous belly. "I could hardly depend solely upon my irresistible charm, not when it comes to you, my shrew."

Tell him to go away, her more logical mind whispered. It was a poor notion to mix business and this potent male. But meeting his dark, smoldering gaze she felt her logic evaporating with astonishing speed.

What could be the harm? She had already made her decision regarding the building. There was little left to do but begin the inventory.

"Very well," she agreed, turning to walk back toward the center of the room. "I am nearly finished here."

Following in step behind her Hellion suddenly gave a low whistle. "Good Lord, this is the old coffeehouse, is it not?"

"It was. It has been empty for the past year."

"Are you intending to reopen it?"

She cast him a startled glance over her shoulder. "Good heavens, no. If Mr. Christian could not maintain a profitable business I should have no hope of doing so."

He frowned as he glanced about the shadowed interior. "Then why are you here?"

"The building was purchased by my father nearly thirty years ago. Now I intend to sell it."

Surprisingly Hellion came to a sudden halt, his brows snapping together.

"You must be jesting?"

Turning to face him Jane regarded him in open puzzlement. "Why?"

"This building is a part of London," he protested. "My father used to entertain me with stories of the days he would devote here, along with any number of nobles and artists and actors. Do you know that Mr. Christian refused to offer more than thirty chairs and when they were filled one was forced to wait in the streets until a seat became vacant? He claimed the only reason he ever rose before noon was to ensure a seat near the window."

Jane smiled rather wistfully, almost able to see the distant ghosts laughing and shouting at passing pedestrians.

"All in the past now, I fear. No one is willing to travel these streets."

"They are a bit shabby, I admit, but . . ."

"Hellion," she interrupted with a hint of impatience, "the buildings on either side are brothels, and just down the street is a well-known opium den. All hint of respectability has been tarnished beyond repair."

Oddly reluctant to concede to her more experienced judgment Hellion gave a lift of his hands.

"What are a few brothels?"

She gave a choked laugh. "Only a man would ask such a question."

"Granted it might be difficult to lure proper ladies to such a neighborhood, but there are few men who would feel such delicate distaste," he insisted. "You must simply concentrate upon a business that caters to gentlemen."

"Such as?"

"A gentleman's club, or a private gambling hell," he promptly retorted.

Jane was caught off guard. It did not seem at all like Hellion to waste his thoughts on something so mundane as an empty building. Perhaps the sentimental value of his father's long-ago stories had stirred a sense of possessive attachment to the place.

Unnoticed by either Jane or Hellion, Mr. Steinman stepped up beside them, his lips pursed in thought.

"'Tis not a bad notion, Miss Middleton," he said.

Jane turned to regard her agent with a frown. "What?"

He nervously cleared his throat. "It would be a shame to see an end to such a long-standing establishment. With a bit of work it could be brought back to its former glory."

She resisted the urge to roll her eyes heavenward. It was obvious both gentlemen were attempting to be of service. Unfortunately neither of them seemed to comprehend the delicacy of her position.

"Perhaps, but it will have to be done by another owner. I will not become involved in such a venture," she said with a crisp finality. "Mr. Steinman, would you please begin with the inventory?"

Familiar enough with Jane to know that her mind had been set, the agent offered a ready bow.

"Of course."

With near military precision Mr. Steinman turned on his heels and marched up the narrow flight of stairs to begin his task. Watching his retreat Jane failed to notice Hellion's tight features and distinct absence of amusement in the dark eyes.

"It is unlike you to be so bloody-minded, Jane. At least when it comes to business."

Instinctively Jane bristled at the implied criticism. Perhaps she was overly sensitive when it came to those questioning her decisions, but dash it all, she had been forced to battle for her right to make her own choices for so long it was not easy to remain indifferent.

"I am not bloody-minded. I simply must make

the decisions that I feel are for the best," she retorted stiffly.

He gave a lift of his brows, his lips thinning. "Are you certain that is all there is to it?"

"I beg your pardon?"

Hellion stepped abruptly forward, his expression impossible to read. "Could it be that you simply do not desire to hear any suggestions from a frippery rakehell?"

She blinked at the unexpected attack. Hellion almost seemed . . . offended. Which did not make sense at all.

"That is absurd."

"Is it?" he demanded. "I have noted that you have never once asked my opinion or included me in your business affairs."

Wondering what the devil had gotten into the man, Jane planted her hands upon her hips.

"You were the one to claim that your only business was pleasure, Hellion. I did not presume you would be interested."

"And if I assure you that I am? Would you be prepared to listen to my advice?"

Jane faltered at the blunt question. She had never actually considered sharing her vast responsibilities with another. Not even her husband. Somehow she had just assumed whomever she wed would be content to run the estate and see to his own interests.

"I . . . would always listen to advice," she cautiously retorted.

As if sensing her reluctance his lips twisted. "Just as long as it did not come from me, eh Jane?"

There was an edge of bitterness to his voice that

made her heart abruptly clench with regret. Although she was uncertain what she had done, it was obvious that his pride had been wounded.

"Hellion, it is not that I do not desire to listen to your advice."

"Then what is it?"

"As a woman it is difficult enough to command respect among those gentlemen I must maintain contacts with. I must always recall that one misstep could ruin everything."

His expression remained as unyielding as granite. "And?"

She waved an impatient hand about the shabby common room. "Can you imagine what the gossips would do to me should they discover I have opened a business next to the most notorious brothels in London? Especially a business that caters solely to gentlemen? There is not a businessman about who would not close his doors to me. And society . . . gads, I would be worse than a wallflower. I would be an utter pariah."

With a restless motion Hellion turned away, his hand lifting to rub his nape as if plagued beyond bearing. Which was ridiculous, she told herself somewhat grumpily. If anyone was being plagued it was she.

"You are right, of course," he said in flat tones. "I did not consider."

It was clear that he was far from appeased by her perfectly reasonable explanation and Jane heaved a sigh of impatience.

"For goodness sakes, Hellion, what is it?"

For a moment he kept his rigid back firmly turned

before at last he swiveled to regard her with a burning gaze.

"It is not about the coffeehouse, although it is a shame to think of this place falling to ruin. It is about the manner in which you allow me to draw close one moment only to have you fade to a wisp of smoke the next."

She blinked at his fierce tone. Gone was the playful seducer and nonchalant gentleman of leisure. In his place was a proud, exasperated male very much at the end of his tether.

"That is not true."

"Yes, it is." He gave a slow shake of his head. "To be honest, I am at a loss. I have attempted every means to win your heart, but it is your trust you continue to withhold. I begin to wonder if there is anything I can do to earn that."

Her hand instinctively reached out as she battled an unexpected flare of panic. Did he mean to walk away from her? Had her hesitancy at last become too much to bear for such a proud man?

"Hellion . . ." she breathed, an odd flare of panic racing through her stomach.

Without warning he pressed the basket into her outstretched hand, performing a stiff bow.

"I shall allow you to enjoy your luncheon alone, my dear. 'Tis obvious how you prefer it to be."

CHAPTER FIFTEEN

From the diary of Miss Jane Middleton, May 25th, 1814:

Dear Diary,
I have always detested those milk-toast females who are incapable of knowing their own minds. They flutter about like butterflies, allowing others to tumble them from one opinion to another and agreeing with everyone and everything. And heaven forbid that they ever be expected to make a decision. They will twitter and dither and vacillate until one longs to throttle them.
Now I discover that I have been harboring a hidden milk-toast within myself.
It is the oddest thing.
Without undue boasting I could claim for myself a most resolute temperament. Even when it comes to the most vital decisions I am capable of reasoning the best course of action without undue agony. How else could I have possibly taken over my father's business?

And yet, when I am now confronted with perhaps the most important decision I have ever faced, I am utterly incapable of reasoning or logical debate.

I twitter and dither and vacillate like the most witless butterfly ever to flutter.

Jane was in a fretful mood.

Hardly a dire situation for most females. It was a natural part of one's existence to stew and brood when life did not go precisely as planned. And of course, when one added a handsome, unpredictable rogue into the mixture there were bound to be a great deal of worrisome moments.

Jane, however, had managed to blaze through life with an inordinate amount of confidence. It was a rare occasion when she discovered herself wavering in indecision.

Which no doubt explained why she discovered the unfamiliar sensations so troublesome.

Pacing the length of her beautiful library, Jane momentarily perched upon the padded window seat, only to hop to her feet again when a vexing shiver of unease raced over her skin.

Damn and blast Hellion, she inwardly cursed.

This was entirely his fault, of course.

He refused to play the game by her rules. Or any rules, for that matter. Which was not at all acceptable to a female accustomed to being in control of every aspect of her life.

What the devil was the matter with him? Last night he had been the wicked seducer she had come to know intimately. He had quite literally made her swoon with pleasure. But this morning . . .

This morning he had been different. Tense. Impatient. And clearly determined to take offense at the slightest provocation.

No, she slightly chastised herself. That was not entirely fair.

She had perhaps been a bit more than merely provoking. Not that it had been in any way intentional. She simply was unaccustomed to sharing her authority or having her decisions questioned.

And as for his claim that she refused to trust him . . . well, it was not so simple as he wished. Not so long as her heart was involved.

Reaching her desk she abruptly spun about to heave an exasperated sigh. Whether at her own ridiculous behavior or that of Hellion she was not entirely certain.

Seated in a leather wing chair, Anna at last broke her self-imposed silence with a click of her tongue.

"Good Lord, Jane, you are a mess."

Jane came to a halt as she flashed her friend a jaundiced frown. "Well, that is very helpful, thank you, Anna. I am so relieved that you called this afternoon."

"I merely speak the truth."

"I know." Jane ruefully grimaced. "It is all that . . . scoundrel's fault."

"Hellion?"

"Is there another?"

The curvaceous brunette gave a lift of her brows. "Quite a few actually. What has he done now?"

"He is . . ." Jane struggled to conjure the words that would explain Hellion's unreasonable behavior. It was remarkably difficult.

"What?"

"He is making me batty" was the best she could do.

Anna offered a charming laugh. "I presumed that was the purpose of all gentlemen. Indeed, it appears to be their one certain talent."

"Very true."

"Has he done anything in particular to make you batty?" Anna demanded.

"Beyond being his usual aggravating, unpredictable, utterly irresistible self?"

Anna's lips twitched with barely repressed amusement. "Exactly."

Realizing how ridiculous she must sound, Jane wrinkled her nose in defeat.

"Oh, in truth it is not Hellion I am angered with, it is myself. I have been such an idiot."

"Absurd," Anna loyally denied. "You have been very brave and daring. There is nothing foolish in taking command of your future."

Jane gave a short, humorless laugh. "But have I, Anna? I mean have I truly taken command?"

"What do you mean?"

She paced restlessly to the center of the room. "I have always prided myself upon being such a logical woman. I thought I was far too sensible to behave like a silly, goose-witted *débutante*. But here I am. As fluttery over a handsome cad as any schoolgirl."

Anna frowned. "I think you are being too hard on yourself, Jane."

"You cannot deny that I have begun to think with my heart rather than my head," she confessed with brutal honesty.

Surprisingly Anna gave an indifferent lift of her

shoulder. As if she did not find Jane's lack of sense in any way disturbing.

"Is that such a ghastly thing?"

Jane stiffened at the soft words. "Of course it is. My judgment has become dangerously clouded."

Without warning Anna came to her feet and moved to stand directly before Jane. Then just as unexpectedly she placed her hands upon Jane's shoulders and steered her firmly backward. Nearly stumbling over the hem of her gown, Jane discovered herself bumping into the low sofa near the fireplace.

"Sit," Anna commanded, pressing upon Jane's shoulders until she toppled onto the brocade cushions.

"Good heavens, Anna, what are you doing?" Jane demanded in some bewilderment.

Crossing her arms over her waist, Anna peered down at her friend much like a governess about to scold a vexing child.

"I wish you to listen to me," she said sternly.

With a lift of her brows at her friend's high-handed manner, Jane gave a faint nod.

"Very well."

"Can you honestly tell me that in all of your business dealings you have never once allowed yourself to be led by more than dull facts and numbers?"

"I . . ." Jane gave an uneasy shrug, already sensing where her friend was going with this. "There are many factors that must be put into a business decision."

"Such as instinct?" Anna pressed. "Or a gut feeling that it was the right thing to do?"

"Perhaps upon occasion," she grudgingly conceded.

"So why is this so different?" Anna demanded. "If your heart tells you that Hellion is the husband you desire, why must it logically follow that it must be mistaken?"

"Because we are so dissimilar," Jane burst out, her fingers twisting together in rare agitation. "How could he possibly be satisfied molding away in Surrey?"

Anna slowly narrowed her gaze. "Do you know what I think?"

"What?"

"I think you are afraid."

Jane gave an offended blink at the accusation. "Fah."

"Oh yes. I think you are afraid because this matters."

"Whatever are you speaking of?"

Anna abruptly dropped to her knees before the chair, taking Jane's hands in a tight grip.

"Just consider, Jane. If you wed some comfortable gentleman who would willingly disappear into the woodwork after providing you with suitable children, you could still maintain your independence and have the family you desire. You would have precisely what you want and all without risking your heart."

It sounded perfectly reasonable to her. Indeed, that had been the plan when she had arrived in London.

Before Hellion had come along to perform his particular brand of bedlam.

"What is so wrong with that?"

Anna smiled somewhat wryly. "There is nothing wrong, except that you will never know the beauty of life with a true partner. A companion is all well and good, but a gentleman you can love with all your heart is something quite special."

There was a throbbing intensity in her friend's voice that caught Jane off guard. As if Anna were speaking from experience rather than spouting the nonsense usually reserved for fools and poets.

"But my parents . . ."

"Founded a relationship that suited them," Anna overrode with firm tones. "It does not necessarily mean that it would satisfy you. You are not your mother, nor your father. You are Miss Jane Middleton. You should choose the future you desire, not one that was wished upon you by someone else."

Jane faltered, her heart squeezing as she forced herself to truly consider a future without Hellion.

No doubt it would be far more peaceful, she acknowledged. And certainly her heart would be safeguarded from disappointment and pain.

But was it also a future that suddenly seemed unbearably empty?

"Gads, why must this be so complicated?" she bemoaned.

"Because you came to London to discover a dull fish and instead landed a Hellion."

A reluctant chuckle was wrenched from her throat at the droll words. "Oh Lord."

"What do you want, Jane?" Anna gave a fierce squeeze of her fingers. "What do you truly desire?"

She did not even hesitate. "Hellion."

"Then you had best tell him. A gentleman such

as Hellion will not allow his pride to be forever trampled."

Jane wavered for a moment more. Bringing herself to the point of admitting that she desired Hellion as her husband was one thing. To actually confess her desire to Hellion, well, that was something else altogether.

Still, as she met Anna's steady gaze she realized that her friend was absolutely right.

Hellion was clearly becoming impatient with her hesitation. Perhaps not without some cause. She had waffled about like the veriest nitwit, encouraging his seduction at one moment and then shying from him the next.

The time had come to behave as a mature woman rather than a quaking child.

"You are right." With a brisk motion she rose to her feet, pulling Anna upright. "Will you come with me?"

Anna blinked at the sudden flurry of movement. "Now?"

Jane wrinkled her nose. "I must. Otherwise I shall manage to convince myself this is all some ghastly mistake."

"True. But . . ."

"What is it?"

Anna gently cleared her throat. "It is not entirely proper to call upon a bachelor's household."

Jane gave a dismissive wave of her hand. "It is if that bachelor is about to become my husband."

"I suppose you do have a point," Anna conceded.

"And you shall be my chaperone."

A sudden smile curved Anna's lips. "My carriage is waiting outside."

"Then let us go before I lose my nerve completely."

Suppressing the urge to dash out of the house like a common hoyden, Jane forced herself to calmly gather her bonnet and gloves while she informed the butler that she would be spending the afternoon with Miss Halifax.

Then arm in arm the two women left the house, pausing to direct the groom to the tidy square not far away as they climbed into the waiting carriage.

Once rumbling down the street, Jane discovered her gaze absently watching the passing houses, her heart not certain whether to race with excitement or to lodge in her throat with dread.

It was ridiculous. She had made her decision. She should be content. That was what she had expected.

Unfortunately a shadow deep in her heart continued to plague her.

"You are very quiet." Anna at last intruded into her brooding.

Pasting a smile onto her lips, Jane turned to meet her friend's searching gaze.

"I am practicing what I shall say," she hastily improvised, not wishing to bedevil her poor friend even further.

Anna gave a startled laugh. "Good heavens, you are not hoping to borrow money from the man. What you say should come from your heart."

"If I should say what is in my heart I should end up sounding like a lunatic," she confessed with all honesty.

"You are supposed to sound like a lunatic, that is what love is all about."

Jane rolled her eyes heavenward. "You are not comforting me, Anna."

Anna merely chuckled. "Sorry. Oh . . . I believe we have arrived."

Not waiting for the groom Anna shoved open the door, and grasping Jane's hand she tugged her out of the carriage and up the narrow path. Stumbling behind the determined young lady, Jane abruptly pulled them both to a sharp halt.

"Wait."

No doubt sensing Jane's inner turmoil Anna turned around to regard her with a fierce glare.

"What is it now?"

Repressing the urge to turn tail and run, Jane steeled her failing courage.

"I hear voices in the garden."

Anna widened her eyes. "We cannot . . ."

Squaring her shoulders Jane headed toward the path that led around the narrow town house.

It was now or never.

"Come along, Anna."

Standing next to the roses that had long ago been left to grow into an untidy tumble of thorns and fading blooms, Hellion frowned at his rat-faced friend.

A part of him knew that he should have refused to allow Biddles to reveal the information he had unearthed concerning Jane and her father's secret dealings. It was one thing to pry and sneak into Jane's past when he was uncertain of her motives concerning him. But now that he was determined to make her his wife, it did not seem at all the thing.

There was another part of him, however, that was

not nearly so concerned with tedious things such as conscience or morals.

This morning Jane had proved she was still just as determined to keep him at a distance.

Dammit all, he had tried everything. Patience. Kindness. Romance. And a seduction that still left him stunned with its power.

There seemed nothing left to do. Nothing but to walk away in defeat.

A notion that made his heart desire to stop beating and his chest so tight he could barely breathe.

Thrusting aside his odd sense of budding panic he returned his thoughts to the tiny gentleman leaning against a crumbling fountain.

"I do not believe it," he said, folding his arms over his chest.

The pointed nose twitched. "I can only offer you what I have discovered, old chap. Remember that I found the contract for the uniforms in Miss Middleton's own desk."

"Yes, but that does not prove they were of inferior quality."

Biddles shrugged. "I spoke with an acquaintance of both Mr. Middleton and Mr. Emerson. He said there had been rumors of fraud."

"Rumors are not facts," Hellion pointed out.

"No indeed, but I also used my connections with the War Department to ensure that the rumors had come from the top. He claimed there had indeed been a scandal, but that it had been nicely hushed."

"Good Lord."

"It seems as if Mr. Middleton decided to add to his fortune at the cost of our soldiers. Not unusual, I fear."

Hellion pulled his brows together. It was not that he doubted the considerable talents of the sly wretch. Biddles could be depended upon to know the darkest secrets in London.

Still, he found it difficult to believe that the father whom Jane held in such loving regard could be so callously indifferent to brave young men being sent into battle. She was too shrewd a judge of character not to have sensed such a fatal weakness, even in her own father.

"Why was he not punished?"

Biddles shrugged, too familiar with the more vulgar aspects of human nature to be shocked.

"Power. Money. An earl as a father-in-law. 'Tis amazing what such things can accomplish."

"It still seems odd," Hellion muttered.

Biddles snapped open a Chinese fan to wave it with a negligent ease.

"Odd or not, Hellion, you desired me to discover a secret that you could hold over the head of Miss Middleton and that is what I have done. Since she was so inconsiderate as to have refrained from indulging in scandalous affairs or peculiar diversions, this is the best I can offer."

Hellion smiled ruefully, realizing he was being wretchedly ungrateful. It was not his friend's fault that he was feeling such an odd sense of discomfort.

"Forgive me, Biddles. It is just that . . ." Hellion abruptly turned his head toward the town house. He had been quite certain he had heard a muffled sound. Something remarkably similar to a sob. "What the devil was that?"

As if in answer to his muttered question a sudden flurry of female fury appeared from behind the hedge and launched directly toward the two startled gentlemen.

Almost instinctively Hellion stepped backward as Miss Halifax barreled forward, although he needn't have bothered. She spared him little more than a venomous glare as she swept past to head directly toward Biddles. Then shockingly she drew back a tiny fist and struck the unsuspecting gentleman directly in the pit of his stomach.

"Why, you weasel-faced, sneaking, lying toad," she shouted as Biddles reeled backward, barely keeping himself from plummeting into the fountain. "I hate you. Do you hear me? I hate you."

Holding his hand to his maltreated stomach, Biddles gave a small cough. "I should think all of London has heard you, my love."

"Is that so. Well I . . ."

Sensing another burst of violence building within the clearly demented damsel, Hellion thought it prudent to intervene. He was uncertain what Biddles had done to cause such hostility, but he was reluctant to allow a vulgar brawl in what was left of his pathetic garden.

"Forgive me, Miss Halifax, but may I inquire what you are doing in my garden?"

She stuck out an insulting tongue toward Biddles before jerking about to stab Hellion with her smoldering gaze.

"I came here with Jane."

Hellion's brows snapped together. "Jane is here?"

"She was, although I do not doubt that she is already on her way home so that she can pack and return to Surrey."

A sudden dread lodged in Hellion's heart. "Why the devil would she return to Surrey?"

"So that she need never again clap eyes upon a gentleman who would stoop so low as to blackmail her into marriage."

"Blackmail?" Hellion blinked, quite certain the woman had run mad. "What the hell are you talking about?"

"We heard you, Mr. Caulfield. You had that . . ." She pointed a dramatic finger toward the silent Biddles. ". . . demon digging up her father's past just so you could hold it over her head. You are despicable. I cannot believe I ever encouraged her to wed you."

Hellion swayed, feeling as if he had just been tossed off the edge of a cliff.

Oh God. She was no doubt feeling utterly betrayed. And wanting nothing more than to put as many miles between them as possible.

He had to stop her. To make her understand that he had never, never intended to hurt her.

"I must go," he muttered, sprinting away before anyone could attempt to halt him.

"Oh no you don't," Anna gritted from behind, clenching her fists as she prepared to follow.

Unfortunately at that moment a strong arm wrapped about her waist to put paid to her efforts.

"Leave it be, my dear," Biddles drawled near her ear. "This is between Hellion and Jane."

Easily spinning in his grip Anna turned about, and as he smiled his wicked smile she promptly acquainted her fist with his distinctive nose.

CHAPTER SIXTEEN

From the diary of Miss Jane Middleton, May 25th, 1814:

P.S. Diary,

I suppose every woman must endure a broken heart at least once in her life. Unfortunate, of course, since I have discovered it a most unpleasant experience. Oh, not just the agonizing pain that is only to be expected. Or the heaviness of spirits that gives a bleakness to the entire world. Or even the ridiculous tears that refuse to be stemmed no matter how sternly one might lecture oneself.

It is more the horrid fear that one has lost some vital part of oneself.

The terrifying emptiness is nearly more than I can bear. How do I go on?

The answer quite simply is that I must.

Life has not halted, nor have my responsibilities vanished just because I desire to crawl beneath the covers and grieve at my stupidity.

Countless women have survived broken hearts throughout the ages; no doubt so shall I.

Yes, no doubt . . .

With her usual precision Jane set about packing her cases.

After a hearty bout of tears that had lasted until she had reached the town house and finally her chambers, an icy numbness had settled within her ravaged heart.

Thankfully her common sense had also managed to survive. A common sense that told her that nothing could be gained by remaining in London.

At the moment she was in no condition to seek another potential husband. The mere thought was enough to make her stomach queasy. And goodness knew, there was nothing else to keep her.

Besides which, she had to admit she was enough of a coward to go to any lengths to avoid accidentally bumping into Hellion. She could not hope the blessed numbness would last, and the thought of breaking down before the treacherous gentleman was something her pride simply could not bear.

No it was best she return to Surrey and consider her future when the pangs of unrequited love had managed to fade.

And they would fade, she told herself fiercely, folding her shifts so neatly the edges could slice through paper. She was not about to pine away for a gentleman who was too foolish not to return her love.

A gentleman who would wed her because it was the simplest solution to his current difficulties.

Gathering her stockings Jane only faintly heard

the sound of her butler's raised voice echoing through the hallway. She presumed that a message arrived for her elderly companion that naturally demanded a shout in her ear to be conveyed, or that the chambermaid was once again caught sneaking off from her duties to lure a kiss from the footman.

It was not until she heard the sound of her door being firmly closed and bolted that she belatedly turned about to discover Hellion regarding her with a fierce expression.

With her knees suddenly weak she reached out to grasp for the bedpost, a wrenching pain wracking her body.

Oh God, to see him standing there. So close she could reach out and touch him, but as distant as the angels in heaven.

It was unbearable.

Taking a step forward Hellion closely studied her pale features until his gaze flicked toward the open case upon the bed.

"Running away, my love?" he rasped.

It would be ridiculous to deny her imminent flight. Not with the evidence piled all about her.

Still it rubbed her wounded pride to be accused of such cowardice.

"I am returning to Surrey," she grudgingly retorted. "It has become obvious that I should never have come here."

"You came here to find a husband."

She stiffened at his audacious remark. Why, the insensitive lout! Did he not possess the least shame?

"Unfortunately no one was kind enough to warn

me that London was filled with deceitful cads who
have no respect for women. Now I know better."

She thought he might have winced at her thrust,
but it was impossible to determine from his grim
features.

"Because of what you overheard in the garden?"

So, he had discovered she was quite aware of his
betrayal. Not so surprising. No doubt Anna had at-
tacked him with a nearby spade.

A pity she seemed to have missed any vital organs.

She tilted her chin to a haughty angle. "I do not
wish to discuss this."

"That is a pity, because I do."

Her teeth ground together. "Get out of my house,
Hellion."

"No. Not until you have heard what I have to say."

He took another step forward and in sudden
panic Jane whirled to pace toward the window.
God, she could not allow him to touch her.

"I have no desire to hear more of your lies."

"More? When have I lied to you, Jane?" he
demanded.

She was certain she could think of a dozen occasions if only her brain was not refusing to work
properly. Instead she could only give a shake of her
head.

"Just go away."

There was a moment's pause, as if Hellion were
carefully considering his words. As well he should.
In her current temper the notion of launching the
nearby chamber pot at his head was not beyond
possibility.

"Jane, what you overheard in the garden is not
what you think."

"You mean that Lord Bidwell was not spying into my father's past?"

"He was, but . . ."

"Then it was exactly what I thought."

A harsh sigh echoed through the room. "Jane, I asked Biddles to discover a secret concerning you when you first approached me with your proposition. I did not know you or if you might have some nefarious purpose in approaching me. It seemed best to have a means of protecting myself."

Her heart clenched. "Is that supposed to make your deception more acceptable?"

"It is simply the truth."

"And you had no intention of using the information to ensure that I said yes to your marriage proposal?" she demanded in soft tones.

She heard him shift impatiently, clearly reluctant to answer her blunt question.

"I do not know. You have me so addle-witted that I can barely recognize myself anymore."

Jane briefly closed her eyes before forcing herself to slowly turn and meet his searing gaze. Perhaps it was for the best that Hellion had arrived before she left for Surrey, she told herself. It would plague her forever if she left, allowing him to believe her father was no better than a common thief.

"Well, allow me to save you the bother of threatening me. My father was not responsible for those uniforms."

This time there was no mistaking his wince as he took a jerky step forward.

"Jane, it does not matter . . ."

"It does to me," she interrupted in fierce tones. "I will not have anyone speak ill of my father."

"Very well."

Folding her arms over her waist Jane willed her voice not to quaver.

"When my father agreed to provide uniforms for the army he was approached by Mr. Emerson. The two were competitors, but they were also friends from childhood. Mr. Emerson told my father that he was horribly near financial ruin. Indeed, he was terrified he might very well end up in debtors' prison if he did not have a means of turning his fortunes around." She grimaced as she recalled her father's kindly heart. "Of course my father agreed to help. He could never turn away someone in need so he allowed Mr. Emerson to manufacture the actual uniforms while my father provided him with the material."

His features softened with a hint of sympathy. "I presume his work was not up to your father's standards?"

"It was utterly inferior. Not only were they poorly cut and sewn, but he had secretly sold the fine wool my father had provided and replaced it with a cheap weave."

He lifted his hand as if to touch her, only to abruptly drop it as she took a hasty step backward.

"Your father must have been very disappointed."

"He was devastated. His friend had deceived him, and worse, he was blamed for the entire debacle. It was only because my father was able to replace the uniforms quite swiftly that charges were not brought against him."

"A most unfortunate incident," he said softly.

"Yes, but my father was innocent."

A faint smile touched his lips. "I must admit that

I found it difficult to believe the gentleman that you hold in such high esteem could have been involved in such a sordid scheme."

Jane arched her brows in obvious disbelief. "Indeed?"

"Of course. It was only . . ."

"Hellion, I am rather busy at the moment," she interrupted in abrupt tones, not desiring to hear any excuses he might have to offer. What did it matter? The fact that he had delved into her father's past had hurt, but it was not the reason she was returning to Surrey. "I think it best if you leave."

Hellion's brows furrowed as his eyes seemed to darken with pain. "For God's sake, I am sorry. I never intended to hurt you, Jane. You must know that is the last thing I would ever want."

The sight of his pleading expression nearly threatened to shatter her fragile composure. Odd, considering she was supposed to be damn well furious with him.

"Please do not," she muttered, turning toward the bed to absently fold a shawl that was already perfectly well folded. "I was a fool to believe for a moment that we could be more than passing acquaintances."

"Passing . . ." There was a moment of shocked disbelief before Hellion was at her side, roughly snatching the shawl from her hands and tossing it aside. "I would say we have been a damn sight more than passing acquaintances. I have the scratches and bite marks to prove it. Shall I show them to you?"

Her cheeks burned at the fierce words, but not entirely out of embarrassment. She possessed a most vivid memory of how he came about those scratches and bites. And the heated pleasure that had been exploding through her at that precise moment.

"That is not what I meant."

His hand reached out to run a light finger down the back of her neck. "I know you better than you know yourself, Jane."

A shiver of pure delight raced down her spine at his touch. Gads, it was so vexingly unfair that the one gentleman she could not possibly have should be capable of stirring such magic within her.

Sucking in a deep breath she forced herself to ignore the desire to lean against the warmth of his male body.

She would not be seduced into making a decision that they would both live to regret.

"And yet you know nothing of yourself," she said in tones that were more sad than angry.

His light touch stilled. "What the devil is that supposed to mean?"

Stepping from the distracting fingers she turned to face him squarely. "Why do you desire to wed me, Hellion?"

"You know why."

"Tell me."

He regarded her closely, as if seeking to determine what words might offer the best comfort.

"I believe we will suit one another quite well. I admire your intelligence as well as your kind heart. More importantly I admire your independent spirit, which is a damn sight more than most gentlemen could claim." His gaze deliberately lowered to her lips. "And of course, there is that undeniable fact that I desire you to the point of madness. It is more than most marriages possess."

She pressed her hands to her churning stomach. Whatever the truth of his words she would not be swayed. Not again.

"Perhaps, but I believe that you have left out the most important reason you desire me as a wife."

His expression became guarded. "What is that?"

"My fortune, of course."

A prickling tension entered the air as he slowly narrowed his gaze.

"You do not think you are being rather a hypocrite to accuse me of wedding you for your fortune when that was precisely the requirement you demanded in a husband?"

"I do not speak of my own feelings upon the matter," she corrected in a low voice, "but yours."

"My feelings?"

"You would never be happy as my husband. Not truly."

"You are so wise you can see the future?" he demanded, an icy anger entering his dark eyes.

Jane unconsciously rubbed the skin of her arms, as if sensing a danger just out of sight.

"Oh for goodness sakes, Hellion, we both know in time you will come to despise yourself for having reduced yourself to a fortune hunter. And in turn you will come to despise me as well."

His hands clenched as he abruptly turned on his heel and paced across the room. For a moment she thought he might simply walk out of the door and wash his hands of her utterly. Then swinging back toward her he stabbed her with a glare.

"You are the one reducing me to a fortune hunter," he said with an awful calm. "It had been my rather absurd belief that I genuinely cared for you.

Obviously I am too stupid to be allowed to know my own heart."

Jane inwardly cringed, not expecting the wounded darkness in his eyes. She surely could not have hurt him? How could she when his heart was not involved?

"Hellion, please . . ."

"Oh no, do not become squeamish at this point, my love," he snarled as he folded his arms over his chest. "If you have any further insults to fling at my head you should do so without hesitation. I should hate to think of you brooding alone in Surrey with the regret that you did not manage to reduce my vile character to utter shreds."

She gave a slow shake of her head, her stomach so tightly clenched that she feared she might be sick. Why was he making this so damnably difficult? It was not as if there weren't dozens and dozens of wealthy *débutantes*, all anxious to toss themselves at his feet.

"That was not my intention at all."

"Then I should hate to think what you could accomplish should you set your mind to it."

Jane heaved a sigh. She had been so furious with Hellion. And rightly so. He had not only pursued her with a relentless determination that had made her behave in a foolish manner, but he had pried shamelessly into her most private affairs.

Now, however, her treacherous heart could not bear for him to believe she would ever think ill of him.

"You are not vile, Hellion," she said softly. "Indeed, you are a wonderful gentleman that shall someday make some fortunate woman very happy. Just not . . ."

"Just not wonderful enough for you," he broke in with bitter tones.

Jane took a step closer, her expression troubled. "Just not until you have accepted that you have no need to depend upon another. Not your uncle. And certainly not me."

"Depend upon?" If anything his expression only became more remote. "Now you are implying that I am weak?"

A flare of exasperation tightened her lips. "You are willfully misunderstanding me."

"Then halt this ridiculous babbling and tell me what you mean."

She bit her lip, not at all certain whether or not to try a sensible conversation when he was in such a foul temper. He appeared remarkably determined to cast her as the villain of this absurd drama. Ridiculous, considering dull, staid spinsters were never the villain.

"Very well," she at last capitulated. And why not? Hellion would not allow her to rest until he had satisfied himself she had confessed all. Resisting the urge to turn away she forced herself to meet his glittering gaze without flinching. "You are strong and intelligent and quite capable of achieving anything you might set your mind to, but not so long as you allow yourself to drift along the path with the least amount of effort."

A flare of heat bloomed along the angular line of his cheeks, as if she had managed to strike a vulnerable nerve.

"That is what you believe I am doing in wedding you?"

"Is it not?"

He abruptly averted his gaze. "You seem to have all the answers, not me."

Gads. Villain, indeed.

"Hellion, if I did not care, it would not matter a wit to me if you might eventually regret the decision to wed me," she said, unaware that her throbbing voice unwittingly revealed just how much she indeed cared. "I could not bear to have you some-day regard me in disgust."

There was a short silence, as if Hellion was bat-tling within himself. Then, with a slow motion he turned his back to her.

"I could never do that, Jane. Not ever. But you have made it obvious I am a spineless creature who is incapable of earning your respect. I will trouble you no further. I hope you discover your paragon of dullness, my shrew. The two of you shall no doubt live in tedious bliss the rest of your days."

His cutting insult delivered, Hellion marched to the door and after fumbling with the lock at last managed to snatch it open. He did not bother to even glance over his shoulder as he left the room, closing the door with a sharp bang.

Jane was relieved that he had not looked back.

The dratted tears she had thought were done were once again streaming down her face. Damn, damn, damn.

This was what came from making wicked propo-sitions to handsome rakes.

Several blocks away the fierce battle that had been waging was coming to a weary halt.

Holding a blood-soaked handkerchief to his wounded nose Biddles held off the vicious hellcat with a reluctant laugh.

My God, but she was glorious, he acknowledged, regarding her sweet features flushed with fury and her eyes lit with a brilliant sparkle. During the brief but delicious struggle her dark hair had tumbled to fall about her shoulders and her gown became disheveled to reveal a glimpse of her ample bosom.

Biddles's already heated blood nearly came to a boil. There was such passion crackling about her that it was all he could do not to jerk her into his arms and drown her in kisses.

Thankfully he was wise enough to resist temptation.

He would dare any obstacle, including hell itself, to have this woman as his own. He did not intend to risk losing her.

"Enough, my vicious beauty," he commanded, taking a judicious step away from her ready fists. "You have already broken my nose."

Far from appalled, Anna offered a superior toss of her head. "I hope that I have. It will perhaps teach you not to stick it in other people's business."

"Or to be a bit quicker in dodging a vengeful woman's wrath," he drawled. "That is quite a wicked right hook you possess."

"You hurt my friend," she charged in return.

With a delicate shudder Biddles tossed aside the bloody handkerchief. "And you broke my nose, not to mention ruining a vexingly expensive coat. I should think we are even."

His logic did little to impress the furious Anna,

who flounced across the overgrown path to seat herself on a bench.

"Fah."

Fiercely relieved that she had not marched out on him before he could make amends, Biddles covertly edged around the lethal rosebushes to stand before her.

"And of course there is the very real danger that my nose shall heal in a grossly crooked fashion," he mused in dark tones. "You might very well have ruined my male beauty beyond repair."

She flashed him a warning glare. "This is not amusing."

"Oh, I quite agree." Plucking a rose from a nearby bush he absently tugged off the petals to drop them into her lap. "Without my dazzling male attractions I shall never win the hand of a fair maiden. You might very well have condemned me to a life of lonely bitterness."

Her lips thinned, although he suspected it was from an effort to disguise her treacherous amusement.

"'Twas my understanding that you preferred the companionship of tarts, in any event."

He scattered another handful of petals as he slowly knelt at her feet. "But a gentleman must marry eventually."

Her lips parted in shock at his soft words even as she struggled to hold on to her righteous anger.

"There is no doubt some female desperate enough to settle for a sly, scheming, disreputable . . ." Her damning litany of his faults was brought to a convenient halt as Biddles leaned forward and kissed her. She stiffened, but thankfully for his bruised stomach and aching nose she did not feel the necessity to strike out. Pulling back he watched as an enchanting confusion rippled over her countenance. "Sir, you must not do that."

"Why?"

"Because . . . because I am quite furious with you."

He trailed a finger down the length of her arm, savoring the dewy softness of her skin.

"Yes, I know."

"You had no right to intrude into Jane's privacy."

"Just as you had no right to spy upon me or follow me about, sweet Anna," he pointed out with a faint smile.

She briefly faltered, clearly not having considered her own actions in any way dishonorable. "I was only attempting to protect my friend."

"As was I."

She rolled her eyes heavenward, as always refusing to be easily persuaded. It was oddly enough one of her most potent charms.

"As if a gentleman such as Hellion would need protection from poor Jane."

His smile was self-mocking. "There is no greater danger to a gentleman than an intelligent, cunning, spirited female. They steal a man's wits and slip into his heart before he realizes he has been well and truly caught."

"What?" Her shock was palpable in the air. Odd, Biddles acknowledged in bemusement. He would have thought Hellion's, not to mention his own, tender feelings should have been obvious to all. Such intelligent gentlemen did not behave as perfect loobies without love having addled their wits. "You surely do not mean to imply that Mr. Caulfield possesses feelings for Jane?"

"Why do you sound so disbelieving?"

She abruptly rose to her feet, sweeping past him in obvious agitation. "Because."

Slowly rising he stepped directly behind her stiff form. "That is not precisely an explanation."

"Oh for goodness sakes, you know perfectly well that Hellion only desired to wed Jane for her wealth."

"That was certainly the excuse that he used."

At his soft words she turned to regard him with a frown. "Excuse?"

His lips twitched. He thought men vastly superior to women when it came to denying what was beneath their very noses.

"Pretending to be a fortune hunter is far less risky than confessing his most intimate emotions. Surely you must know that a gentleman will go to the most appalling lengths to protect his fragile pride?"

Anna sputtered in confusion. "But that is absurd. If he loves her then he must tell her so."

"It would, of course, be the logical thing to do," he drawled. "Unfortunately logic rarely goes hand in hand with love. Besides which, I fear that Hellion is not yet prepared to admit his feelings. Not even to himself."

"Then he is bound to lose her," she ground out in aggravation.

"Perhaps."

"Perhaps?" Her hands landed upon her deliciously rounded hips. "That is all you can say? This is a tragedy."

His brief interest in Hellion's muddled heart was

seared away as his gaze swept over the woman who had somehow become as necessary as breathing.

Unlike his friend he had no intention of risking his future happiness. Not for pride, not for fear, not for anything.

"What it is, my sweet, is out of our hands," he murmured, reaching up to lightly stroke her shoulders. "It is up to Hellion and Miss Middleton to resolve their difficulties."

"Yes, but . . ." Her determination to continue arguing was easily halted as Biddles leaned forward and covered her lips with a brief, possessive kiss. It was not that he did not take great delight in crossing swords with the intelligent minx, it was simply that at the moment he preferred that she have her thoughts utterly concentrated upon him. Reluctantly pulling back he watched her give a bemused blink. "Sir, you really must halt your habit of kissing me whenever you might feel the urge."

"Why is that?"

Her tongue peeked out to touch her lips in a revealing motion. "It is not at all proper."

"We could make it proper." His hands slid down her arms to grasp her hands. "Proper enough for even the highest sticklers."

He felt her stiffen beneath his touch. "Whatever do you mean?"

Now that the moment had come, Biddles discovered that it was not nearly so difficult as he had once supposed. Indeed, he could not imagine anything being more right.

"If you were my wife I could kiss you whenever I please."

Her eyes widened as she struggled to disguise her

shock. "I . . . I might have something to say about that, sir."

Biddles chuckled softly, tugging her close enough to feel the heat of her skin.

"You, my love, would have everything to say about it."

Bewildered and struggling to accept that he had just offered her a proposal, Anna gave a slow shake of her head.

"You truly desire to marry me?" she husked, her gaze searching his face as if seeking to discover if he were playing some sort of cruel hoax. "I am not at all beautiful or wealthy, or even a comfortable sort of female. Indeed, my aunt assures me that I am well on my way to becoming a harridan."

Biddles felt a flare of irritation that anyone would dare to insult his beloved. Someday soon he would have a lengthy chat with Anna's relative. She would learn to treat his fiancée with unwavering respect.

"Let us get one thing perfectly clear right from the beginning," he growled. "You are never again to tell me that you are not beautiful. As far as I am concerned you are the most beautiful, most desirable, most intoxicating woman ever to be born."

Her lips parted in astonishment. "Oh."

"And as far as wealth, we shall manage to muddle along in whatever style you desire. I am a very resourceful sort of chap."

A tentative happiness began to glow in her lovely blue eyes. "And the fact that I am a harridan?"

Biddles abruptly locked his arms about her, not intending to let go any time soon.

"I happen to find it your finest quality."

Her hands gently touched his chest. "You must be mad."

"Absolutely," he readily agreed. "Will you share this madness with me?"

A smile that pierced his very heart curved her lips. "I suppose I must. Who else will keep that prying, crooked nose out of trouble?"

Sweet joy flooded through Biddles. A joy far too precious to put into mere words.

Instead he lowered his head to reveal his feelings in the most intimate manner possible.

CHAPTER SEVENTEEN

From the diary of Miss Jane Middleton, September 15th, 1814:

Dear Diary,

I am quite determined to be satisfied with my current situation. After all, I have returned to my beloved home where I am quite comfortable. My business dealings are the envy of hardened merchants throughout all of England. My numerous friends have devised any number of entertainments to welcome me back to Surrey. And the servants are determined to pander to me with such smothering devotion that I can barely rise from my bed before they are hovering about with anxious loyalty.

There are few women who can boast such a peaceful, utterly independent existence.

Besides which, I would never be so weak-willed as to waste my days with futile self-pity and remorse.

I am not some tragic figure from a Shakespearean play. I am an intelligent, mature woman who will overcome whatever obstacles may come my way.

Even if that obstacle is a broken heart that refuses to mend.

Hellion was seated in the cramped office above the old coffee shop. Or what had once been the old coffee shop.

Few could recall now that a mere four months before the building had been an abandoned ghost of the past. Especially not the elegant young blades who thronged to the most popular establishment in all of London.

It had taken weeks of unrelenting work and not an inconsiderable amount of money to transform the shabby establishment into an exclusive gambling den.

Hellion's Den, to be exact.

A flare of pride raced through him as he carefully tallied the considerable profits from the past week.

He knew without undue vanity that much of the success of the club was entirely his doing. Not only because of the endless hours he had devoted to his newfound business, but because it was his scandalous reputation that had lured the gentlemen from their more comfortable establishments.

All desired to be known as companions of the most notorious rake in London.

Oh, there was still much to be accomplished. The gaming rooms were far too cramped even after the kitchens were converted to make room for the faro tables. Soon enough he would be forced to use these private chambers on the second floor for the more elegant subscription rooms.

Which meant he would have to locate apartments

for himself since he had moved into the attics after selling his town house to have the funds necessary to refurbish the old building.

Tedious details he would deal with at a later date, he assured himself with a faint smile.

At the moment he had a far greater accomplishment to occupy his thoughts.

Locking the money box, Hellion placed it in the bottom drawer of his desk when the door to the chamber was suddenly pressed open. He lifted his head to watch Biddles enter with a grimace.

"Egads, I feared I would never battle my way through the crush," he complained, producing a lacy handkerchief to brush at his blinding yellow coat. "It seems Hellion's Den truly is all the rage."

Settling back in his chair Hellion steepled his fingers beneath his chin. His eyes were narrowed as his friend approached the desk.

Most would no doubt presume the rat-faced gentleman was here to ensure that his investment was running smoothly, but Hellion did not believe he could be so fortunate. Although Biddles had been invaluable in creating Hellion's Den he rarely could be seen without his devoted wife at his side, even here. Not unless he had been commanded by Anna to try and convince Hellion once again of the error of his ways.

"Yes, so it would seem," he drawled.

Pretending not to notice Hellion's dry tone Biddles offered a faint sniff. "Although not everyone is pleased with our success, I must confess. The madam next door tossed a chamber pot out the window when I passed by."

"Are you certain she was not merely offended by that ghastly coat?"

"Ghastly?" Biddles conjured a wounded expression. "I will have you know that this particular shade of yellow is the very height of fashion."

"I cannot imagine where it would be the height of fashion, unless you refer to the savages that run rampant through the colonies?"

"Philistine." Biddles held up the small basket he had hidden behind his back. "I have every notion to leave without offering you the treat I have brought with me."

"What treat?"

Setting the basket on the desk Biddles peered within. "Roasted pheasant, potatoes in cream with fresh mushrooms, cheese, warm bread, and grapes."

"Quite a feast."

"And one you will consume before I leave this room," Biddles commanded, clearly not missing Hellion's faint grimace as the rich smells filled the small room.

Hellion heaved a resigned sigh. The Lord save him from meddling friends.

"Bloody hell, Biddles, you are not my mother. I do not need you fussing over me."

"And I have no desire to fuss over you, my aggravating friend," the elegant gentleman mocked. "Unfortunately Anna is quite convinced you are in the throes of a horrid decline and I will have no peace until you recover your spirits."

Hellion groaned. If a meddling friend was annoying, a meddling female was an out-and-out curse. God knew the kindly but stubborn Anna would not leave him in peace until he was married or driven to Bedlam.

It would never occur to her that he could manage either quite well enough on his own.

"There is nothing the matter with my spirits."

"Nothing beyond the fact that you are obviously fagged to death, you have lost weight, and I have not seen you step foot outside this damnable building since you purchased it."

Hellion shrugged. "Hardly a source of astonishment. I have discovered it is rather tiresome to create a successful business."

"And that is all there is to it?"

With a smooth motion Hellion rose to his feet, his expression tight with displeasure.

"Biddles."

The tiny man gave a flutter of his handkerchief. "Glare at me all you desire, I will hold my tongue no longer. Whether you will admit the truth or not you are pining for Miss Middleton."

In spite of himself Hellion could not halt his lips from twitching with reluctant amusement.

"Pining? Are you not being rather melodramatic?"

"Do you deny it?"

"You intrude in matters that do not concern you."

"It would not be the first occasion, as we both know."

This time he laughed out loud. Had there ever been a greater understatement? That pointed nose had been stuck into more people's business than anyone would ever know.

"True enough."

Allowing his frivolous manner to disappear Biddles regarded his companion with a hard stare.

"For God's sake, Hellion, just go to the woman and confess that you love her."

Hellion did not even flinch. He had long past accepted his feelings for Jane. Ridiculous considering that had he been wise enough to search his heart when he should have then he could have avoided the misery of the past months.

Still, in some ways he accepted that he had earned his suffering.

Jane had been absolutely correct to accuse him of fearing to stand upon his own. For too long he had allowed his uncle's bitter accusations to rule his life.

He was a hellion tainted by the blood of his feckless parents. He was doomed to bring nothing but shame to his family. He could offer nothing but scandal and betrayal to those he loved.

It was not until he had truly stood upon his own feet that he had at last banished the wounds that had never fully healed.

He might very well be a hellion, but he had far more to offer than mere scandal.

A wondrous realization, but one that might very well have come too late.

"It is not quite so simple," he admitted with a sigh.

Biddles gave a lift of his brows. "Actually I have discovered much to my surprise that it is precisely that simple."

"Not with Jane." A pain wrenched through his heart at the mere mention of her name. "From the beginning I attempted to command and bully and manipulate her. I claimed to admire her independent spirit even as I sought to seduce her to my will."

There was a short pause as his friend closely scrutinized his grimly set features.

"So you believe it more noble to condemn her to a life with a gentleman who could never possibly love her as you do?"

Hellion resisted the urge to lash out. Biddles was only concerned for him. And it certainly was not the poor gentleman's fault that Hellion had managed to make such a hash of things.

"I believe it more noble to give her the freedom to decide if she wishes to hear my words of love."

Biddles made a sound that adequately revealed his disgust at such a chivalrous gesture.

"She can hardly make such a decision while she is in Surrey. Since you have forbidden Anna to reveal our little enterprise she might very well presume that you are currently seeking your fortune with another heiress."

Just for a moment Hellion struggled to breathe. It was a risk he was vibrantly aware of. In truth, the fear that she might have already condemned him to the netherworld in favor of a dull, tediously loyal farmer made him break out in a sweat during the dark hours of the night.

It was only by recalling her fragile features and eyes darkened with pain during their last encounter that kept him from rushing to Surrey and simply tossing her over his shoulder.

Thus far he had done everything wrong that could be done wrong in dealing with Miss Jane Middleton.

For once he was determined to do matters right.

Clearing his throat Hellion sent his friend a rueful smile.

"Actually I possess high hopes she will soon be returning to London."

"Are you daft?" Biddles demanded. "I should

think she would sooner toss herself from the nearest cliff. Her previous visit could hardly have inspired a love for the city."

"We shall see," Hellion murmured.

Biddles abruptly paused, his gaze narrowing as he watched Hellion absently straighten the candlestick upon the desk.

"I recognize that expression. What are you plotting, Hellion?"

Well aware the cunning little ferret would sniff out the truth within moments if he did not take care, Hellion deliberately settled his features into a stark warning.

"Nothing nefarious on this occasion," he retorted. "I have merely offered Jane an opportunity to reveal if she has washed her hands of me for good or if she still cares. We shall discover the truth of the matter within a few days."

The pointed nose twitched with pained curiosity, but for once in his life Biddles seemed to realize that his interference would not be tolerated.

"I wish you luck, my friend," he at last conceded to the inevitable.

"Thank you." Hellion smiled wryly. "When it comes to Miss Middleton I shall need all the luck I can muster."

The hotel was one of the finest in London.

Well situated in a quiet neighborhood it catered to those wealthy patrons who preferred a peaceful elegance during their brief stay in the city.

Not that Jane particularly cared that her chambers were furnished with highly polished mahogany, or that the servants had been trained to meet her needs without so much as stirring the air.

She was in London only for one purpose.

To confront Hellion and discover why he had returned the five thousand pounds she had paid to him.

Pacing across the floral-patterned carpet, Jane absentmindedly shredded the handkerchief in her fingers.

She had been utterly shocked when the servant had arrived at her home in Surrey. She had not expected Hellion to attempt to contact her. Not after their less-than-harmonious parting. And she most certainly had not expected to be handed a package containing the small fortune.

Why would he do such a thing? Anger? Pride? A need to banish her utterly from his life?

Whatever the cause Jane had discovered herself consumed with a fierce, unexplainable fury.

Was it not enough that he could not return her love as she desired? Or that he remained so sharply seared into her heart that she could not even imagine wedding another? Or that she felt so alone she physically ached?

Did he also need toss away her one gift as if it were utterly meaningless?

It was unbearable, she had decided. And so, refusing to give herself the opportunity to consider her actions, she had hastily packed her bags and taken off for the city.

She wanted to see Hellion. To hear from his lips his explanation.

Arriving at the hotel the previous evening she had immediately sent a note to Hellion's town house. Somehow she had expected a response by the time she had awakened this morning. Not that she was vain enough to suppose he would rush to her side in a flurry of anticipation. Hellion would never be so gauche. But surely he would be at least mildly curious at her sudden arrival?

The day had passed, however, with not the slightest indication that Hellion had received her message and a new fear had bloomed within Jane's heart.

What if he ignored her missive? What if he decided that she was not worth the effort of meeting?

Her heart clutched at the mere thought. No. Dear God, no. She had endured so much over the past months. She could not bear to discover that Hellion would deliberately cut her.

The day passed with a ghastly silence and she had worked herself into such a state of nerves that when the knock at last fell upon her door she nearly leaped from her skin.

"At last," she gritted, tripping over the hem of her plain gown in her haste to pull open the door. "I had begun to think . . . oh." Her eyes narrowed as she gazed at the uniformed servant who stood in the hallway. "What is it?"

"Good evening, Miss Middleton." The servant performed a deep bow. "Mr. Caulfield sent me to meet you."

She gripped the door as her heart threatened to break in two. "He is not coming?"

"He requested that I take you to him. I assure you that it is not far."

She blinked in surprise. This was not what she had expected at all. And indeed, she was not certain that she shouldn't be a tad offended by his cavalier treatment.

Still, she had traveled all the way to London to meet with him. It would be ridiculous to waste the journey just because her pride had been pricked.

"Very well."

Turning about Jane gathered her straw bonnet as well as her gloves and the small packet upon a low table before stepping through the door and closing it behind her. In silence they descended to the lobby of the hotel and out the door to where a polished black carriage awaited her.

With a sense she was losing command of the situation she allowed the groom to settle her upon the leather seat before they were abruptly moving through the thick London traffic. Alone with her thoughts Jane sternly attempted to dismiss the faint ball of tension that had settled in the pit of her stomach.

There was nothing to make her uneasy, she sternly reminded herself. She would return the money to Hellion and be on her way. A simple transaction.

Oh yes, quite simple, a voice mocked in the back of her mind.

The last transaction she had conducted with Hellion had cost her heart, her future, and any hope for the convenient marriage she had hoped to contract.

There was absolutely nothing simple when it came to Hellion.

Lost in her thoughts Jane paid no heed as they slowly weaved their way through the narrow streets. She did not even glance out the window when they at last pulled to a halt and the groom was helping her alight.

It was not until a slender gentleman attired in a modest black coat and breeches came forward to take her arm that she at last bothered to take notice of her surroundings.

What she discovered made her eyes narrow in confusion.

"Good heavens," she muttered, easily able to identify the old coffeehouse despite the obvious changes. "There must be some mistake."

"No, there is no mistake," the young man insisted with a smile, steering her firmly through the open door. "Mr. Caulfield is expecting you."

Far too bemused to argue Jane discovered herself stumbling over the threshold, her eyes widening at the sight within.

Gone was the shabby air of neglect and forlorn emptiness that had haunted the building. In its place was a warm, decidedly masculine club with polished teak paneling and a vast crowd of elegant gentlemen standing or lounging about the various tables.

She barely had the opportunity to study the loud, decidedly boisterous guests as she was firmly steered toward the narrow stairs and led upward.

"Do not fear, Mr. Caulfield is in his private chambers," the young gentleman murmured close to her ear.

She gave a baffled shake of her head. "Is this a gambling hell?"

"Yes, miss." An undoubted expression of pride settled upon the slender features. "The finest in all of London. Most nights a gent cannot get through the door."

That much was obvious. As a businesswoman she fully appreciated the undoubted eagerness of the crowd gathered about the room. But it did not explain what she was doing here.

"When did this open?" she demanded, knowing it had to have been recently. After all, she had sold the property only a few months before.

"Mr. Caulfield opened the doors just three months ago."

Jane stumbled upon the stairs, her heart halting in shock. "Hellion? This belongs to Hellion?"

"To him and Lord Bidwell," he clarified.

Jane struggled to accept the astonishing confession. Hellion. The owner of a gambling hell? It seemed impossible. Utterly unthinkable.

Oh, it was not that she did not realize Hellion was perfectly capable of such an accomplishment. She had told him of her belief before she had left London. And of course he had revealed a decided interest in the coffeehouse when he first visited the establishment.

But . . .

What?

Could it be that she had not truly expected him to forge so brilliantly forward while she still brooded upon the past?

Could it be that she was so petty as to begrudge his obvious success?

"Good God," she muttered, realizing that she was indeed that petty.

Thankfully misunderstanding her muttered exclamation her companion offered a pleased smile.

"Quite astonishing, is it not?"

Her own smile was stiff. "Words fail me."

Reaching the landing, he led her to the far door and pushed it open. "Here we are."

Before she was prepared he offered a bow and turned to disappear back down the stairs. Left on her own Jane momentarily wavered. Damn and blast. It had all seemed such an easy matter when she had packed her bags in Surrey. Now she wondered if she had not made some horrid mistake.

Still, she could not hover in the hallway forever, she sternly chastised herself. She had no choice but to go forward.

Squaring her shoulders she forced her feet to take her over the threshold, already prepared for her heart to stop beating and her breath to catch as Hellion rose from behind a desk and moved toward her.

God. He was just as achingly beautiful as she remembered. His hair a perfect gold. His eyes dark as sin. His male features blessed by an angel. And his elegant form enough to make any woman flutter in pleasure.

And flutter she did.

And ache.

And curse the fate that had brought this gentleman into her life and into her heart only to snatch him away.

"Ah . . . Jane." With an oddly searching gaze Hellion led her across the room, removing her bonnet and then her gloves with gentle movements since she seemed quite incapable of dealing with the mundane tasks on her own. Then with a firm insistence he pressed her into a cushioned chair. "May I say you are appearing as lovely as ever?"

Giving a shake of her head Jane struggled to regain her shattered composure.

"Thank you."

He leaned against the desk, his leg brushing her own in the cramped space. Jane gritted her teeth at the sharp flare of pleasure that jolted through her.

"I pray you will forgive me for not calling upon you as you requested," he said smoothly. "I have discovered it is devilishly difficult to leave the club when business is so brisk."

"Yes." She was forced to halt and clear her throat. "Your servant revealed that you own this establishment."

"Along with Biddles."

"But . . . how?"

He smiled ruefully at the blunt question. "Like any other investor, I would imagine. I purchased the property at quite a reasonable rate, as you must know, and sold my town house for the initial costs. After that it was sheer luck that made Hellion's Den the favorite among the gentlemen of the Ton."

His offhand manner did not fool Jane for a moment. She learned the art of trade before she had cut her teeth. No one knew better than she the difficulties involved in creating such an enterprise.

"No," she said slowly. "Success in business is never a matter of luck.' Tis obvious you have a gift."

He folded his arms across his chest, a worrisome expression upon his countenance.

"You seem surprised," he murmured.

Surprised. Stunned. Utterly befuddled. That about summed it up.

"I suppose I am just caught off guard."

"It was you who claimed that I could achieve whatever I set my mind to," he reminded her.

"I . . . Yes."

"Of course I did not believe you at the time. No doubt because I was utterly furious with you, and my feelings more than a bit wounded." His lips twisted at her small wince. "Once I had time to soothe my ruffled pride I decided I could do no worse than fail. A fate that suddenly did not seem quite so frightening as it once did."

Her eyes dropped to the forgotten packet in her lap. "I am quite pleased for you."

"I am pleased as well," he retorted. "For the first time, in a very long time, I feel quite proud of myself."

Absurdly his words seemed like a dagger through her heart. Stop it, she told herself fiercely. She was the one who had urged Hellion to stand on his own. To discover the strength he possessed within.

Only a despicable wretch would wish he were as miserable as herself.

"You should," she forced herself to mutter. "You have obviously achieved a success that anyone would envy."

"I do not know about envy, but I have managed a newfound independence." He gave a soft chuckle. "And best of all my uncle is nearly foaming at the mouth at the thought that I have sullied his name with such a sordid enterprise."

With an effort she lifted her reluctant lashes and offered what she hoped would pass as a smile.

"So, you had your revenge after all."

He gave a lift of his slender hand. "Not the way I had anticipated, but it is sweet nonetheless."

Jane swallowed heavily. Dear heaven, this was unbearable. She had not realized just how difficult it would be to be in his presence again.

Or perhaps she had known and simply chose to ignore the warnings of her heart, a small voice whispered.

Just maybe she had been so desperate to see him once more that she had refused to ponder the consequences of her hasty flight to London.

The shocking thought was enough to make her squirm in her seat. Go. She should go. Preferably before she managed to make even more of a fool of herself.

But first she had to complete the duty that had brought her here.

"I suppose I should not keep you when you are so busy," she muttered.

Hellion did not move, but Jane easily sensed the tension that hardened his elegant frame. Much like a tiger coiling to pounce.

"I am in no hurry," he drawled, his gaze glittering from beneath his half-lowered lashes. "Although I must confess an interest in what brings you to London. As I recall you once said you would rather face the hangman's noose as to return."

She frowned at the unnecessary reminder. "I would not have if it were not a matter of some import."

"A business matter?"

"In a manner of speaking." Before she could question the wisdom of her decision she jerkily reached out to thrust the packet into his hand. "I have come to return this."

Oddly his gaze did not waver from her strained features, as if he were utterly indifferent to the mysterious bundle loosely gripped in his fingers.

"Why?"

"It is the five thousand pounds you sent to Surrey."

She was uncertain what she had expected. Surprise? Relief? Frustration?

At least something beyond the mild lift of his brows. "You traveled all the way to London to return money that rightfully belongs to you?"

Somehow his bland question made her feel as if she had foolishly overreacted.

"We had a bargain," she gritted with a tilt of her chin.

"A bargain that failed, if you will recall. You did not discover a husband." His lips twisted in a humorless smile. "At least not one you desired."

A painful heat crawled beneath her skin. Blast. He was not supposed to mention such an awkward subject.

"Our agreement was simply that you bring me to the notice of society. You fulfilled your duty and I must fulfill mine."

He appeared remarkably unimpressed with her well-rehearsed speech. "And if I tell you that I do not desire your money?"

"I would say that it is not my money, it is yours. What you do with it is your decision."

"Good." With an unexpected flick of his wrist he tossed the packet back into her lap. "What I want to do with it is give it to you."

Her teeth snapped together. She had not forgotten his heart-stopping beauty. Or the manner in which his presence could send delicious shivers over her skin. Or even the male scent that had haunted her dreams for months.

Somehow, however, she had managed to forget just how easily he could annoy the devil out of her.

"Why are you being so aggravating about this?" she snapped.

There was a moment's pause before he slowly straightened from the desk. In the flickering candlelight his expression seemed uncommonly somber.

"Because I do not wish to have that fortune, or any other fortune, standing between us any longer."

Jane's heart faltered at the fierce edge in his voice. "I do not understand."

Holding her gaze with astonishingly little effort he reached down to knock the money to the ground. Then, while she was still in shock at his bizarre behavior, he grasped her hands and firmly tugged her to her feet.

"Why did you come to London, Jane?" he demanded.

She barely heard his low question. How could she? They were standing too close together. Far too close. Her entire body felt scorched by his male heat. And those wicked fingers were brushing up her arms and over her shoulders. She was lucky she could continue to breathe, let alone think.

"I told you . . ."

"Rubbish," he interrupted her stammering, audaciously resting his thumb against the frantic pulse at the base of her throat. "If you desired to return the money you could have easily sent a bank draft, or requested your man of business to offer me the funds. There was not the slightest need for you to come all the way to London."

Of course there had been need. Great need. Unfortunately she simply could not recall why at this precise moment.

"It was because . . . because I . . ."

His features softened as she struggled to maintain a shred of sanity among the poignant longing that threatened to drown her.

"Because you desired to see me again?"

"Why would I desire to see you again?" she whispered.

His hand shifted to splay at the curve of her back, gently pressing her against the wickedly firm muscles of his thighs.

"I hope it is because you love me," he said with astounding simplicity. "Just as I love you."

If he had not been holding her so tightly Jane was quite certain she would have toppled to the floor. As it was, she swayed against him in shock.

"What did you say?"

He smiled with an aching tenderness. "I said that I love you, Miss Jane Middleton."

"But . . . you cannot."

His arm about her abruptly tightened. "Oh no. You have attempted to tell me what is in my heart before. On this occasion I will be the one to tell you."

Her eyes widened at his stern command. It was utterly unlike the nonchalant, urban rake he usually revealed.

"Indeed?"

"Indeed," he growled. "I love you. I love your indomitable spirit and your unwavering courage. I love your intelligence. I love the manner you find society ridiculous and prefer to be in your library rather than Almack's. I love your intelligence. I love your scent. And I most certainly love the taste of you." His eyes probed deep into her own, as if willing her to believe the sincerity of his husky words.

"I love you, my sweet shrew, and it has nothing at all to do with your appalling fortune."

On this occasion she did not even bother to try and recall to breathe. What was the point when her heart was lodged in her throat and her head reeling?

It was a dream. A wondrous, unbelievable dream. And one she had no intention of waking from.

"Oh, Hellion," she breathed. "I have been so miserable."

"Forgive me." Bending down he rested his forehead against her own. "I was a fool. I was so terrified to admit even to myself that you had become more important to me than life itself that I risked losing you forever."

Ridiculous tears nearly blinded her. "I have behaved somewhat foolishly myself."

His chuckle brushed over her cheek. "My logical, always sensible shrew? Never."

She clutched at the lapels of his coat, indifferent to the fact she was crushing the superfine material.

"I cannot imagine I could ever have thought I could settle for a dull, comfortable husband."

"True."

She pulled back to meet his glittering gaze. "Hellion."

His expression was unbearably smug. "Well, 'tis obvious even to the meanest intelligence that only a scandalous rake would suit you."

Sweet, near unbearable elation filled her heart as she pressed even closer. Not even in her wildest fantasies had she allowed herself to believe he could ever return her love. It had seemed such an impossible dream.

Now she slowly allowed herself to trust in the happiness that was within her grasp.

"And of course, a highly successful businessman," she teased.

As if sensing the unquestioning faith that was slowly filling her soul, Hellion's dark eyes abruptly smoldered with a wicked fire. With a swift motion he swept her into his arms and was headed toward a nearly hidden door leading to a second chamber.

"Hellion, whatever are you doing?"

His smile was filled with all sorts of wicked intentions. "I am about to negotiate a new proposition."

"I see." An intoxicating heat was flowing through her blood, tingles of pleasure stirring in the most wicked places. "And what would this proposition entail?"

"Just one thing."

"And what is that?"

He came to a halt as he studied her flushed features with a vulnerable expression.

"That you love me."

Her hand instinctively lifted to rest against his cheek. "I believe that I can meet your terms, Mr. Caulfield," she said, the fierce love she felt for him evident in her husky voice. "Although, we must officially seal such a bargain."

"My thoughts precisely," he whispered, his steps once again carrying them toward the shadows beyond. "Of course this bargain is to be for quite some duration. An eternity, in fact. I shall have to conjure something quite special."

Her fingers lightly outlined the sensuous curve of his mouth. "I trust in you, my love."

A strangled groan was wrenched from his throat

as he regarded her with eyes shimmering with an immeasurable love.

"Ah, my beautiful shrew."

"My wicked Hellion."

Please turn the page for an exciting sneak peek of
Deborah Raleigh's next historical romance
SOME LIKE IT SINFUL
coming in May 2006!

CHAPTER ONE

It was a typical spring evening in London.

Damp, foggy, and exquisitely miserable. The sort of weather that should have made any reasonable gentleman consider staying tucked nicely by the fire. Or better yet, of immigrating to India with all possible speed.

Of course English gentlemen were a rare breed.

While they might be incapable of tying their own cravats, or removing their boots without a small legion of servants, they would not so much as bat an eye at braving the most formidable weather. Earthquake, flood, or monsoon—nothing was allowed to interfere with the nightly round of entertainments.

Especially when that entertainment included a few indulgent hours spent at Hellion's Den.

Once a coffee shop that had catered to the various artists spattered about the capital, the narrow, decidedly shabby building had been purchased by Hellion Caulfield and Lord Bidwell to create an exclusive gambling club.

Since its opening last year it had become a favorite

gathering for the gentlemen of Society. Dandies, rakes, rogues, and a sprinkling of hardened gamblers were stuffed into the smoky interior.

And then there was Rutherford Hawksley.

No one could claim him a frivolous dandy, nor did rake or rogue entirely suit him. Oh, he was handsome enough to make any woman forget to say no. Quite often they forgot to say anything at all. Drooling and swooning was by far the more likely response.

Perfectly reasonable.

His features were lean and perfectly carved. He possessed a long, aquiline nose; a broad forehead; and high cheekbones that gave a hint of exotic beauty to his countenance. His eyes were an Indigo-blue and surrounded by a fringe of black lashes. And as if he were not blessed enough, he possessed a set of dimples that could flash with devastating results.

But while women had always, and would always, lust after him, and more than a few knew the pleasure of his intimate touch, the past months had wrought a change in the once devil-may-care Hawksley.

No longer did he tease and charm his way through Society. No longer did he shock London with his madcap dares. No longer was there a ready smile and hint of laughter in the astonishing blue eyes.

Instead there was a hard edge to his features and a hint of ruthless determination about him that kept the women casting longing glances from a safe distance and wise gentlemen stepping out of his path.

On this evening he was attired in his familiar black with his long raven hair pulled into a queue with a satin ribbon. In the muted candlelight a diamond flashed on his ear with cold beauty and the scar that ran the length of his jaw was thrown in sharp relief.

Seated at a private table, he sprawled in his seat with elegant ease. An ease that did nothing to disguise the air of lethal power in his lean form.

He looked precisely what he was: coiled danger ready to spring.

Unfortunately Lord Pendleton, who was currently in the chair across the small table, was far too infuriated to appreciate the risk of baiting the young nobleman. In one short hour he had lost three hundred quid. Not such a terribly large sum, but one he could ill afford to hand over—especially since his harridan of a wife had threatened to tell her father of his gambling habits. The clutch-fisted old gudgeon was bound to pull the purse strings even tighter, God rot his soul.

Tossing his cards onto the table, he glared into Hawksley's unfashionably dark countenance. His annoyance was not lessened by the fact that the . . . the dastard was utterly impassive despite the stack of vowels piled indecently before him.

"You seem to be in luck yet again, Hawksley," the older man growled.

"So it would seem."

"Some might even say unnatural luck."

Hawksley narrowed his gaze. He had sensed his opponent's frustration early in the game. The fool had been well outmatched, but like most noblemen, he had been too proud to admit his incompetence. For such a gentleman it was far preferable to blunder along, somehow hoping that lightning might strike and avert the inevitable disaster.

Rather like clinging to a horse as it tumbled off a cliff.

As a rule Hawksley was content to toy with such prey and move on when they began to twitch. Why bleed a poor bloke dry? It only provoked an ugly scene. And besides which, there were always a ready supply of dupes anxious to hand over their allowance. On this evening, however, he did not possess the luxury of time.

During the past fortnight he had devoted his nights to shadowing a certain Lord Doulton through the fashionable balls, routes, and assemblies of London—not to mention the less fashionable brothels that clogged the Dials. It had left precious little opportunity to earn his livelihood.

Now he was without money, without credit, and his rent was due. He needed a bit of the ready if he wasn't to be tossed into the streets of the stews, a fate that did not suit his current plans.

And the blustering Pendleton had been the perfect pigeon.

Folding the vowels in his slender fingers, Hawksley tucked them into the pocket of his jacket. "I prefer to think of it as skill rather than luck," he drawled.

"Skill?" The older man's face was becoming an ugly shade of pink, as if his cravat were choking him. "I could name another word for it."

"Take care, Pendleton. My temper is rarely dependable and I should take great offense if you were to cast dispersion on my honor."

"Arrogant pup, I shall say whatever I damn well please."

Hawksley smiled his cold smile. "Only if you happen to be anxious for a dawn appointment."

There was a moment of shock at the blunt warning. "Are you threatening me?"

Hawksley shrugged. He was in no mood to soothe the twit's wounded pride. He had the man's money; now he wanted him to leave.

"Merely clarifying your options, Pendleton. You can accept your loss and walk away with a bit of dignity, or we can meet tomorrow on the field of honor."

The pink countenance became puce and then an intriguing shade of purple. For a crazed moment the older man seemed on the brink of utter stupidity. Thankfully the moment passed and he awkwardly rose to his feet. "Fah, you aren't worth the cost of a bullet."

Having devoted a lifetime to disappointing and aggravating others, the insult slid off Hawksley without drawing so much as a wince. "That seems to be a common conclusion among most who know me."

"Bloody sharp," Pendleton muttered even as he backed away with something just short of an all out run.

Hawksley did not even bother to watch the rather amusing retreat. Instead he silently sipped at his whiskey as he contemplated what to do with the remainder of his evening.

It was too late to pick up on the trail of Doulton, and in truth he was weary of the fruitless effort. He could always move onto another gambling hell. His luck was in and he could always use the blunt; that, however, held little appeal as well.

He sipped more of the whiskey.

If he were being perfectly honest, nothing seemed to hold appeal. Oh, perhaps a luscious armful of willing women. That usually managed to lift a man's spirits. Unfortunately he had no current mistress and no desire to go to the effort of locating one.

Bloody hell. He leaned back in the seat. He was weary.

Weary and frustrated and so sick at heart that there were times when he wanted nothing more than to crawl into his bed and never leave.

The bleak thoughts were interrupted as a thin, rat-faced gentleman attired in a shocking pink coat and yellow waistcoat slid into the vacant seat across the table.

A faint smile, genuine on this occasion, tugged at Hawksley's lips.

He acquired any number of casual acquaintances since being tossed out of his father's home and traveling to make his fortune in London, but there were few he actually considered a friend, and even fewer that he trusted.

Lord Bidwell, better known as Biddles, was one of those few.

Although now a properly married gentleman with the task of ensuring Hellion's Den kept him disgustingly wealthy, Biddles had once been England's most proficient spy. Intelligent, cunning, and possessing the sort of morals that allowed him to climb into the sewers with the best of them, he had done as much as Wellington to save England from defeat.

His retirement from the War Office had been a decided blow for his country but a blessing for Hawksley.

Never one to allow his talents to fall into waste, Biddles kept himself entertained by turning his attentions to those closer to home. There was nothing that occurred in London, be it in the most elegant ballroom or the seediest back streets of the stews, that Biddles was not aware of. Which was why Hawksley had turned to him the moment he realized he needed assistance.

"Ah, Hawk, you are in your usual charming mood, I see," Biddles mocked as he raised a lacy handkerchief to dab at his pointed nose.

Hawksley shrugged. "I find it difficult to be charming when I am being accused of cheating."

"Then you shouldn't win so often, old chap. It makes gentlemen peevish."

"It makes me peevish when I cannot pay my rent."

The pale eyes narrowed as Biddles regarded him with a shrewd thoroughness. "Difficulties?"

Hawksley choked back a humorless laugh. He could write an epic on difficulties: a father who detested him; bill collectors yammering at his heels; a title and duties hanging about his neck like a yoke; a murdered brother; oh, and an investigation that had produced precisely nothing. Well, nothing more than a lingering headache and a bad taste in his mouth.

"No more so than usual," he retorted in wry tones.

"You know I always stand prepared to offer assistance if you find yourself in need," Biddles murmured.

Hawksley gave the faintest nod. He did know, and it offered him a comfort he rarely found these days. "Not necessary at the moment, although I do appreciate the offer."

Biddles gave a small smile. "I believe I have something you will appreciate even more."

Hawksley lifted his brows. "Is she beautiful?"

"I fear it is not a woman."

"A pity," he drawled. "Now that I have a bit of blunt I could use some companionship."

"A swift means of not having your blunt for long."

He briefly thought of the luscious, dark-haired widow who had been on his scent for the past weeks. And the slender blond actress who had offered all sorts of intriguing possibilities. Either would do.

"Ah, but what more delightful means of becoming a pauper?"

Biddles gave a soft laugh. "I must refrain from answering such a leading question. I am a married man after all and I prefer my head not to be placed upon the platter."

"Where is your charming wife?"

The expression of sardonic amusement faded as a frown of annoyance marred the thin countenance. Hawksley noticed that frown quite often when men spoke of their wives. Only one of a dozen reasons he was not wed.

"She was decidedly pale this morning and I left strict orders that she was to stay home this evening to rest." Biddles grimaced. "Of course that only ensures that she will be gadding about to every assembly and ball in Town. She possesses a remarkable dislike for orders."

Hawksley sipped his whiskey, his lips twitching. "Perhaps you have not been stern enough in teaching her who is master."

"Master?" Biddles tilted back his head to laugh with rich amusement. "I would suggest you not say such a thing in Anna's presence."

"You believe it would be my head upon the proverbial platter?"

"Without a shred of doubt."

"That is the trouble with wedding a spirited woman."

"Ah no, that is the pleasure," Biddles corrected with a wicked glint in his eyes.

Hawksley briefly thought of the actress again. She was spirited in all the right ways, and without the bother of a wedding ring; unfortunately he wasn't entirely certain she was worth the effort or the money. A thought that entered his mind far too often of late.

Bloody hell. Obviously the sooner he ended this frustrating search for the truth the better. Another few months and he'd be a damn eunuch.

"I should be on my way. Pendleton is no doubt drinking himself into a rage in some corner and I have no desire to have to shoot him."

Biddles glanced about the crowded room. "If you are not in a desperate hurry I think you should join me in my office."

"Office?" Hawksley grimaced. The word was enough to conjure up his father's large study where he had regularly endured endless lectures, sermons, and an occasional beating, none of which had done the least good. "That sounds tediously dull."

"Actually I think you will find it of great interest."

Interest? Hawksley narrowed his gaze. "I suppose I could spare a few moments."

Together they left the table and climbed the narrow stairs to the upper floor. Out of habit Hawksley glanced about to ensure he was not being watched. He had taken care to hide the fact he was searching for his brother's murderer, but he was never foolish enough to lower his guard. Satisfied that the crowd below was suitably entranced by the turn of cards and rattle of dice, he allowed himself to be escorted into a barren room that was notable only for its lack of space.

Giving a lift of his brows he glanced over the desk and lone chair that managed to consume the small chamber. "Not quite what I expected from the notorious Hellion," he murmured, referring to Biddles' partner who had once been the most successful rake in all of England.

Daintily dusting off the edge of the desk, Biddles perched himself upon the worn wood. "His wife has ensured that he is not nearly so notorious these days."

Hawksley leaned against the paneling, crossing his arms over his chest. "Poor blighter."

"He wouldn't agree, I assure you."

He offered a dramatic shudder. "Lord save me from happily married gentlemen."

Biddles chuckled. "We are a dull lot, are we not?" Reaching behind him, the slender gentleman produced a bottle to pour Hawksley a measure of the amber spirit. "I think you will find this to your taste."

Accepting the offering, Hawksley took an experimental sip. Ahh. A smoky fire slid down his throat. Whiskey, of course; Hawksley always drank whiskey. "Excellent. Your private stock?"

"Of course."

Beyond his skill in spying, Biddles always managed to procure the finest spirits—another reason to like the man.

"I would ask where you purchased it, but I have a feeling you have no desire to share your source."

Biddles held up his hands in a helpless motion. "I

must have something to maintain my intriguing air of mystery."

He gave a bark of laughter. "You become any more mysterious and Parliament will have you locked in the Tower. Prinny already complains you need to have a bell tied about your neck to keep you from lurking about and sticking your nose into places it has no business being."

"My poor nose"—Biddles fondly stroked the pointed end—"it is sadly abused."

"It is a lethal weapon."

The pale eyes glittered in the candlelight. "You will not be near so condemning when you discover what this nose has managed to sniff out."

"You have information for me?"

"Not precisely the sort you requested, but I think you might find it interesting."

Hawksley did not move but every muscle in his body tightened in anticipation. Biddles would not have approached him if he didn't think the information was something he could use.

"Tell me."

"There is a rumor floating about the stews that a certain Lord Doulton approached Jimmy Blade with an offer to pay him one-hundred quid."

Hawksley abruptly set aside his whiskey. He could not deny a measure of surprise at the information. Although he suspected that the elegant Lord Doulton dabbled in all sorts of nasty business, the man had always been careful to keep his reputation spotless. He preferred to hire others to wallow in the muck.

"He has need of a thief?"

"A highwayman."

Well, this just got more interesting by the moment. "Why?"

"It seems there is a carriage on its way to London from Kent that Lord Doulton does not wish to arrive."

Hawksley narrowed his gaze even further. "There is something in the carriage he desires?"

Biddles grimaced. "Actually there is something in the carriage he wants dead."

An icy fury flared through his heart. Damn the ruthless bastard. One day he would overplay his hand and put himself in Hawksley's clutches—and that day would be his last.

"Who?"

"A Miss Clara Dawson."

Shock made him catch his breath. "A woman?"

"Yes, is she familiar to you?"

"I have never heard her name before. Bloody hell, why would Doulton want this woman dead?"

Biddles shrugged. "Well the prig is too much a cold fish to have it be for the usual reasons a gentleman might wish to do away with a woman—love, hate, jealousy—so it must be that he either owes her money or that she has information he does not care to have spread about."

Hawksley shoved away from the wall. Unfortunately there wasn't the necessary room for a good pacing. He took two steps to the chair and then back to the wall; still by the time he turned, he had made his conclusion.

He had already discovered that Doulton possessed an astonishing fortune, too much fortune for a man who had inherited a crumbling estate and a pile of bills. The nobleman could easily afford to pay off any trifling debt.

"Information," he said firmly.

"That would be my guess," Biddles offered.

"You said the carriage was coming from Kent?"

"Yes."

A silence descended as Hawksley debated how best to use his unexpected windfall.

He could lay a trap for Jimmy and force whatever information he might possess out of him. Not a bad plan except for the realization that the likelihood of Doulton sharing his reasons for wanting the woman dead was about as likely as a pig sprouting wings.

No, Jimmy would know nothing. But the woman . . . ah yes. She knew something—something Doulton was willing to kill to keep secret. "Where is Jimmy to attack?" he abruptly demanded.

"Westerham, just past the King's Arms."

"When?"

"Tomorrow afternoon."

Hawksley gave a slow nod, then with a lethal smile he reached out to lay his hand upon Biddles' shoulder. "I owe you yet again, old friend."

Biddles grasped his arm before he could move away, his expression somber. "What do you intend to do?"

A grim determination hardened his already hard features. "Get to the information before Jimmy Blade can make it disappear."

Biddles took a moment before he slowly released his arm. "Take care."

CHAPTER TWO

It was not until she had hired the carriage and was well on her way to London that Miss Clara Dawson discovered she was not at all suited to long journeys.

The swaying carriage made her queasy and the relentless jolting made her head ache. Even worse, her unsettled stomach made it impossible for her to read, or work upon her needlework, or even count the blasted cows as they passed. She was a prisoner in the cramped confines with nothing to occupy her restless mind.

Who could have known?

Having lived in a small village for all her six-and-twenty years she had always used her God-given feet to take her about. And the few times she had resorted to accepting a ride by a kindly neighbor, the distance had been short enough to avoid any hint of her weakness.

Besides which it was not as if she were one of those timid, easily distressed creatures who was overset by every situation that might come her way. While she might barely stand five foot and weigh little more than a feather, she was a sturdy, sensible woman.

Most would say far too sensible. Or even annoyingly sensible, despite the fact she'd had no choice in the matter. When a woman was left on her own at the tender age of seventeen with a mere pittance and no family to speak of, she either learned to confront life squarely or she found herself begging in the streets.

Still it was perhaps best that she had not realized just how great her discomfort would be, she acknowledged as another pain shot through her head. As much as she wished to ease the curiosity that had plagued her for the past fortnight, she sensed she would have been far less likely to leap into this carriage and head off so willy-nilly if she had known the nasty surprise awaiting her.

At least she had the comfort of knowing they were less than two hours from London, she told herself. And the small sherry she had enjoyed at the posting inn had helped to ease her heaving stomach. She was bound and determined to survive.

It was, after all, what she did best.

Chancing a brief glance out the window, she noted the sun was slanted toward dusk. It would be dark by the time she arrived at the hotel, but at least the weather was cooperating. After a week of endless rain, the sun had struggled through the clouds to chase away the gloom—she would not be forced to make her first appearance in London wet and bedraggled. Queasy and weary was bad enough.

Leaning against the worn leather squabs, she resisted the urge to close her eyes. The swaying was horrid enough with her eyes open—with her eyes closed it was unbearable; she barely dared to blink.

They slowed as the plodding team approached a curve, then oddly she felt them being pulled to an abrupt halt.

Clara frowned. There was no toll gate along this road that she was aware of, and certainly there was no traffic to impede their progress. Had something gone wrong with the carriage? They had hit enough bumps to rattle any number of vital things loose.

Not one to sit about and await problems to be smoothed away, Clara reached up to push open the hatch in the top of the carriage.

"Driver, why have we stopped?" she demanded.

There was a muffled curse from above. "Hold, miss."

Clara's frown deepened. "What is happening?"

"Trouble."

Not at all satisfied with the vague response, Clara reached out to push open the door. If the driver had halted to have another drink from his flask, she would have his hide. Her hand, however, found nothing but empty air as the door was wrenched open without warning.

Nearly tumbling off her seat Clara was forced to steady herself before she could glance up to regard the large form standing in the opening.

When she did her heart momentarily halted.

Even with his tall form cloaked in a caped driving coat and a hat covering his hair, there was no doubting the stranger was very large—and very, very male. Precisely the sort of ruffian a woman did not desire to encounter on a lonely stretch of road.

Her mouth went dry and her blood rushed, but she refused to give into panic, that would surely accomplish nothing. Instead she sternly forced herself to view the man with the logic she had learned from her father.

Breathing deeply, she first studied the coat that was frayed but clearly of good quality. Good enough quality to boast gold buttons and an exquisite tailoring that fit the muscular form to perfection; not the sort of thing one would expect a highwayman to possess.

Her gaze lifted higher, taking note of the dashing diamond earring and then the hard edged features of his countenance. He was handsome, she easily decided. By far the most handsome man she had ever encountered. But there was a grimness in his expression that halted him just short of beautiful. At last she forced herself to meet his glittering gaze.

Her heart once again halted, only on this occasion she could not blame it on fear. Sweet heavens, she had never seen such astonishing eyes: the blue was as rich as the finest velvet and rimmed in black, while the startling long lashes framed them with artistic perfection. They were the sort of eyes that women would kill for, but there was nothing effeminate about them; instead they shimmered with a cold intelligence that sent a small chill down her spine.

Clara gave a vague shake of her head at her ridiculous reaction.

If her inspection had told her nothing else, she did know for a certainty that this man was no mere highwayman. From the top of his beaver hat, to the tips of his polished Hessians, he spoke of noble breeding. No doubt a bored aristocrat out on a lark, she told herself with a disgusted sigh. She had heard that many gentlemen who considered themselves Tulips enjoyed daring one another to the most outrageous antics, including holding up carriages and demanding some sort of token for proof of their foolish courage.

Waiting for him to finish his own survey of her slender form, Clara folded her hands neatly in her lap. "Sir, may I inquire what this is about?"

"Get out of the carriage."

Clara blinked. Not so much at the soft purr of his voice, although it was deliciously compelling, but more at his astonishing demand. It was one thing to pinch a fan or even a kiss, it was quite another to haul her off to prove his daring.

"Get out of the carriage? Why should I?"

A raven brow flicked upward. "For the simple reason that I told you to do so."

Clara decided his voice was not so nice after all. "I did hear you, despite my advanced years I am not deaf."

He paused, as if caught off guard by her response. Not surprising. Clara had learned long ago that she tended to catch others off guard. Not in a good way, but in an aggravating, longing to gag her, sort of way.

"If you heard me, then why are you still sitting there?" he growled.

"I am not about to be ordered about by a perfect stranger."

His eyes narrowed and he slowly reached into the pocket of his coat to withdraw a pistol. With an ease that was not at all reassuring, he pointed it at her heart. "Perhaps this will convince you?"

No doubt it should have, but Clara was busy

noticing that the pistol was much like the rest of him. Sleek, lethal, and very expensive. Just the sort of thing a dandy on a childish lark would carry.

"That is a very fine dueling pistol." She leaned forward to inspect the detailed workmanship. "I notice it even possesses ivory inlay. No doubt you had it crafted at Manton's?"

The faux highwayman gave a muffled cough. "Bloody hell, have you been drinking?"

"Of course not . . . oh, that is not entirely true." She gave an unconscious grimace. "I did have a small sherry at the posting inn. I possess a very sturdy constitution, but I have discovered that it does not care for long journeys. My stomach becomes very queasy."

"I . . . see." The eyes held a growing hint of bemusement, as if the man was not quite certain what to make of her. "You are not about to sick up, are you?"

Clara gave the matter serious contemplation before offering a shake of her head. "No, I do not believe so. Not at the moment in any event."

"I cannot express the depth of my relief." He took a step back. "Now, I am in something of a hurry so I must insist that you step out of the carriage."

"You still have not explained who you are or why you wish me to leave this carriage."

"And I have no intention of doing so." An edge had entered that honey voice as he gave a wave of the gun. "Get out or I will be forced to use this."

Clara leaned further back in her seat. She was not opposed to this man having a bit of fun, but she was tired of this dismal journey and not at all in the mood to play—especially not if he wished to display her to his cronies like some sort of trophy.

"I do not believe you will pull the trigger."

The slender fingers tightened on the pistol. "What?"

"Well, if you truly wanted me dead, you would have shot the moment you opened the door. I cannot imagine a cold-blooded murderer seeking to indulge in conversation, which leads me to presume that you desire to keep me alive."

"A desire that is waning with every passing moment," he muttered.

A wry smile touched Clara's lips. "Not surprising. I tend to have that effect on most people."

Again there was that startled pause. "You are a most . . . unusual young woman."

She flicked a pointed glance over his elegant attire. "And you are a most unusual highwayman."

"One who does not possess time to wrangle with you. Forgive me, but you leave me no choice."

"What do . . ." Clara's words ended in a startled shriek as the stranger reached into the carriage and wrapped an arm about her waist. With surprising ease she discovered herself being hauled from the carriage and slung over the man's shoulder. "Sir."

He paid no heed to her protest, not even when she beat her fists upon the broad width of his back. Instead he calmly moved to a massive black stallion and smoothly vaulted into the saddle.

Real panic flared through Clara. Not so much at being kidnapped since she still did not believe this man intended to harm her, but at the thought of riding over the man's shoulder. Sweet heavens, she was guaranteed to be violently ill.

As if sensing her distress, the stranger tugged her downward, settling her across the hardness of his thighs and clamping a firm arm about her waist.

Clara discovered her new position somewhat of an improvement: at least her head was not dangling downward and her stomach threatening a revolt. But she had to admit she was not entirely pleased with her awareness of the hard muscles that pressed into her legs. It did not seem entirely respectable to be so conscious of the warm sensations that flushed through her body.

Barely given time to catch a glimpse of the two gentlemen who were seated on horses and pointing guns at her poor driver, she felt the horse taking off with a sharp leap. Clara bit her lip, ridiculously glad of the strong arm that kept her from tumbling onto the ground. She may be furious at being hauled off in such a manner, but falling from the huge beast seemed a somewhat worse fate just at the moment.

In silence they thundered down the narrow lane, and then without warning, the man tugged on the reins, angling them toward the shallow ditch before plunging straight into the trees.

Out of necessity the galloping nightmare was forced to slow its pace and Clara took her first breath since being hoisted onto the horse.

She had not fallen and been trampled to death. That had to be a good thing.

As her heart slowed to something approaching bearable, her simmering anger was allowed to resurface. Blast it all, what was this man doing? She was never going to get to London.

More Regency Romance
From Zebra